KU-538-464

THE PRIVATE BLOG OF JOE COWLEY

OXFORD
UNIVERSITY PRESS

Great Clarendon Street, Oxford OX2 6DP
Oxford University Press is a department of the University of Oxford.
It furthers the University's objective of excellence in research, scholarship,
and education by publishing worldwide in

Oxford New York

Auckland Cape Town Dar es Salaam Hong Kong Karachi
Kuala Lumpur Madrid Melbourne Mexico City Nairobi
New Delhi Shanghai Taipei Toronto

With offices in

Argentina Austria Brazil Chile Czech Republic France Greece
Guatemala Hungary Italy Japan Poland Portugal Singapore
South Korea Switzerland Thailand Turkey Ukraine Vietnam

Oxford is a registered trade mark of Oxford University Press
in the UK and in certain other countries

© Ben Davis 2013
The moral rights of the author have been asserted

Database right Oxford University Press (maker)

First published 2013

All rights reserved. No part of this publication may be reproduced,
stored in a retrieval system, or transmitted, in any form or by any means,
without the prior permission in writing of Oxford University Press,
or as expressly permitted by law, or under terms agreed with the appropriate
reprographics rights organization. Enquiries concerning reproduction
outside the scope of the above should be sent to the Rights Department,
Oxford University Press, at the address above

You must not circulate this book in any other binding or cover
and you must impose this same condition on any acquirer

British Library Cataloguing in Publication Data

Data available

ISBN: 978-0-19-273675-8v
1 3 5 7 9 10 8 6 4 2

Printed in Great Britain
Paper used in the production of this book is a natural,
recyclable product made from wood grown in sustainable forests.
The manufacturing process conforms to the environmental
regulations of the country of origin.

Internal photography:
Empire State – Matt Apps/Shutterstock.com
Rhino – Aaron Amat/Shutterstock.com
Bowling Pins – nikkytok/Shutterstock.com
Warthogs – Albin Ebert/Shutterstock.com
Flowers – JeniFoto/Shutterstock.com
Chihuahua and Macaw – Eric Isselee/Shutterstock.com
All other images OUP

THE PRIVATE BLOG OF JOE COWLEY

WRITTEN BY
BEN DAVIS

OXFORD
UNIVERSITY PRESS

Dear Reader,

Please note that all artwork and design is rough at this stage, except for the first 20 pages which I managed to finish last night when I should have been doing my Chemistry homework.

I would have done more except I've been pretty busy lately dealing with a series of catastrophic life events. You'll see what these are when you read my blog.

Yours sincerely
Joe Cowley

Sunday 1st January

RIGHT. Here we go.

This thing is set to private isn't it? It'd be just my luck if it went viral.

OK, it's definitely on private.

So here's the thing. I've decided to start writing a blog. A private one. Kind of like a diary but not a diary because diaries are for girls.

The idea is that it'll help me clear my head and sort my life out, because quite frankly, it can't get much worse.

In just the past year this CATALOGUE OF MISERY happened:

1 Mum and Dad got divorced.

2 Dad shacked up with Svetlana, who is like a million years younger than him and is Russian.

3 Mum started seeing Jim the plasterer, and yet the crack in my bedroom ceiling grows bigger with every passing day.

4 I nearly got to snog Louise Bentley at the fair, but ended up throwing up all over her after the waltzer made me nauseous.

5 I gained the nickname 'Puke Skywalker' at school for the above reason.

6 That idiot Gav James ramped up his campaign of torment against me, once even dunking me in a bin upside down and making me stay there for the entire lunch break.

THE CANNOT GO ON. I have to do something, or I'll end up like Mad Morris down the park who thinks he's Jesus.

By the end of next term, I'm going to be a **COMPLETELY DIFFERENT PERSON**. And I'm going to do the following to make that happen:

- Get Gav back for all the crap he's done to me.
- Become more respected.

Kiss a girl. **<u>A REAL LIVE GIRL.</u>** A lot of other fourteen-year-old lads have snogged loads of girls, but I haven't managed any. If I do this, then surely I will become more respected, and random people won't slap me around the head in the corridor every day. But it has to be a real girl. The back of my hand does not count.

My other goals include teaching my stupid parrot, Syd to say 'Joe is the man' and saving up enough money so me, Harry and Ad can finally go to *BUZZFEST*. Easy.

Lisa Hall   Lisa Hall   LISA

Lisa
Hall

Lisa Hall

Wednesday 4th January

I'm thinking when we go back, it wouldn't hurt to try Louise Bentley again. I had already made a bit of headway with her, before the spewing incident behind the waltzer. Perhaps she's ready to forgive and forget?

The problem is, she's not the girl I really like. Not properly. I have been obsessed with one girl since forever. **Lisa Hall.** Just writing her name fills my head with heavenly choirs singing. She is <u>PERFECT.</u>

But she always goes for bad boys and idiots, like now she's with that chimpanzee Gav James. Every time I see them together, it's like being hoofed in the stomach. I know I would be so much better for her.

I doubt she even knows I exist, though. In four years I think we've exchanged maybe ten words. The closest I get to her is in General Studies, where I just stare at the back of her head. I know that sounds creepy, but what else can I do? Whenever she talks to me, it's as if my tongue glues itself to the roof of my mouth. Once, she turned around and asked me the time, and I replied, 'September'. It was April.

I don't know what's wrong with me. I can think clearly, but somewhere between my brain and my mouth it all gets mixed up and I end up either rambling like an idiot, or saying something offensive.

The only way I've ever been able to express myself properly is through my drawings. I reckon I'll stick some of them in this blog in case I struggle with words on here as well. In fact, maybe I should give up talking altogether, and just carry my sketchpad around at all times, and communicate like that? No, I'd end up with wrist ache.

Now, this is going to sound stupid, but for some reason, I imagine that there's this control room in my brain, full of computers and dials and blinking lights, a bit like the bridge of the **USS ENTERPRISE**, and it's operated by these little men in lab coats.

The main man in the control room is this bloke I named Norman. He wears glasses and is going bald, but he's sensible and keeps me from doing anything crazy. But recently, another control room worker started to have more of a say. He's younger than Norman and has shaggy hair, and for some reason, is American. His name is Derek.

MY BRAIN

I was on holiday in Spain a couple of years ago. Mum and Dad were having a row in the room so I went down to the pool by myself. After a while, this girl came over and started chatting to me. She was dead fit and my heart was beating so fast I could feel it in my nose. IN MY NOSE!

She asked me where I was from. I immediately thought, *Tammerstone* because that's where I am actually from.

But then one of the control room blokes chipped in. *She probably hasn't heard of Tammerstone. You should mention someone famous from around there.*

But Norman disagreed: *I think a better approach would be to say where it's near to give it some context.*

Derek got up from his desk where he'd been napping. *Bullcrap! Tell her you're from somewhere different. Somewhere exciting. You're only going to see her on vacation, so what the hell does it matter?*

So from the initial *Tammerstone*, I somehow ended up saying, 'I'm from New York City! Yeah, New York, New York. That's what they call it. Great town. Never sleeps, apparently. I wouldn't know about that, I mean if I don't get my eight hours I can get a bit cranky! But can't we all, let's face it? We all need our beauty sleep. I'm not saying you do, by the way. You need very little. I bet you're a light sleeper. So, yeah, as I was saying, I'm from the Big Apple.'

'You don't sound like you're from New York,' said the girl. Norman threw his clipboard down and turned on Derek.

I can't believe you told him to lie! What do you expect him to do now?

Just ride it out, my man, said Derek. *Put on a New York accent and tell her you're in with the mob. Chicks dig dangerous guys. Bada bing!*

Don't listen to him, Joe, said Norman. *He's got you into enough trouble already. Just come clean.*

'Yeah, I'm actually from Tammerstone,' I said. 'Which is sort of near Birmingham. No Mafia there as far as I'm aware. Famous people from this region include William Shakespeare and Ozzy Osbourne. Both mad! "To be or not to be!" "Sharon!" What's all that about?'

She couldn't tell me what all that was about because she was too busy swimming away as fast as she could.

I should point out that this thing doesn't make me one of those schizo-whachamacallits. I'm aware that the control room men aren't real. At least, I think I am.

My mate Harry tells me that the key to stopping my big, fat mouth getting me into trouble is to get more self-confidence. Well, he does walk around with a pipe in his mouth like some kind of Victorian detective, so maybe he has a point. It's all down to how you carry yourself, and your ability to talk to girls without sounding like someone on day release.

I googled **'How to be more confident'**, but all I got were pages and pages about how to make me 'bigger in the trouser department'. I don't need that.

« Older posts

At least I don't think I do.

How can there not be a tape measure in this entire house?

Thursday 5th January

On the way round to Harry's I took a detour past Lisa Hall's house. This doesn't make me a stalker. It was only a mile out of my way.

As I went past I glanced up at her window and saw her. She looked at me and I don't know, but I think she smiled. I smiled back, then slipped on my bum in some ice.

Found an article about how to impress girls on the internet. It was on a website called Men's Domain. It looked useful so I bookmarked it. These are the tips it gave.

how to impress girls| Search

FIVE WAYS TO IMPRESS GIRLS...

1. Be well-groomed.
2. Have a good sense of humour.
3. Be a good listener.
4. Respect her ideas and opinions.
5. Be confident.

1. Be well-groomed

« I'd like to think I'm pretty well-groomed. Having said that, Mum did say I had hair like a bird's nest. My own mother. I sneaked into her bedroom and took a pot of Jim the plasterer's hair gel. I experimented in front of the mirror for a while and I think I've found a style that suits me.

2. Have a good sense of humour

« Check. Obviously.

3. Be a good listener

« I'm an excellent listener. It's talking that's the problem.

4. Respect her ideas and opinions

« I can do that. Unless it's her opinion that I stink. Or that in the battle of the *Star Trek* captains, Kirk is better than Picard.

5. Be confident

« Now, this is the biggy. Google is still no help on this subject so I'm going to have to think for myself. Maybe I need to embrace my inner Captain Picard and approach every situation as if I am the master. That's it. As of tomorrow, I am Picard. Only less bald.

Jim is staying over again tonight. He's been around loads lately. He bought me an MP3 player for Christmas and told me to listen to it at night. 'Turn it up nice and loud, son,' he said. What a weirdo. Fell asleep listening to (the best band in the world ever) Pink Floyd, and woke up in terror when it switched to Motörhead.

« Older posts

Friday 6th January

Mum asked me to take the Christmas decorations down while she was at work. Harry and Ad came over to help. Ad says he'll do anything for my mum. I don't know what he means by that but I'm sure it's not good.

The three of us have been friends since forever. In Year Seven Harry wanted us to do one of those blood brother things, but I opted out on hygiene grounds and Ad accidentally severed a major vein and had to be airlifted to hospital.

While we were up in the loft, Harry sprung one of his topics on us. **'OK, if you could have any super power, what would it be?'**

'Invisibility,' I said without even thinking about it.

'Invisibility, you old dog?' he chuckled. 'I see what you're thinking. Girls' changing rooms perhaps?'

'Yeah, maybe,' I said. 'But mainly it would mean me being able to walk around school without being given an EPIC WEDGIE by Gav.'

He nodded. 'How about you, Ad?'

'Definitely X-ray vision,' he said, twiddling his glasses.

Harry laughed. 'OK, now I know you must be thinking about the girls' changing rooms, old son.'

'Nah,' he said. 'I'd use it to win *Deal or No Deal*. Then I'd be so minted that I could, like, pay girls to strip for me or something.'

Me and Harry looked at each other.

'You know, old boy, in some ways you can be very wise,' said Harry.

Ad said thanks then fell head first into some fibreglass and had to go home with a prickly face.

Watched an old **STAR TREK** episode after. I don't care what Harry says, Picard is superior to Kirk in every way.

Saturday 7th January

Stood in the kitchen saying 'Joe is the man' to Syd for an hour. Nothing. Like talking to a brick wall with feathers. I asked Mum if he was still under warranty as he's clearly

« Older posts

defective. She said parrots don't have warranties. I am sceptical.

Jim gave me a fiver and told me to go out for a bit. Bought a comic and a can of Coke and sat in the park. Big fat Greeny from 10d walked past and asked if I was reading a girl's magazine.

'No, actually, it's *Batman*,' I said.

'Yeah, 'cause you love staring at muscly geezers in kinky outfits, don't you?' he said, and then waddled away cackling to himself like a hyena with learning difficulties.

One of these days I'm going to think of a brilliant way of getting my own back on him. Like tying him to a fence and dangling a Mars bar just out of his reach.

Went to Griddler's cafe with Harry and Ad to discuss fund-raising ideas for *BUZZFEST*. Ad suggested getting in touch with this Nigerian prince who'd been emailing him, trying to give him a quarter of a million US dollars. We tried everything to convince him it's a scam but he still doesn't get it.

Harry reckons we should stick with *OPERATION BLOOPER*; a scheme to fake a funny video and send it off to *You've Been Framed* for the £250 prize. I keep telling him it's too dangerous and that Ad has the scars to prove it, but he won't listen.

I had a double cheeseburger instead of my usual panini, because I could do with bulking up. Maybe if I get bigger,

I won't be such an easy target and I'll be more respected. Either that, or there'll be more of me to aim for.

The greasy burger made me feel properly sick, and Harry insisting we play WOULD YOU RATHER? straight afterwards didn't really help.

'Alright, alright,' he said. **'Would you rather . . . have a motorbike for a penis, or no penis at all?'**

'Depends.' Ad slurped down the rest of his chocolate shake. 'What type of bike?'

'What difference does it make?' said Harry.

'Big difference,' said Ad. 'If it's like a crappy moped thing then no, but a Harley-Davidson Fat Boy; I might consider it.'

'Interesting,' said Harry. 'So what would your choice be, Joe?'

'No penis at all,' I said. 'What good's a bike going to do down there?'

'Well, none, but at least it'll look bad ass,' said Ad.

'It wouldn't look bad ass, it'd look like the world's crappiest Transformer,' I said.

'True,' said Harry, puffing on his empty pipe. 'But how bad ass would you look without a pecker?'

'Well, Action Man doesn't have one and he's pretty tough,' I said.

I was considering Ad's so-wrong-I-don't-even-want-to-write-it-down WOULD YOU RATHER? topic when I saw someone familiar walk in. It took a few seconds to register,

« Older posts

but then I remembered. It was Kyra Critchley, my old babysitter. I hadn't seen her in years. She looked amazing. I consulted the control room about my next move.

Stay where you are, Joe, said Norman. *Just give her a friendly nod.*

A friendly nod? said Derek. *Right, the babes love friendly nodding. 'Oh yeah, my date with Joe was great, we just sat there and nodded at each other all night. Man, my neck is so sore from all that NODDING we were doing.' Gimme a break. Get over there and talk to that fox, Joe. You're supposed to be confident, remember? Like Picard?*

That settled it. I got up and strutted over there as confidently as I could.

'H-hi, Kyra, remember me?'

She turned and squinted at me.

'Joe Cowley?' she said.

'That's me!' I said. 'The very same! All grown-up, like a, um, big . . . man thing. I know, I've changed quite a bit.'

'I should hope you have,' she said. 'I mean, you're pretty old to still wee yourself with fright at the *Teletubbies.*'

'Well Kyra, it was nice catching up,' I said, before scurrying back to my seat and hoping Harry and Ad hadn't heard.

They stared at me for a few seconds, then shouted, **'EH OH!'**

Damn.

Sunday 8th January

I hate Sundays, mostly because it's the last day before going back to crappy school, but also because it's the day of my weekly court-appointed visit with Dad.

His flat is depressing, everything is expensive and shiny and I'm pretty sure Svetlana hates me. What a cheek. She split up my family. She should be kissing my arse. Not literally.

Dad's changed since he moved in with her, too. For one thing, he's suddenly got more hair and his teeth are whiter. And he's started listening to rap. Two words. **Trag. Ic.** I'm glad he didn't see this picture I sketched of him while he was scrolling through his new iPod.

DAD

'Hey dude,' he said to me. 'Have you heard Titchy Stryder's latest joint? It is off the hook. Wicked fresh.'

'Um, no.'

'Ah, you're just not down with the sounds of today like I am,' he said. 'Oh actually, it's not Titchy Stryder, it's Titchy Temper. It's still well banging, though. Sorted. Proper raving. You chief.'

I stared at him until it got awkward. Then he offered me a drink.

'I'll have what Svetlana's drinking,' I said.

'This is vodka.' She peered at me sideways. 'You are not old enough to drink it.'

'That may be true,' I said. 'But I'm not entirely convinced you are, either.'

'Ah, come on, son, don't be like that with Svet,' said Dad. 'She'll be your stepmum one day.'

Svetlana pulled a face like someone had just shoved their collection of fresh turds under her nose. Dad didn't see this because he was in the kitchen making me a drink with a cocktail umbrella in it. That made me laugh because it reminded me of the time Ad shoved one of them up his nose for a bet and had to go to A & E when it got stuck. The nurse wouldn't remove it though because the umbrella was open and she was too superstitious.

They've got a new dog too; a little Chihuahua thing called Hercules. You might as well just have a rat running around the place. I think Svetlana's trained it to hate me as well, because it keeps attacking my shoelaces and giving me evils. Pointy-eared little git.

The worst of it was when he sat right in front of me and started licking his nuts as if they were a meaty treat.

'Can't you make him stop that?' I said. 'It's disgusting.'

'Ah, you're only jealous,' said Dad.

'Why would I be jealous? I don't want to lick the dog's nuts.'

Svetlana tutted.

'He'd better make the most of them while he's still got them, anyway,' said Dad. 'He's having the old snipola soon.'

'Why?' I crossed my legs.

'Well, Svet likes to take him out in her handbag, and she went in there looking for her lipstick, and let's just say when a dog gets excited, it's an easy mistake to make.'

I nearly spat out my drink. Svetlana scowled at me.

Other than that, the entire day was miserable. Every time I'm there it reminds me of the whole divorce thing: me having to turn the TV up extra loud to drown out the rows, then Dad leaving and Mum crying all the time.

Dad kept asking about Jim, and how he treats Mum and me. I was tempted to say that he whips me and makes me eat dog food, but I decided against it. Kind of wish I had now. Might have made the day more interesting.

Dad made tofu casserole for dinner. It was rank. Dog food would have been tastier.

Monday 9th January

First day of school. First day in the life of Joe 2.0. It's going to be hard, but I'm ready.

See, the thing about Woodlet High is that it's like a jungle. To survive, you have to be tough, or at least able to pretend you are. The foodchain is like this:

PREDATORS

People like Gav James, the love of my life **Lisa Hall** and her friends Ellie and Chloe, as well as chumps like Pete Cotterill, who goes around singing vomit-inducing love songs all the time. They are top of the pile and no one messes with them. The best you can hope for is that they ignore you. There is also a sub-section within this group who are only there because they are useful to the real predators. This is people like Jordan Foster and the Blenkinsop twins, Brains and Bruiser, who are unbelievably thick, but could probably rip you in half without even thinking about it.

PARASITES

This is people like Greeny, who are so _desperate to be predators_ that they will do anything to get in their good books. I'm not saying he literally lives in Gav's digestive tract but I bet he would if he could.

MONKEYS

Your average, ordinary person. They might get a bit of attention due to their cuteness, or ability for _throwing their poo_ around, but they will generally go by unnoticed.

THE FOODCHAIN

HERBIVORES

This is the category I'm in, along with Harry and Ad. As much as we try to hide in the undergrowth, we are _prime targets_ for predators, who will hunt us down again and again and feast on our entrails. Sometimes they will toy with us, and make us think we have a chance of escape, before dealing the lethal blow. Parasites will try and bring us down to impress the predators, but it rarely works.

CRITTERS

These are the weirdest jungle inhabitants. People like Jason Downey, who keeps getting excluded for _drawing swastikas_ on his face. They don't get as much trouble from predators as the herbivores because of the slight possibility that they may return to school one day with an Uzi. This is where the jungle metaphor falls down.

I got up early to go through my strategy. Harry's big on that kind of thing. I remember when he developed a master plan to sneak us into an 18 film. **Obviously**, it didn't work and he ended up sneaking us into a *My Little Pony* movie by mistake. Ad wouldn't leave though.

'It's gonna get raunchy any minute now, lads,' he kept saying.

There's no way I can tell Harry about my goals, though. He'll just laugh at me and say he's snogged loads of girls, when he quite clearly hasn't. I mean, for one thing, it'd require him to take that stupid pipe out of his mouth.

After Mum left for work I went into the bathroom with Jim's gel and worked on my do. I don't know why but it didn't come off quite as well as it did the other day. It kind of stood up on top of my head. I think I might have used too much. It didn't look great but as I squinted at myself in the mirror, I did kind of look like a confident person. Kind of.

When Harry saw me, he laughed so much he nearly inhaled his pipe. But that's not the worst: as soon as I walked into school, Gav James shouted **'Grease boy!'** at me and slapped his hand down on top of my head, obliterating my quiff and making me look less like a confident guy with a cool hairdo and more like a nerd who's been cacked on by a seagull.

I was about to say something, but then the Blenkinsops looked at me like they wanted to javelin me out of the window.

Not to be put off, I saw Louise Bentley sitting alone at lunchtime and went over. Time to activate phase one. I had a word with the control room and told them to keep quiet and leave it to me and my prepared lines. Derek didn't look pleased.

'Hi Louise.' My heart jackhammered against my chest.

'You're not coming to puke on me again are you?' she said.

I laughed a bit too loud. 'No, Louise, I'm not,' I said. 'My regurgitating days are behind me.'

'Good,' she said. 'Because you ruined my best jacket.'

'I was just wondering if you wanted to, you know, do something again?' I said.

She looked at me like I'd suggested going bungee jumping without a bungee.

'After what happened last time? Are you mental?'

'Perhaps,' I said. 'But, but maybe I just want another chance. It's not my fault I suffer from waltzer-related motion sickness. It's a medical condition! If you come out with me again, we'll go somewhere that couldn't possibly happen. A waltzer-free zone.'

She smiled a little bit. Must have been my new confidence.

'Where would we go?' said Louise.

'I don't know,' I said. 'Maybe we could go to the cinema and grab something to eat afterwards?'

'And you promise not to throw up on me?' she said with a smile.

It was all going so well.

'Well, there'll be no waltzers, so yes, I promise,' I said. 'But then, you never really know what made me vomit on that particular night. It may have been the dodgy hot dog I ate, or all that candyfloss. Who knows, it may have been the idea of kissing you for the first time.'

The slap really stung my face and before I could gather my thoughts, she was storming away.

'LOUISE,' I yelled after her, 'I didn't mean it like that! I meant I was nervous! In a good way! Louise!'

Why do I say these things? What is wrong with me?

Tuesday 10th January

PE today. Mr Boocock made us roll in the mud 'to get us used to it'. When I pointed out that he was breaching my human rights, he made me do ten laps. Me and my big mouth.

Still no further in my quest for a snog. Gav saw me reading a book at break time and called me a 'book turd'. Witty.

« Older posts

Wednesday 11th January

Jim wants to know what happened to his gel. I'm saying nothing. He's been off with me ever since I pointed out that ridiculous inaccurate apostrophe on his new business cards. (Wall's? I mean, really?)

At school, Harry asked me if I knew anyone that needed DJs in the near future. He says he's trying to get the SOUND EXPERIENCE back up and running.

'Harry, I wouldn't inflict yours and Ad's mobile disco on my worst enemy,' I said. 'Don't you remember the Year Seven Christmas party?'

'Of course I remember it, old boy,' he said. 'It's not our fault if the little tykes failed to appreciate the magnificence of Swedish grindcore music.'

'Eight of them had to go to hospital with perforated eardrums,' I said. 'It was so loud it broke Mr Dalton's glasses.'

'Yes, so as I say, soldier, let me know if you hear anything,' he said.

Not cocking likely.

Read a few more articles on **Men's Domain** It says a good way to meet girls is to go on a blind date. My only fear is she'd get there, take one look at me and wish she was blind.

I suppose another version of this would be internet dating, but at least with that you can see a picture of them first. I might give it a go.

Syd is still mute. Useless bird.

Thursday 12th January

Harry and Ad called for me this morning and insisted on walking through the park to school.

'I'm afraid you have been immortalized again, old son,' said Harry, pointing at a bench with his pipe.

I didn't have to get close to see it. The words 'JOE COWLEE IZ A BUMLORD' stood out in big, black letters. It wouldn't take Sherlock Holmes to figure out who did it either, because on the seat of the bench, in exactly the same handwriting, it said 'GAV JAMES WOZ ERE LUVIN DA LADYS'.

Hmm, I wonder if Lisa knows about this.

'What am I going to do?' I said. 'I can't have the whole town thinking I'm a bumlord. What is a bumlord anyway?'

'Fear not, old boy, I've got you covered,' said Harry. He took a marker pen out of his pocket and carefully crossed

out the word **'BUM'** and replaced it with **'TIME'**.

'See, now you're like Dr Who,' he said. 'Now all I have to do is add a **"D"** to **"LADYS"** and we're ship-shape'.

'LADDYS?' I said. 'A bit subtle for Gav, isn't it?'

'You're right, old bean,' said Harry, and we walked away a few seconds later, happy in the knowledge that anyone who sits on that bench from now on will know that Gav had already been there, **'LUVIN DA THAI LADYBOYS'**.

Even so, I'm still steaming with him. What gives him the right to do things like that? One day I will have my revenge. God knows how, but I will.

I didn't have time to think about him too much though because we ran into Mad Morris by the bins. I hate it when he gets too close because he's got stuff in his beard and I can't make out what it is, but I bet it's disgusting.

'REPENT!' he yelled. **'FOR THE RETURN OF CHRIST IS UPON US!'**

'Sequels are rarely as good as the originals, old son,' said Harry.

'Yeah, we have to be off now, Morris,' I said.

'SILENCE, EVILDOER!' he screamed. 'You have the number of the beast!'

'Ah wicked, can I have it so I can drop her a text?' said Ad.

We walked by the creepy old bunker on the edge of the park. There's always been rumours about that place being haunted by the ghosts of soldiers, but really, it's a load of

« Older posts

old bullcack. I mean, if you were a ghost and could go any-where, would you hang around in a park with a load of tramps and thugs?

Harry says the bunkers were built in the Second World War to house anti-aircraft weaponry. He knows everything about the war. If he went on Mastermind, it would be his specialist subject. Mine would be **STAR TREK,** and Ad's would be . . . I mean come on, what would Ad be doing on Mastermind in the first place?

Got to sit next to _Lisa Hall_ in English today. I couldn't even look at her, partly because I was so nervous, and partly because I thought Gav might pound my face in if I did. My best pen (Captain Picard bobblehead topper) ran out and she gave me her spare!

'Th-thanks,' I said. My eye started twitching.

'That's all right,' she said, and smiled.
SMILED!

I went to return it to her at the end but she told me I could keep it. Then she smiled at me again! I almost floated to my next lesson, where Gav himself was waiting to give me a brutal wedgie.

I have no idea what she sees in him.

Friday 13th January

I'm feeling pretty cocky right now because I have avoided the curse of Friday the thirteenth. I'll never forget that last one, when we were on a field trip to the zoo and a chimp torpedoed his poo at me.

Anyway, forget that, because Lisa smiled at me again (I think) when I told her that her pen's still working. Little does she know I keep it in a small box in my top drawer at home.

Then Gav came over and put his arm around her. I swear I saw her roll her eyes a little, but I couldn't be too sure because he dragged her away while the Blenkinsops rolled me up and stuffed me under a chair. I'd say that all considered, makes the day pretty even, rather than unlucky.

Got home and logged onto a site called **Teenmeet**, which apparently helps you find friends. I made sure to specify 'girls only'. I had to fill in this questionnaire to get me started.

« Older posts

About you:

Name:	Joe Cowley
Age:	14
Location:	Tammerstone, Warwickshire
Interests:	Star Trek, books, music, parrot husbandry
Favourite TV Show:	Duh! Star Trek
Favourite film:	Star Trek: Generations
Favourite music artist:	Pink Floyd
Favourite colour:	I don't know. Burgundy?
Biggest ambition:	To snog a girl before I die
Biggest phobia:	None. Definitely not the Teletubbies
Pet hate:	Idiots called Gav	

I've got to leave it now while they find me some matches. I don't want to go downstairs because Mum and Jim are down there, holding hands and calling each other cutesy names and doing other stuff that makes me be a little bit sick in my mouth. The saga of the missing gel is still ongoing.

11.30 p.m.

Checked **Teenmeet** and somehow dropped the laptop on my foot.

THE CURSE OF FRIDAY THE
THIRTEENTH STRIKES AGAIN!

Saturday 14th January

Checked the *BUZZFEST* fund in the jar on top of the fridge. So far I have £27, which when added to Harry and Ad's savings gives us the grand total of £59.93. One weekend ticket is £180. At this rate the first Buzzfest we'll be able to go to will be Buzzfest 2035, where we'll eat overpriced burgers in pill form and sleep in hovertents.

8 p.m.

Jim got his new business cards out at dinner.

'How about this, Mr Smartypants,' he said. 'I've had some new cards printed with that apostrophe you were moaning about taken out.'

'Yes you have,' I said, inspecting the card. 'And although I appreciate that N is right next to J on the keyboard, I don't think you really meant to say "no nob too small" on here. Or did you?'

Honestly, the foul-mouthed outburst he let fly after that would have made a sailor blush.

10.15 p.m.

Looked at *Lisa Hall's* Facebook profile. I don't have my own account so I couldn't see it all, most annoyingly a photo album named 'holiday pics'. I considered setting my profile back up again so I could see, but then I remembered the incident that drove me off it in the first place: Greeny

AWESOME PRODUCTIONS presents:
BUZZFEST
2035
TATE OF THE ART
OVER TENTS!
BURGER PILLS!
SAT-SUNDAY. 8 AM - WHENEV'R.

setting up a fake account and sending me a link to what I thought was a trailer for the new *Batman* film but what turned out to be a website for nudist pensioners.

Monday 16th January
PANIC STATIONS!

Jim found his missing gel in my room this morning.

'What I don't get is that you've clearly not been using it on your hair,' he said, eyeballing my early morning head thatch.

You've been caught, Joe, said Norman. *It's only fair that you apologize. I mean, how would you like it if someone took something of yours?*

Derek nearly choked on his coffee. *Are you kidding me? You don't have ANYTHING to apologize for. He's just ragged on your hair, man. Plus, oh my God, he's dating your MOM. Hello? You're the man of the house, Joey boy. Show him who's boss.*

'Well, Jim,' I said. 'From now on, why don't you keep your hair gel in your house, where you live?'

Mum went **BALLISTIC** at me for that, but come on, I've got a point. I mean, Jim's OK really, but he's here way too much. Plus, there's something about his face I just don't like. He reminds me of someone.

The two of them have been acting weird lately as well: talking quietly and shutting up whenever I enter the room. I know they're talking about me. Maybe they're thinking of ditching me?

Looked into acquiring a bugging device off the internet. It would take up too much of the Buzzfest fund, so will concentrate on developing ninja-like stealth instead.

8.00 p.m.

I need ninja stealth fast. Mum made me go down the shop to get some eggs and milk, and I cut through the park on the way home.

Bad idea. As I walked around the corner, I saw Gav and the Blenkinsops hanging around by the bench. I tried to sneak away, but they must have heard my carrier bag rustling.

'Hey, pukeboy,' Gav called after me. 'Where you going?'

'Oh, nowhere,' I said. 'Just going for a walk. With my bag. Just walking my bag.'

'Come here.'

I sighed. The control room men stood up and watched. What now?

'I'd rather not if it's all the same to you,' I said.

'Yeah, well it ain't all the same to me,' said Gav. 'So come here, I want to talk to you.'

'If you don't we'll come and get you, yeah?' said one of the twins.

I turned around slowly and walked over to them. I scanned the park for a responsible adult. The closest thing was Mad Morris, who was busy having an argument with a dog poo bin.

'So,' I said, swaying slightly from side to side. 'What's happening?'

'What's happening?' said Gav. 'This is what's happening.'

He grabbed me by the arm. I squirmed, but one of the twins grabbed my other arm.

'Please!' I squeaked. 'I-I've got eggs!'

They laughed and jerked me over to the bench.

'So what's this, man?' said Gav. 'You saying I love thigh ladyboys?'

'That wasn't me!' I said. 'And it's pronounced _Thai_.'

'He's saying you're a bummer, Gav,' said the twin holding my arm.

'Yeah, he's mugging you off, man,' said the other.

'No!' My eye started to twitch. 'I've never mugged anyone, off or on. Now please, let me go.'

'I should mess you up for this,' said Gav. I felt his smoky breath on my cheek.

'But I didn't do it!' I said. 'And anyway, you wrote stuff about me being, you know, a "Bumlord". Does that mean gay? And anyway, who cares if I am? Because this is the twenty-first century and you are totally committing a hate crime.'

« Older posts

His face screwed up like a balloon knot. But I just couldn't stop.

'Similarly, if you enjoy the company of ladyboys, or, to give them their correct term, transgendered people, then that's fine. Each to their own, that's what I say. And let's face it, you've got the best of both worlds haven't you? Yeah, if you haven't already, you should look definitely into it.'

I got home with eggs splattered on my back, in my hair and down my pants. When Mum saw me she nearly had a coronary.

'What the hell happened?' she said.

I remembered the last thing Gav said to me before I got away:

'This never happened. If you tell anyone, we'll get you, you know what I'm saying?'

'Sorry, Mum,' I said. 'I fell over.'

'Oh, Joe,' she said. 'Can't you even do a simple thing like go to the shops anymore?'

'Apparently not,' I said.

10.30 p.m.

I'm lying on my bed now. I've showered all the egg residue off. I'm trying to relax. Looking at the glow-in-the-dark stars on my ceiling usually works. I remember Dad putting them up there when I was little.

Everything is quiet. Everything is neat. My books, CDs,

and DVDs are alphabetized. Can't relax if they're not. My 'Most Merits' trophies from Years Seven, Eight, and Nine have been polished, too. This is my room. The only place I can be truly safe.

I can feel sleep coming so I think I'll stop now.

Tuesday 17th January

Ad brought balloons to school today. He inflated one and then sucked the air back out. I tried to explain that the balloons need to be filled with helium to give you a squeaky voice, but he didn't get it.

I asked Harry how I could develop ninja-like stealth. He said, 'Just be quiet at all times.' I said, 'Is that it?' He said, 'Shhhh.'

I had Biology while Ad and Harry had Chemistry. Ad was *finally* allowed to do practical again after the eyebrows incident. I can't remember learning much biology, but then I was slightly distracted by the bits of rubber Gav kept flicking at me. I turned around to confront him, but I spun too quickly and fell off my stool, landing face first on a work bench.

In other news, Ad is once again banned from Chemistry practical after trying to fill his balloons with butane gas. I would have laughed at this but my lips were too swollen. Even if a girl begged me for a kiss, I couldn't rise to the occasion.

« Older posts

7 p.m.

Mum and Jim stopped talking when I walked in again today.
Need to work on my stealth.

Wednesday 18th January

Arrived at school to find a picture of me stuck to the form-
room door. I'd been Photoshopped to look like the girl from
that old film *The Exorcist*, puking green stuff everywhere.

   Greeny hid around the corner laughing so hard his moobs
jiggled. He's always doing these Photoshop things, the cretin.
His dad's apparently a special-effects man for a low-budget
horror film company, so he knows how to do all that crap.
   'So this was you, was it?' I said.
   'I'm saying nothing,' he said.

'Who told you to make this?' I said.

'That's private and confluential,' he said, then gave Gav and the Blenkinsops a thumbs up.

They probably used the money they nicked off me to pay for it. It's like the circle of life, only soul-shatteringly depressing.

'You'd do anything for money, wouldn't you?' I said. 'How about if I paid you to jump off the roof? Would you do that too?'

Greeny laughed before asking how much.

I collected all my puking posters, then when I was home I shredded them and put them in Syd's cage. He's still as talkative as your average turnip.

8 p.m.

Teenmeet emailed me with my matches. I'm a bit disappointed, to be honest. How can there only be three girls in the whole area who like *STAR TREK?* Out of the three, I picked two. The one I left out was called Crysstal DuBois xxx. Probably a fifty-year-old bloke. I've messaged the other two: Natalie Tuft and Sally Harper. Now to play the waiting game.

10 p.m.

Sally Harper messaged me to say she'd rather date a pig. I'm going to think of something really witty to send back.

11.30 p.m.

I'm stuck.

12.30 a.m.

OK, how about, 'Yeah, well why don't you go and look in a mirror or something?'

1.30 a.m.

You know what? I think I'll maintain a dignified silence.

2.00 a.m.

I wonder why Natalie Tuft hasn't replied yet.

Thursday 19th January

Harry called after school, trying to get me to take part in *OPERATION BLOOPER*. I told him no. I've been wary of it since the last attempt when Ad had to be taken to A & E. I told them before they started: pogo sticks and trampolines are a deadly combination.

As I lay in bed, the battery on my MP3 player ran out and I heard Mum and Jim talking outside my room.

'How will we tell him?' said Jim.

'I don't know,' said Mum. 'He's such a sensitive boy, he's bound to overreact.'

What's she on about? I never overreact.

Friday 20th January

Aaaaaaaaargh! That's all I can say at the moment. I'll come back to this later when I can express myself better.

12.30 a.m.

Aaaaaaaargh! No, still not ready.

1.15 a.m.

OK, I'll try it now. Today has been the worst day of my life. Aaaaaaaargh! No, I still can't do it.

3 a.m.

Right, it's 3 a.m. and I'm sitting in the airing cupboard writing this on my phone. I have to get today's events down because if I don't, the truth may never be heard because I will have become a shambling tramp who screams at traffic.

Gav and the Blenkinsops were following me down the corridor at lunch. I tried to ignore them, but they were throwing Skittles and they kept catching me on the backs of my ears. It really stung. Everyone thought this was the wittiest thing ever and started following Gav as if he were some kind of mentally challenged Pied Piper.

Ignore him, Joe. Don't lower yourself, said Norman.

I tried, but then Derek threw his coffee mug at the wall and kicked his chair over.

God dammit. Do you want him to be a victim all his life?

« Older posts

It's time to man up, Joey boy! Look 'em in the eye and ask 'em what their freakin' problem is!

Before I knew what I was doing, I found myself spinning around and confronting them.

'Hey!' I said. 'Why won't you just leave me alone? What do you want from me, anyway?'

I was trying to sound tough, but my fat lip from my desk faceplant the other day made me go all lispy and everyone laughed.

'I want to know,' said Gav, 'if you like geezers.'

The corridor fell silent. The crowd seemed to lean in closer, all wanting to know how I was going to deal with it.

Gav stepped closer and smirked out of the side of his big, stupid face. I scopped the corridor for an escape and saw none. Trapped.

'All right, if it's so important to you, it's true,' I said, my mouth moving but my brain having no idea what it was saying. 'I'm gay! I love man-love! I love willies! Happy now?'

Everyone stared at me. Then they started laughing.

Gav opened another bag of sweets. Fresh ammo. My eye twitched like a fly in a glass of lemonade. What could I do? My first attempt to get rid of him had been an epic failure. I knew it needed an extra push. Then it came to me. Or rather Derek brought it to me. A stone-cold classic, fresh from the database of killer comebacks. A zinger so devastating, people would talk about it for years to come.

They would carry me out of that stinking school on their shoulders and I would rule them like a king. Then I'd show them. I'd show all of them. I took a deep breath.

'I must be gay,' I said. 'Because I shagged your dad!'

I grinned and waited for the adoration of the crowd. Nothing. No reaction. No one cheered, no one laughed and no one carried me out on their shoulders. Just a heavy silence. Some people looked at the floor, others bit their bottom lips. I wouldn't have been surprised if some tumbleweed had blown past. Gav's eyes looked like they were going to pop out of his head. Somewhere in the distance a train sped by. I wished I was on it.

After what felt like a thousand years, a laugh burst out somewhere on the other side of the crowd. Then someone else joined in. Then someone else. Soon, everyone was laughing. Some were even crying. Derek had finally come up with the goods. I was about to order them to bow to their new king when Gav grabbed me by the neck and threw me up a locker.

'You think that's funny?' he said, covering my face in spit. 'Well, let me tell you something, freak, no one talks crap about my family and gets away with it.'

I squirmed in his grasp but I was stuck. The Blenkinsops stood behind him. He gripped my collar with one hand and drew the other back. I thought he was going to pulverize my face with his sovereign-ringed fist until he opened a locker next to me.

'Time to go away, freak,' he said as he pushed me towards it.

I cried out for help, but the same crowd that laughed at my comeback were now desperate to see me shut in a locker. He grabbed the back of my head and tried to force me inside. I gripped the side so tight, I swear I left imprints in the metal. If he shut me in there I'd never get out. They'd discover my skeleton years later and probably just huff it into a skip or something.

'Push him in! Push him in! Push him in!'

My grasp started to weaken, when through the shouting and laughing and chanting I heard a voice. A girl's voice.

'Gav!' it said. 'What the hell are you doing?'

He took his hands off me and turned around. I did too, and saw Lisa standing there. She looks gorgeous when she's angry. My knees went weak, although that may have had more to do with the attempted locker-stuffing.

'What's up?' said Gav.

'I want you to know if it's right what I'm hearing,' said Lisa.

'About what?'

'About you giving Leah Burton a lovebite last night.'

Gav loosened his grip. I thought about making a run for it.

'Nah, man, course it ain't,' he said.

'Don't lie to me, Gav,' said Lisa.

'Hey, come on, babe,' he said. 'How about we talk about this somewhere private?'

'Don't babe me, you pig,' she said. 'I hate you.'

He laughed. 'Well, if that's how you're gonna be, you can do one, innit?'

She cried out in frustration and stormed off. For a millisecond, I was overjoyed, then terrified as to what Gav would do to me. He stared after her. No-one knew where to look. I tried to move away, but he got me in a death grip.

'See what you did?' he said.

'What I did?' I said. 'What did I do?'

'You know . . . '

I couldn't speak.

'I'm not going to get you here,' he said. 'But you are going to meet me round the back of the D&T rooms after school and we're going to have a little chat, yeah?'

'Chat?' I said. 'But surely we can chat here, where there's plenty of witnesses?'

'Be there,' he said, and walked away.

I must have seemed distracted at lunch. I'd barely touched my smiley-face potato waffles.

'Cripes, old son, you're shaking,' said Harry. 'What

happened? Did you see something that reminded you of Tinky Winky?'

I shook my head and told them what happened.

'You've got to fight Gav James?' said Harry. 'The Gav James?

'Yep,' I said. 'What can I do? He'll kill me. Literally kill me to death.'

'This is quite the quandary, old boy, quite the quandary,' said Harry, chewing on his pipe.

'Why don't you just tell a teacher?' said Ad.

'Don't be stupid, Ad,' said Harry. 'If Joe tells, Gav will come down on him harder, and if he can't, he'll send one of his goons to do it for him. He's like the Mafia.'

I nodded. Gav told me as much after the egging.

'If we are to get you out of this, we'll need a brilliant strategy,' said Harry. 'But what? What can we accomplish in such a short time?' He stroked his chin.

Hot fingers of panic gripped my throat. If Harry couldn't figure it out, no one could.

'I've got it,' he said, sitting up. 'Ad, do you still have those balloons in your bag?'

'Yeah, loads,' said Ad. 'Why, are we going to make water bombs?'

'Not exactly, old boy,' said Harry. He pulled some coins out of his pocket. 'Go and buy as many drinks as you can, and drink them fast.'

'Why?' said Ad.

'Because today, soldier, you are making our ammunition.' He sat back with his pipe.

'I don't get it, Harry,' said Ad.

'Just do it,' he said.

I couldn't concentrate in the first lesson after lunch. Harry's idea circled around my head. Simple but brilliant. Would it work, though? What if it went wrong?

I thought about Lisa. Why has she stepped in? She could just as easily have got him another time. Maybe what tipped her over the edge was finding him picking on me? I told myself off for even thinking that someone like Lisa would care about me.

But hang on a minute. What about the pen? What about when I offered to give it her back and she told me to keep it? What about when I saw her and I was like 'Yeah, the pen's great!' And she was all like, 'Good!' Maybe it wasn't such a crazy idea. Maybe she was tired of mouth-breathers like Gav and wanted a sophisticated young gentleman?

Go for it, said Derek. *You've been listening to these losers for too long.*

I pulled out my knackered *Star Trek* pen and rubbed Picard's bald head for good luck. He looked back at me as if to say **'MAKE IT SO'**.

« Older posts

As soon as the bell rang, I launched myself out of my chair and ran to the General Studies room. The perfect situation. Gav won't be there because he's excluded from General Studies for stealing sex education DVDs and selling them to Year Sevens.

When I got there, Lisa was already outside. She was alone, looking at the floor with her arms folded. I leaned against the opposite wall. Now is the time. No excuses.

'H-h,' was all I could manage before my voice gave out. I tried to make it seem like I was clearing my throat, but then I really did start coughing and stood there hacking my lungs out until my eyes watered. Why does this kind of thing never happen to James Bond? I shook my head and tried again.

'Hi Lisa,' I said.

She looked up and pushed her hair out of her face. I love her hair. It's the colour of sunshine.

'What do you want?' she said.

'I just wanted to say thanks,' I said. 'So this is me saying it: thanks.' *OK, now stop talking.* 'Thank you kindly.' *That's enough.* '*Merci beaucoup.*' *Oh sweet Jesus.*

She looked at me blankly. 'What for?'

What for? Surely she couldn't stop that many kids from being stuffed into lockers by Gav?

'For, you know?' I said, wishing my eye would stop twitching. 'Stopping Gav from . . . putting me in a locker.'

'Oh,' she said, as if it was nothing. 'Don't worry about it.

I'd been getting sick of him for a long time. I realized I need to start spending more time with people who actually get me, do you know what I mean?'

I nodded like an idiot while Derek went into overdrive.

This is it, your way in. She's sending you signals. The smile, the pen, the locker, and now saying she wants to be with people who get her. You definitely get her, man. It's all coming together like a jigsaw puzzle. Not like the boring ones you do with your dad and Svetlana, but like a . . . a sexy jigsaw puzzle. Anyway, enough about jigsaws, the girl of your dreams is offering it to you on a silver platter and now all you have to do is reel her in.

Wait a minute, said Norman. *Is this a fishing metaphor or a puzzle metaphor?*

Shut up, Norman!

There was a moment of doubt when I remembered Gav, but I thought if he was going to kill me later anyway, I might as well get my money's worth.

'So,' I said, trying to stop my voice from drifting into 'castrated chipmunk' range, 'you're single now then?'

'Well, yeah.' She twirled a strand of her hair around her finger.

'So, you know,' I said, only able to look at a place on the wall above her head. 'Would you like to—' I stopped and pulled a face which in my mind meant 'go out with me'.

'Would I like to what?'

« Older posts

I sighed and blinked hard. Just talking to her took up all my energy, but having to actually finish my sentences was an eventuality I hadn't prepared for.

'Would . . . you . . . like . . . to . . . do . . . something . . . some . . . time?' I left long gaps between each word and when I finally dragged the last one out of my screaming brain, I collapsed against the wall, exhausted.

'With you?' she said.

'Well,' I said, desperately trying to think of someone else I could have been asking for, 'yes. Me.'

'I wouldn't have thought so,' she said.

What about the signs? The smile, the pen, the locker, dumping Gav? What about the jigsaw? It was at that moment I realized it wasn't a jigsaw. It wasn't even Bucka-roo. It was a Jenga tower with the last vital piece removed. It was a pile of Jenga blocks.

'Oh right,' I said, suddenly unable to think about anything but Jenga.

'I'm just, like, not ready for another relationship right now,' she said. 'And I don't know, maybe you're not my type. Sorry.'

'No, no, it's fine,' I said. 'Fine-a-rooni.'

I tried to laugh but what came out sounded more like a fat bloke sitting on an accordion.

She looked at me as if I were a tramp in a tinfoil helmet and walked away, pretending to answer her phone.

I wondered if I could blame this latest humiliation on the table faceplant on Tuesday. Some kind of brain trauma. I mean, what has happened to me? Before now, I wouldn't have dreamed of asking a girl like Lisa out. I would blame Derek but he's not even real.

I looked up and saw Greeny standing at the end of the corridor holding his phone.

'What are you doing?' I said.

He grinned at me like a D-grade Cheshire cat. 'Just watching a video.'

'Oh yeah?' I said. 'What video?'

'Nothing you'd be interested in: it's got girls in it.'

I sighed. 'You going to call me a bender now aren't you?'

'Nah,' he said as he walked away.

About five seconds later, my phone buzzed in my pocket. Text from unknown number.

'Where did you get my number?' I yelled at Greeny, who by now was leaning on the reprographics hatch and laughing.

« Older posts

'Off the toilet wall,' he said. 'It says, "If you want gay love, call Joe on this number."'

'And you wrote it down?' I said.

'Er, yeah?' he said, his stupid grin fading.

'Well,' I said. 'I think we've learned a little bit about who's a "bender" and who isn't, haven't we?'

His mouth fell open. I thought shutting him up would have made me feel better, but arguing with Greeny is like kickboxing a five year old: you'll win, but you won't feel good about yourself.

Then he said something really quick that I couldn't catch.

'What?' I said.

'Ahhhhhhh!' He pointed at me victoriously. 'Bender.'

I facepalmed. I'd just fallen for the 'onlybenderssaywhat' trick. Not only the oldest trick in the book, it's so old, it predates the book. It's probably painted on the inside of a cave somewhere.

Why is he so obsessed with me being gay, anyway? It's weird. I mean the bloke who plays Sulu in **STAR TREK** is gay and he's twice the man Greeny is. Not size-wise.

General Studies was horrible. Lisa wouldn't even make eye contact with me, and I kept thinking about what Gav would do to me behind the D & T rooms if Harry's plan didn't work. It had to work. He's a military genius. I noticed Ad wasn't in the lesson. He must have been hiding in the toilet, making our stockpile.

I met Harry and Ad at what Harry called the rendezvous point. Harry had his best pipe out and was pacing around clutching a carrier bag.

'Have you got the ammo?' I said.

Harry smiled. 'Plenty,' he said. 'Ad was weeing like a stallion, weren't you, old boy?'

Inside the bag a healthy collection of piss balloons jiggled like a disgusting jelly.

'Brilliant,' I said.

'I have formulated a plan of action,' said Harry. 'In t-minus two minutes, Private Ad and myself shall make our way onto the roof of that disused mobile classroom with our weapons cache. When the targets arrive, we shall commence bombardment from behind that vent. When said targets have been neutralized, we will retreat through the gap in the fence to a safe position. Any questions, soldier?'

'Can't I come with you?' My eye started twitching again.

'Negative,' said Harry. 'You must remain here to act as bait. It's the classic decoy tactic, as utilized by Allied Forces in Operation Fortitude, 1944.'

'But,' I said, 'what if I get wee on me?'

'That's a risk I'm willing to take, Private Cowley,' he said. 'But don't worry, we are excellent marksmen.'

I looked at Ad, who was staring at the balloon in his hand and squeezing it. Harry noticed too and took it off him.

« Older posts

'I hope you appreciate the trouble I'm going to for you, old son,' said Harry. 'Because this type of operation is not my usual approach.'

I nodded.

'Because even though I'm a military man, I believe in non-violent solutions first,' he said. 'Like Gandalf.'

'You mean Gandhi,' I said.

'No, I'm on about that old boy who wears rags,' said Harry. 'Gandalf.'

'He's right you know, mate,' Ad said to me. Well if Ad says it's right, it must be. God.

I took a deep breath and scanned the horizon as Harry and Ad climbed onto the roof. Still no sign of Gav and his goons. Harry fastened his tie around his head and gave me a thumbs up.

I glanced at my Enterprise watch. A minute to go. I started listing the things I'd never done. Kissed a girl. Collected every *Star Trek* annual. It was only then I realized that my obsession with the latter must have hurt my chances with the former.

A voice from behind jolted me out of my thoughts.

'There he is,' said Gav, strutting over with the twins in tow. 'Thinks he can ask my girl out and get away with it.'

'Bu-but—'

'Don't even bother denying it, Greeny showed me the video,' he said.

If I die, I'm going to poltergeist that lardy cretin.

'Ready for the pain, freak?' Gav cracked his knuckles. It was so loud, it sounded like gunfire.

Before I could reply, I saw a balloon out of the corner of my eye. It looped through the air and smacked one of the Blenkinsops on the nose. He went down on his knees, heaving.

'What the—?' The other one turned around and caught one in his stomach and then another on his head.

Gav sniffed the air. He turned to run. Ad's balloon exploded on the pavement next to him. Harry lobbed another one with more force which caught him right on the back of the head. He ran away with the twins not far behind. **WE WON!**

'Hey, Joe!' said Ad. 'You can get him, catch.' He threw a balloon, which exploded against my chest, sending warm wee running down my body.

'Cocking hell, Ad!' I yelled, as they climbed off the roof and ran away.

I bombed home, hoping to stick my uniform in the wash as soon as I got in, but Mum and Jim had other ideas. They were sitting together on the settee. The TV wasn't on. It was just like the day Mum and Dad told me they were getting a divorce.

'What's the matter?' I said. 'Not splitting up are you?'

Mum raised her eyebrows at me. I probably shouldn't

have sounded so happy about it. 'No,' she said. 'But we do need to talk to you.'

'Yes, sit down, son,' said Jim. Son? What a cheek.

I carefully sat down in the chair furthest away from them. 'Go on,' I said.

Mum took a deep breath and fiddled with a cushion. My mind fizzed with questions. Were they running away to Vegas? Did Jim have some kind of incurable disease? Had Leonard Nimoy AKA Mr Spock finally replied to my fan letter?

'As you know,' said Mum, 'Jim and I have been seeing each other for some time now.'

'Seeing' each other? Ha!

'And in that time we've become very close.' She stopped. I noticed Jim give her hand a squeeze. 'What I'm trying to say is—Jim has asked me to marry him.'

I sat up.

'And I've said yes.'

'Oh,' I said.

'We've had a talk about our living situation, and we don't want to uproot you, especially when you're so busy with school. So we're going to stay here, in this house. Together.'

'So he's moving in here, now?' I said. I wondered how much stress a human could possibly take in one day.

'Well, yes,' said Mum.

'But . . . but,' I said, 'what about all my stuff?'

'What stuff?'

'You know?' I scanned the room. 'Books, DVDs . . . Lego.'

'Look, Joe, I know Jim's not your dad—'

'Good, because I couldn't take another one,' I said.

Mum shot me that deadly look, all raised eyebrows and tight mouth.

'All I ask is that you give it a chance,' she said. 'I really think the four of us will be very happy.'

'Four?' I said. 'Are you counting that imbecile parrot as a person again, Mother?'

'Oh God,' she said. 'Where is my mind today? I forgot to tell you, Jim's son will be joining us.'

'Son?' I said. 'Cocking . . . son? Jeez, does he have any aunties he wants to bring as well?'

'I realize this is a lot for you to take in, Joe,' said Jim. 'And I'm sorry. But my lad's mum is moving to Scotland, which means I have to look after him permanently now. I'm sure you'll . . . ' He trailed off and sniffed the air. 'Can you smell wee?'

'Wee?' I said. 'Who could think about wee at a time like this?'

'Yeah, I can smell it, too,' said Mum. She looked at me accusingly.

'Oh Joe,' she said. 'I thought you'd grown out of that phase.'

'Phase?' I said, giving her a 'shut up' look. 'What phase?'

« Older posts

Before she could answer there was a loud knock at the door.

'That'll be him now,' said Jim.

He got up and answered.

'Hello son!' he said. 'Bloody hell, you stink of wee as well!'

My life is over.

Saturday 21st January

I will never get over the horror of the past twenty four hours. The person who makes my entire high school experience a living hell now shares my house. And not just my house, but my bedroom too. The spare room is being used to store all of Jim's crap. It's like letting a lion into the gazelle enclosure.

The control room were no help. They were too busy running around trying to stop the equipment blowing up.

When I emerged from the airing cupboard at four in the morning, Gav was asleep on my bed in his boxer shorts. Something was poking out of them, and now the image is permanently burned into my mind. I lay on the fold-up mattress on the floor and looked at the glow-in-the-dark stars on the ceiling. I cursed a universe that would allow such a thing to happen.

When I woke up this morning, the first thing I saw was Gav standing over me. At least he had trousers on.

'Um, hello,' I said.

'Shut up.'

'OK.'

'You been a busy boy, ain't you?' said Gav.

I tried to sit up but he ordered me to lie down and listen. Like the world's most intimidating nurse.

'What do you mean?' I said.

'Asking my girl out, covering me in piss.'

'As much as I hate to be pedantic,' I said, which was a lie, because I love it. 'When I asked her out, you'd already split up. And I certainly didn't cover you in piss, I mean, I was standing right in front of you.'

He smirked. 'But you was involved, wasn't you?'

I didn't know what to say. The closest exit was the window. If I jumped out and slid down the sliding roof I might have been OK.

'So there's gonna be consequences, you get me?' he said.

« Older posts

Consequences? Where did he learn that word?

'What are you going to do?' I said.

Gav laughed. 'What can I do? We're brothers now. We've got to get on, innit?. But let me tell you something, freak. This ain't gonna last. And when it all comes crashing down, I'm coming for you. 'Cause I got a long memory, you know what I'm saying?'

I said yes but I bet he doesn't know pi to a hundred decimal places or anything like that. He means a long memory for stuff that relates to violence.

'And another thing,' he said. 'No one finds out about this. No one.'

6 p.m.

I escaped to the park in the afternoon. I thought about telling Mum and Jim about mine and Gav's history but Derek talked me out of it. Plus, they're too busy cooing over each other to listen to me, anyway.

Harry called and asked if I was up for Operation Blooper. He said he'd had a good idea involving a shed and a bowling ball. He got all narked when I declined.

'Remember what I did for you, old boy,' he said. 'I sorted your problem right out.'

'Oh yeah, everything's FINE now!' I screamed back at him.

Later, I saw Greeny walking through the park and confronted him about the video.

'That wasn't me,' he said, through a mouthful of Twix. 'And that photo on Facebook with you as Jabba the Hutt and Lisa as Princess Leia, that wasn't me, either.'

'CURSE YOU, GREENY,' I said.

'CURSE YOU AND YOUR ROTTEN PHOTOSHOP.'

I plan to learn how to use it so I can make him look stupid. More stupid than he already is. Stupid Greeny. If anyone's Jabba, it's him, the tubby git.

I'm writing this entry on the toilet. When I left Gav he was lying on my bed and wiping bogeys on my *Star Trek* poster. Picard looks on, not letting it get to him. Good man, Picard.

« Older posts

Sunday 22nd January

After hardly any sleep last night, Mum sent me to Dad's with a solemn promise not to tell him about the engagement.

'I need to tell him myself,' she said. 'But it'll take time.'

Whatever. I was too busy thrashing him at Scrabble anyway. He even tried to argue that 'chillax' is a word. One day, I'm going to make 'infidelity' on a triple word score and properly show them both up.

Still, it was the first time I didn't want to go home at the end of the day. I went into the spare room when I got back, but the sheer amount of crap in there means clearing it would be a two-person job.

Maybe I should ask him?

No. He'd probably bury me in it.

Monday 23rd January

Gav woke me up in the night. I was having a beautiful dream. I'd won the lottery and used my winnings to build a rocket to blast him into outer space. Well, they used to do it with chimps all the time.

'Oi,' he said through the darkness.

'Yes?'

'You didn't really shag my dad did you?'

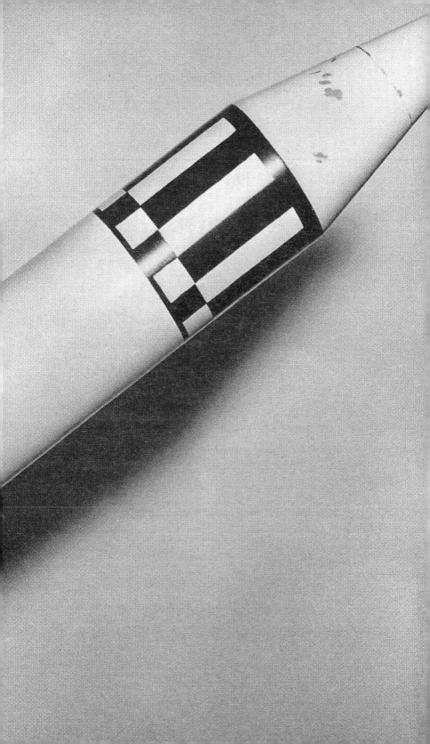

I stood in the kitchen this morning, still numb with horror, waiting for Harry and Ad to call for me. I wondered if the whole weekend had just been a really vivid nightmare. To test this theory I slammed my hand in the fridge door. This experiment confirmed two things:

1. I'm not dreaming.
2. It takes a long time to pick up my fridge magnet alphabet when one of my hands is bruised.

I heard a knock at the front door. Every day Harry knocks the rhythm of a different movie theme, but I couldn't figure out if it was Superman or Jurassic Park, because I was frozen in terror at the sound of Gav's footsteps coming down the stairs. Then, answering the door.

'But you're?' said Harry. 'Is this? Is this the right house?'

The silence was painful.

'Well, we'll be off, then.' I heard them running away. So much for non-violent solutions, Gandalf.

Gav sloped into the kitchen looking and smelling like a Yeti in a tracksuit, muttered something about my loser friends going without me and then drank some milk straight out of the carton.

I got out of there when he started feeding Marmite on toast to Syd. Marmite, I thought. How like him. Not in a love him or hate him way, but in a he's slimy and thick kind of way. I realize that's not the wittiest thing I've ever thought of, but give me a break, I'm angry.

« Older posts

I found Harry and Ad at the top of the road.

'We thought you were dead, old son,' said Harry.

'I might as well be,' I said.

'Gav James was in your house, Joe!' said Ad, grabbing me by the shoulders. 'And you tried it on with his girl!'

'I did no such thing!' I lied.

'Then who's that on Facebook?' said Harry. 'Your evil twin?' *Stupid Greeny.*

'Never mind that,' said Ad. 'What was he doing in there?'

I told them everything on the walk to school and swore them to secrecy.

'Sweet, sweaty, swinging gorilla gonads,' said Harry, taking quick puffs on his pipe.

'So does this mean you're like brothers now, or something?' said Ad.

I frowned at him. 'How would that work?'

'I don't know,' he said with a shrug. 'I mean, you look nothing like each other.'

We walked in silence for a while, trying to digest Ad's spaceman logic.

'Anyway, old boy,' said Harry, 'whatever happens, may I be the first to congratulate you on your ballsy attempted pick-up of Lisa.' He plucked one of those grass dart things and threw it into my hair. 'In terms of pure ambition, that's like Ad going on University Challenge by himself.'

I threw the dart back but it missed and went down a drain.

I noticed Lisa wasn't in school today. Has the shame of being associated with me made her move schools? It wouldn't surprise me. When I got home, Gav confronted me with her pen. He must have been going through my drawer.

'How do you know it's hers?' I said.

'It's got her name on it,' he said.

So he can read.

Tuesday 24th January

Lisa was back today, but keeps blanking me. I mean, it wasn't me who did that video! If I wanted to be humiliated on camera I'd audition for the *X Factor*.

Me and Gav are avoiding each other. I agree with him on one thing. This has to remain a secret. Imagine if it got out. It'd be hell.

The one positive to come out of this is that he isn't bothering me as much at school. But what if people notice? What if they get suspicious? Oh God, the secret is eating me up inside. I know how this is going to end, with me going mental and smearing cack all over the walls and screaming about the government trying to steal my thoughts. I can see it now.

6.30 p.m.

When I got home, I climbed into the loft with my laptop. It's the only place I can get any peace. I looked at the box of Christmas decorations and realized I should have savoured last Christmas because Gav will be here every year from now on, probably setting fire to the Christmas tree and doing unspeakable things to the turkey.

I logged onto Men's Domain and saw two new articles. The first one was titled, 'How to get kick-ass glutes'. What the hell are glutes, anyway? The second article seemed more useful. It was called 'Chicks don't dig deadbeats—get a job!'

Maybe that's what I need to get myself taken seriously by 'chicks'? A job. And maybe I'll be so good at my job that I'll earn enough money to afford my own place. Either that or a live tiger to release into the house when only Gav is home. Thinking about it, I compiled a list of my top five dream jobs:

1. CAPTAIN OF THE USS ENTERPRISE
2. CHIEF OIL BOY AT NUTS MAGAZINE
3. KING
4. COMIC ARTIST
5. INVISIBLE MAN

I know that invisible man isn't exactly a job, but it would be good. Here is a list of jobs I am actually qualified to do:

1. PAPER BOY

I called Mr Singh at the newsagents and asked him if he had any vacancies. He said they did, because the kid who did the Heath estate had quit. I asked him why and he mumbled something about a pitbull. Great.

Anyway, I start tomorrow at six, and then have another shift after school. Excellent, walking around the most dangerous part of town in the dark. Ah well, they say girls like scars, don't they?

10 p.m.

Gah! I've had a reply from Natalie Tuft! And it's a nice one! She says I look 'really friendly'. Which is odd because the photo is of me scowling at Syd. It was the best one I could find.

She looks nice too, from what I can make out from the low-res photo. Pretty. Not Lisa Hall pretty, but then, who is? She's got purple hair and wears black lipstick, though. Does that make her emo? If I snogged her, would I look like I'd been eating blackjacks? Ah, who cares? She's a girl and she actually wants to talk to me!

I sent her a message back, asking her about herself. If she likes school, stuff like that. Now I await her reply.

12 a.m.

Nothing yet. I should probably go to bed. Not that I want to, because Gav's up there and I can hear him snoring.

« Older posts

2 a.m.

Keep hitting F5 but nothing comes up. She's probably asleep. I'll try resetting the internet connection, just in case.

2.10 a.m.

No, she hasn't replied. I'd better call it a night. Work in the morning.

2.20 a.m.

One last check. No. Bum.

2.30 a.m.

Just got into bed. My pillow smells funny. What's he done to it?

Wednesday 25th January

Cocking hell, if this is what employment is like, no wonder most people hate their jobs. The alarm went off at half five. I had about an hour's sleep. Gav threw his trainer at me and I dragged myself off the portable mattress.

It was still dark outside and the freezing air brought tears to my eyes. Mr Singh grunted and huffed a bag at me. Obviously not a morning person either.

It weighed a ton. I was loaded down with copies of the *Sun*, the *Star*, and the *Daily Mail*. My spine was like a crushed can.

My first street, Rainscar Way, was confusing. Numbers one to ten were facing a bike track, with twenty-seven to thirty-five opposite. Then, for some reason, number eighty was next door. Most of the other streets were the same. It was light by the time I finished.

'Where the bloody hell have you been, kidder?' said Mr Singh when I got back. 'I ain't paying you extra, you know.'

I had just enough time to run home and throw my uniform on before school. I was so knackered I fell asleep in French class. What's worse is, I had one of those dreams where I'm at school wearing just my pants and when I woke up there it made it all too real.

I tried to speak to Lisa but she ignored me. I started to think that maybe I died in French and the reason she ignored me was because I was a ghost, but then Greeny waddled past and called me a 'knob lover', so unless he's the world's thickest psychic, I'm alive.

After school, I had to deliver the local paper, the **_Tammerstone Times_**. God knows why, no one reads it.

I was nearly at the end of my round, my hands black with ink and stinging with paper cuts, when I delivered the paper to a rundown house at the end of a row. I knew it was bad because there was a washing machine in the front garden and the Christmas decorations were still up. But that's not the worst part. The door opened, and the

« Older posts

Blenkinsops stepped out.

'Hey, look!' said one of them. 'It's that freak!'

'He's a paper boy!' said the other one. 'Paper bender!'

'Paper bender,' I said. 'That's brilliant. Because I do have to bend the papers to get them through the doors, so . . . double meaning. Very clever. Anyway, I'd better be getting on, so . . . '

They looked at each other, then at me. Then they started running. I turned and belted away, having no idea whether I was running to safety or a dead end. I weaved in and out of bins and discarded TVs until I somehow ended up on a canal towpath. The brothers surrounded me and one of them grabbed my bag.

'Hey!' I jumped up, trying to get it off him. 'Give it back!'

'Give it back! Give it back!' they said, in high voices that sounded nothing like me.

They threw the bag to each other and I ran from side to side, trying to catch it. One of them swung it round his head and let go. The papers tumbled out, straight into the canal.

'What have you done?' I yelled, my voice coming out really high. They laughed and walked away.

If Mr Singh finds out about this I'm finished.

Got home to find Gav walking around with Syd on his shoulder. So not only is he mute, but he's also a traitor. That's the last time I form a friendship with an exotic bird.

Despite barely being able to keep my eyes open, I checked my emails. MESSAGE FROM NATALIE!

>> Teenmeet home >>Messages >>New message

Back

New Message
From: Natalie Tuft

Reply

Hi, Joe!
School sucks. I go to St Ethel's All Girls' School just outside Tammerstone. Everyone there hates me and I can't wait to get out. We're taught by nuns and some of the old ones think I'm the devil! I try and stay cool about it, like Picard would. (By the way, he is SO the best captain)
Msg back soon,
Nat
X

OH MY GOD, I THINK I'VE FOUND MY SOULMATE.

Thursday 26th January

I woke up at 5.30 a.m., taking another trainer to the head. I wondered how much longer I'd be able to keep this up. Turns out not much. Mr Singh sacked me for dumping papers in the canal.

To be honest, I'm glad. I couldn't have stuck that job for long, anyway. Early mornings, lugging stuff about? No thanks. Maybe the moron twins did me a favour. Manual labour is not for me. But I do still need a job. It's important for the mature image I'm trying to create.

« Older posts

'Jobs are few and far between in today's economy, old bean,' said Harry on the way to school. 'The way forward is entrepreneurship, like me and Ad with the Sound Experience. Start your own business.'

I hoofed a pebble at a lamp post. 'What can I do?'

'You could sell pictures of your mum,' said Ad. 'I'd buy 'em.'

I punched him on the arm.

'I've got it,' said Harry. 'Take some out-of-focus shots of Gav and tell the press you've spotted Bigfoot.'

I smiled as I imagined an angry mob waving flaming torches and pitchforks at Gav. I even drew a doodle of it during Geography.

'You could work for my dad,' said Ad. 'He needs a new assistant 'cause the last one he had was useless.'

'Weren't you his last assistant?' I said.

'Yeah.'

A phone call later and it's settled. I'm helping Ad's dad out in his meat van. I'll do a day's trial on Saturday, and if I'm any good, he'll take me on permanently.

I was in a decent mood until after lunch. We had to go down to the sports hall for a special assembly with Mr Pratt, the head teacher, just so he could moan on at us about our conduct being 'below the benchmark set by the educational authorities'.

I couldn't really concentrate on what he was saying anyway, because I was sitting in front of Gav and the Blenkinsops and they kept stealing stuff out of my pockets and kicking the back of my chair. It wasn't until I met Harry and Ad that I found out I had a sign saying 'Im a freek-show' stuck to my back.

To take my mind off things, I wrote a new email to Natalie when I got home. I wondered if it was too soon to get flirty. Then I realized I have no idea how to flirt. If I tried, I'd probably end up saying something really pervy and wrong. Anyway, she messaged me back straight away with a new picture. (Nice!) She then suggested that we Skyped at some point. I like the idea of Skyping with a fellow Trekkie because we could pretend one of us was on the Enterprise. She said she's not quite ready to do it yet though, because she has a zit on her chin and she feels self-conscious.

I was about to reply when I heard a giant crash down-stairs. I ran down to find that either Gav or one of the Blenkinsops had kicked a ball through the kitchen window. They responded by doing the grown-up thing and running away.

« Older posts

When Mum and Jim got home I told them what happened and then wondered whether I'll have to go into Witness Protection.

9 p.m.

Just earwigged on Jim and Gav having a row. Jim said Gav would have to pay for a new window. Gav said he's got no money. I found this funny until he took my *Star Trek* annuals and tried to sell them down the park. He found no takers so I bought them back off him for a fiver.

I HATE my life.

Friday 27th January

After school, Mum and Jim tried to get us to come out for dinner as a 'family'. At least I had the decency to pretend to have a stomach ache. Gav just walked out.

While they were out, Gav took over my bedroom and smoked and blasted his crap music, which I'm sorry, just sounds like someone shouting and kicking a bin. I shut myself in the bathroom with my *Star Trek* annuals. Later, Jim knocked on the door and demanded I come out because he needed to, and I quote, 'drop anchor before the ship slides out of port'. Now I see where Gav gets his charm.

Another message from Natalie. She wants to Skype this

Monday! What will I wear? More importantly, what if I say something terrible?

I can't let that happen. I have to be master of the control room. And if it goes well, maybe I'll get to kiss a real live girl after all. I decided to practise on the back of my hand to be safe. I was really getting into it when Gav walked in and caught me.

'Yeah, well it's the closest thing to a girlfriend you're ever gonna have,' he said.

Sometimes I just want to smash his face in with a large hammer.

Saturday 28th January

DISASTER!

A SPOT has appeared on my forehead overnight. Not just a SPOT, a monster! It's as if I'm growing a horn. No time to worry about it too much though because today is my first day at the meat van. Wish me luck!

11 p.m.

Maybe work isn't for me? Perhaps I'll just stay at home for the rest of my life and wait for my teeth to drop out until I eventually get the call from Jezza Kyle to take a DNA test, and I say I can't be the father because I've never even kissed a girl, and then a load of housewives boo me and Jezza calls me a disgrace to the human race. That doesn't sound so bad.

I got to work at 7.30 a.m. The meat van was parked in front of the church in the marketplace. It's not really a van, more like a giant lorry with a big hatch on the side. On the side, it says

The smell inside was as overpowering as the one in my room when Gav leaves his pants out. I found Ad's dad, Malcolm, lugging steaks onto the counter. He's a big jolly bloke with a beard. I think he's originally from Newcastle, because he talks like Ant and Dec's granddad.

« Older posts

'Y'alreet, Joe lad?' he bellowed. 'Welcome to the theatre of meat!'

He gave me a long white coat and a hat, which hid my mega-zit, but rubbed it and made it sore.

It was amazing watching Malcolm work. He wore this headset mic but he shouted so loud he didn't even need it.

'These, love,' he screamed at an old lady, 'are the best Cumberland sausages money can buy. Now, normally, they'd go for eight quid, but because you've got a lovely face, they're yours for four. Now go on, get out of here, you're robbing me blind!'

He gave her a wink and you could tell she was loving it. All I had to do was bag up the sausage and take her money. Easy. How could Ad have messed it up?

I don't know, but he somehow managed to mess it up for me, too. Malcolm was halfway through selling a topside of beef to another old dear when he got a phone call.

'Bloody hell, Joe,' he said. 'That son of mine has got his head stuck in the revolving doors down Sainsbury's again.'

'OK,' I said, as if it was no big surprise. 'So are we closing the van for a while?'

He looked at me as if I'd suggested dealing crack as a sideline. 'Close the van?' he said. 'On a bleeding Saturday? Not a chance. You're going to have to take the reins until I get back.'

'But . . . '

'You'll be fine.' He put his giant hand on my shoulder. 'Talk to the customers, don't go any lower than the deals I've got written on the sheet, and you'll have no problems. Just do what I do: pretend you're doing 'em a massive favour. And most importantly: be confident.'

Confidence, I thought. I can do confidence.

« Older posts

'Er,' I said, adjusting the volume to stop the mic making a horrible squealing sound, 'we've got meat over here. Lots of meat. Cheap as well. Very reasonable.'

I stunk as a meat salesman. I scanned the horizon for signs of Malcolm coming back but he was nowhere to be seen. Then I saw something on the other side of the square that made me want to throw my headset down and run. Gav.

'Hey look!' he said to the Blenkinsops. 'The freak's got a little job!'

They laughed. 'Yeah, what a freak.'

They sat on a bench opposite, watching me.

You don't have to take that, man. Show those sons of bitches you can do it.

'You're right, Derek,' I said, and then remembered the mic was still on and I must have sounded mental.

'Roll up, roll up,' I cried. 'We've got steaks, sausages, bacon, chicken breasts and legs—you name it, we've got it!'

A crowd started to gather. I pointed at a woman with a shopping trolley at the front.

'What can I get you, pet?' I said. I remembered that Malcolm was always calling women that, and they seemed to like it.

'How much for that turkey crown?'

I scanned the price list.

'Well, pet,' I said. 'We should be selling it for twenty quid, but you know what, for you, I'll do it for twelve.'

You should have seen her face. You'd think she'd won the cocking lottery.

I felt myself getting into it. Gav and the Blenkinsops being there only pumped my adrenaline up further. Derek kept screaming encouragement.

'Next!' I yelled. 'You, pet, what can I do you for?'

'How much for three sirloin steaks?' said the old dear.

'Well, my love, my boss says I should sell them to you for a tenner, but for you, because you've got a lovely twinkle in your eye, I'll do it for eight.'

'Ooh, I don't know,' she said. I scanned the list for the best deal I was allowed to offer.

'All right, all right,' I said. 'Seven fifty.'

She didn't respond. Time to ramp it up.

'OK!' I yelled. 'You've got me. You've stitched me up like a kipper! I'll give 'em to ya for six ninety-five and I'll throw in five rashers of bacon. Now get out of here, you're taking the food out of me kids' mouths, you thieving cow!'

She stared at me open-mouthed. So did the rest of the crowd. So did Gav. And Malcolm, who'd just got back. The silence was awful. Behind the van, the church bells tolled.

Maybe it would have helped if I'd winked.

Malcolm sat me down at the end of the day and paid me my thirty quid.

'Well, son,' he said, 'I think that's the end of your meat-

« Older posts

selling career.'

I sighed. 'Is it because I called that old lady a thieving cow?'

'It is, aye,' he said. 'And I know I shouldn't have left you on your own, so it's partially my fault. I'd love to give you another chance but these old codgers are my most loyal customers and they'd never come to me again.'

So that's another title for me. Joe Cowley: repeller of girls, target for menaces, and now, scourge of the elderly.

When I got back I asked Mum if I could sleep on the settee. She said no because, and I quote, 'I don't want my living room stinking of boys.' Then I asked if they would ever get around to clearing out the spare room. She said, yes, at some point.

It is UNBELIEVABLE how little she cares for me. I could die, and they'd only notice when my corpse started getting too smelly for Gavin.

Exchanging a few messages with Natalie before bed cheered me up. She thinks the *Star Trek* remake was over-rated too!

3 a.m.

Can't sleep. Keep thinking about meat.

Sunday 29th January

Woke up this morning depressed about my unemployability. Went round Harry's on the way to Dad's and told him what happened. He said he could get rid of Gav if I wanted him to. When I asked him how, he said he 'knows people'. Yeah right, the only people he knows are me and Ad. Then he tried me to take part in Operation Blooper again but I refused.

Visited Dad. Still sworn to secrecy about engagement. Svetlana still hates me. I still hate Svetlana. Hercules has nothing to lick but his stitches. Dad offered to take me a ride in his convertible IN THE MIDDLE OF WINTER. I said I'd rather wear cheese-grater underpants than be seen in that thing. Don't think he heard me.

Monday 30th January

O, **M**, and indeed **G**, I'm about to Skype with Natalie! I have never been this nervous before. I'm trying to hold my eyelid open to stop it twitching.

Thing is, I'm not a big Skype person. The only time I've ever really done it was with Granddad Cowley who lives in Tenerife, and that was no fun. He's so tanned and wrinkly; it was like talking to a giant prune. With Natalie it'll be different, I know it will. She's funny, pretty, and we seem to agree on nearly everything. Except the Floyd, but we can get around that. I think.

I'm breathing deeply and trying to slow my heart rate. I won't say something stupid. I won't say something stupid. I won't say something stupid. I have lines written on a pad in case I get stuck. Everything is going to be **FINE**.

« Older posts

I've paid Men's Domain one last visit. Mum and Jim are visiting Jim's mum and Gav is out with the Blenkinsops, probably throwing cats at old ladies or something like that, so I know I won't be disturbed. I'm ready. Except for one minor detail. The mega-zit. My fringe isn't long enough to cover it and I look a tit in hats, so I haven't even got that option. What to do? Oh crap, she's just logged on. Talk to you later!

8 p.m.

I wonder if I murdered Gav, I'd get off for mitigating circumstances? I mean, who wouldn't want to kill him?

9 p.m.

My heart rate is slowing a bit now. Maybe I can get down what happened without throwing the laptop out of the window.

Straight after she logged on, Natalie popped up on my screen. I was stunned. She looked great. I mean, she still had black lipstick on, and there were scary-looking posters of men wearing make-up on the wall behind her, but even so... She's easily as fit as the girls who don't give me the time of day at school.

'Hi!' she said with a nervous smile.

'H-hello,' I said.

'Are you all right, Joe?'

'Yeah, great,' I said.

'It's just, you're holding your forehead.'

It was the only thing I could think of to conceal the mutant zit from outer space.

'Oh, I'm fine,' I said. 'It's just—'

'Just what?'

'Promise you won't laugh?'

'Promise.' She smiled.

'I've got a zit on my forehead,' I said. 'It's huge—like a third eye.'

'Oh, it doesn't matter,' she said. 'I had one on my chin, remember?'

'Yeah, but this is massive,' I said.

'It can't be that bad,' she said. 'Take your hand away and let's see it.'

I looked straight into the webcam and grimaced. 'All right,' I said. 'But don't freak out.'

I took my hand away. There was a moment's silence.

'Wow,' she said.

« Older posts

'I know.'

'I would love to squeeze that,' she said.

I looked into the camera.

'Oh God, did I just say that?' she said, pushing her purple hair out of her eyes. 'I am so weird.'

'I'd let you squeeze it,' I said. 'It might be, you know, fun.'

She laughed. 'Cool, you're weird, too. That's a relief.'

We chatted for ages, about music, *Star Trek*, school, films, everything. I hardly got tongue-tied at all and didn't ramble on about crap, either. I was in control. I even made her laugh a few times, and not because I did something stupid. At least, I don't think so.

'I was really nervous about today, you know,' she said.

'Me too,' I said.

'I mean, really bricking it,' she said. 'I think it's because I get loads of bitchy comments at school and I don't know, I expect everyone to be like them.'

'You shouldn't listen to them,' I said. 'I think you're—'

But before I could finish the sentence, the door swung open and Gav strutted in.

'Hey, who's this?' he said.

'Nobody,' I said, trying to cover the screen. 'Can you just go away for a minute?'

He wrenched my hands behind my back.

'No way, man,' he said. 'I know you said she was a munter, but that is ridiculous.'

My eyes nearly popped out of my head and hung on their stalks.

'No!' I cried. 'I didn't say that!'

But she was gone. The last thing I saw was this really hurt look on her face. It was the most horrible thing I've ever seen.

Gav walked away, laughing to himself.

I ran after him.

'How could you do that?' I said. 'What's wrong with you?'

He pushed past me, downstairs and back out of the door.

I went back to the computer and tried to connect to her again, but she was offline. I quickly wrote a message, telling her I'd never say that and he's just an idiot, but it all sounded so made-up. I don't think I'll wait up tonight for a reply.

11.30 p.m.

She's not going to reply, is she? I've just spent five minutes looking at my pillow and Gav's snoring face. No, I'm not capable. Besides, I could never survive in prison. I'd be someone's bitch in five minutes flat.

12.45 a.m.

Goodnight, Natalie. Hope you're OK.

« Older posts

Summary of January.

Kisses with real live girls: None

Girls asked out: One (unsuccessful)

Jobs gained: Two

Jobs lost: Two

Buzzfest fund: £67

High point: 'Meeting' Natalie

Low point: Take your cocking pick

Natalie hasn't replied to any of my messages. (Yes, I sent a few more.) Asked Mr Boocock if I could be excused from PE because of my broken heart. His reply was, 'That won't be the only thing that's broken if you're not in that changing room in two seconds.'

What's worse was, after the lesson, Gav tripped me and I landed in a puddle, creating a massive brown stain on the seat of my trousers. If I had a pound for every time I had to say, 'No I have not crapped myself,' I'd have enough money to buy a new pair.

Played *Streets of Chicago* when I got home. Found a background character that looks just like Gav and spent the evening designing dozens of violent and ingenious ways to murder him. It really gets the aggression out. I feel like I'm in a better headspace now.

Wednesday 1st February

I may have done something a bit mental today.

What am I saying? I'm a criminal. I am guilty of the following atrocities: truancy and stalking. What am I becoming?

I couldn't get Natalie off my mind, if that's any excuse. The liquorice laces in the tuck shop reminded me of her lips and Mr Fuller's big purple nose reminded me of her hair.

At lunch, Harry caught me hanging around by the doors.

'Where are you off to, old son?' he said. 'Have you finally broken and joined Gav's hiding-in-the-woods-and-smoking-during-school-hours club?'

'I'd rather join the Japanese Kamikaze squadron,' I said. 'No, it's something else.'

Harry looked me over and puffed on his pipe with his wise Yoda expression. 'I know what this is,' he said. 'It's a girl, isn't it?'

'How did you know?' I said.

'I can read you like a book, old boy.' He pointed at me with the slobbery end of his pipe. 'And not even a hard book. An easy one, like The Very Hungry Caterpillar. Is it Lisa again?'

'No.'

'Then who is it?'

'You don't know her,' I said. 'She goes to the All Girls' School on the other side of town. I need to go and see her.'

'All girls, eh?' Harry's eyes went huge. 'Maybe I should come with you. For moral support.'

'I don't think that's a good idea,' I said, but before I could debate him any further, he dragged me down the corridor to the school nurse's office.

'Greetings, Nurse Snitterfield,' said Harry. 'Myself and Joe here would like permission to leave school, if you please.'

Old Nurse Snitterfield slammed her crossword book down and scowled at us over her glasses. 'Why?'

'Well, we both have the squits, Miss,' he said. 'If you'll pardon my *français*.'

She huffed and wrote something on two bits of paper. 'Fine,' she said. 'Go.'

'Thanks, Miss,' he said. 'Anyway, we'd better run. Race you to the latrines, Joe!'

'What was all that about?' I said, as we ran down the corridor. 'Couldn't you have thought of something less embarrassing?'

'Always go with the runs, old boy,' he said. 'They'll accept it, no questions asked.'

We bustled through the lunchtime crowd outside the gates and waited at the bus stop on the main road. My eye started to twitch.

'I shouldn't be doing this,' I said. 'It's against the law.'

'Relax,' said Harry. 'It's all above board. The nurse has signed our slips.'

Even so, I still felt as if I was about to be caught out.

'The thing I'm most worried about is what Ad will do in our absence,' said Harry. 'I'm just glad there aren't any revolving doors in the school for him to get his head stuck in.'

I couldn't believe how full the bus was. We had to sit in the seats reserved for pregnant women. I could feel every pair of eyes on us, questioning why we weren't in school.

About halfway there, a pregnant woman got on and stood in the aisle. I felt like I should make an effort to be a responsible citizen, so I stood up and offered her my seat. She just glared at me.

'Do you not want the—'

'No, I can stand, thank you.'

Why didn't I sit back down?

'Oh,' I said. 'I thought you were . . . you know.'

Everyone on the bus winced at the same time. You could actually hear it. I quickly sat back down because the woman looked like she wanted to throw me out the window.

'And there I was wondering why you had women troubles,' said Harry.

Luckily, the non-pregnant woman got off a few stops later and I could relax slightly. I told Harry what had happened with Natalie and Gav and how I had to see her.

'Well, if it gets nasty and loads of girls start fighting you, I will step in,' he said. 'And suggest we settle our differences with a hot-oil wrestling match.'

« Older posts

We arrived outside the school. I couldn't believe how posh it all was with its landscaped gardens and vines creeping up the walls.

We crept around to the gates to get a better view. It looked like their lunch break was coming to an end. Harry surveyed the scene like a lion watching a herd of wildebeest at a watering hole.

'Girls,' he said. 'As far as the eye can see.'

I scanned the crowd. She had to be there. If nothing else, I was worried about her. It didn't help that they were all dressed exactly the same in their immaculate uniforms. Not like at scummy Woodlet, where we're allowed to have our ties really stubby and wear our own jackets instead of blazers.

I was about to give up hope when I saw something purple glinting in the corner of the yard. There she was. Sitting alone on a bench, reading. She still had the black lipstick on, but looked different, wearing a smart uniform like that.

'There she is,' I said to Harry.

'Nice,' he said. 'I didn't realize you went for the emo type, old son.'

'I need to get her attention,' I said.

Harry smiled. 'Leave it to me.' He put two fingers in his mouth, and did one of those big whistles.

'HEY!' he cried. 'NATALIE! OVER HERE!'

Natalie stood up and looked over at us.

Straight away, other girls started shouting things.

'Ooh, which one's your boyfriend, Dracula? Is it the geek or the one with the granddad pipe?'

She looked right at me—that same look I saw the other night on Skype.

'Just leave me alone, Joe,' she said, and then ran inside.

I was about to give the bullies a piece of my mind when Harry cried out, 'NUNS! RETREAT, RETREAT!'

I turned around and saw two old nuns chasing us, their habits blowing out behind them. I've never run so fast in my life.

'No boys at this school!' one of them shouted. For some-one who's married to Jesus, she didn't sound very forgiving.

We sat in silence on the bus home. Seeing what Natalie had to go through at school was horrible. And it was there, sitting in a seat reserved for pregnant women, looking at a woman standing up, who I think was actually pregnant, but I was too scared to ask, that I realized that I had to forget about her.

I'm not crying, I've got something in my eye.

Thursday 2nd February

God help me. It's got so bad, I've even written a poem for her. It was quite easy because loads of things rhyme with her name.

Oh Natalie,
I've been thinking about you latterly.
Although the other girls behave so cattily,
I think you dress nattily,
And they're jealous because they dress tattily.
The proper term for stamp-collecting is philately.
Oh Natalie.

It's good, but it needs work.

As I walked around school like a zombie, my thoughts kept turning to Natalie, again and again. Like a boomerang of pain. I went on Men's Domain after school and clicked on a page called 'Rejection—how to deal with it'.

> ## 'REJECTION–HOW TO DEAL WITH IT
>
> Been rejected? Don't sweat it. It happens to the best of us. But it's not all about being rejected, it's about how you deal with it. If the girl has been firm, don't keep bothering her, or she might take out a restraining order. Just move on to the next one. There's plenty more fish in the sea!

Yeah, well that metaphor doesn't stand up, because even if there are plenty more fish in the sea, what good is it if they all hate me? I won't be able to catch them no matter how big my rod is.

I've just realized that last sentence sounds a bit rude.

Saturday 4th February

Let it not be said that I don't know how to have a good time. I spent Saturday night lying on my mattress, reading and listening to the Floyd. Rock and roll.

I didn't mind, though; it helped take my mind off things and stopped me getting too miserable about Natalie. That is until Gav walked in, grabbed the book off me, and farted in it.

I was determined not to lower myself to his level so I waited until I was sure the smell would have dissolved and reopened the book. Sure enough, the eye-watering stench was still there. Gav thought it was hilarious, but I was reading Dickens and the smell really brought the streets of Victorian London to life, so in a way, the joke's on him.

« Older posts

When he turned the Floyd off and put a mix CD on with some idiot shouting over the top of it, I decided to tackle the spare room myself.

I marched in there and yanked at a curtain in the middle of a huge floor-to-ceiling pile. It seemed to lurch over in slow motion, before clattering down on top of me. As I lay there, buried by a mountain of drawers, sheets, books, and boxes, I thought about how much I needed to work on my Jenga technique.

Sunday 5th February

Dad forced me to go bowling with him and Svetlana. She was crap at it because she wouldn't put her fingers in the holes in case she broke a nail. I wasn't doing much better, until I started imagining Gav's face on all the pinheads.

After that I got five consecutive strikes.

Monday 6th February

I thought I was getting over Natalie, but then her favourite band, Oh, Inverted World came on MTV Rocks and I found myself blinking back tears. GET A GRIP, MAN!

Mum and Jim were looking at wedding clothes online tonight, too. God help me.

'Here, this is what you'll be wearing, Joe,' said Mum, pointing at some white and gold monstrosity on the screen.

'Great,' I said. 'I'll look like a demented ice-cream man.'

She and Jim laughed for ages after that, but I didn't. The idea of Gav as my stepbrother is becoming a reality. It is nut-shrivellingly depressing.

On the plus side, though, the mega-zit has finally gone.

Tuesday 7th February

I'm so excited I think I might actually explode!

I hadn't listened to a word of what was being said in General Studies today. I was too busy thinking about running away and joining the circus. Then I remembered that I'm allergic to straw and scared of clowns. Or is it allergic to clowns and scared of straw? Either way, the idea's a dead end.

I was wondering how bad being a tramp could be when I noticed Miss Tyler standing over me, holding a container.

'What are you waiting for, Joe?' she said. 'Put your hand in my bucket.'

« Older posts

On the other side of the room, Greeny exploded with laughter. I gave him the stinkeye and asked Miss Tyler what it was for.

'It's to pick your partner for the project,' she said.

I sighed and half-arsedly reached into the bucket, expecting to pull out someone like Greeny or Jason 'Heil Hitler' Downey. But when I unfolded the paper and read it, I thought I was going to have a heart attack.

'OK, Joe, you'll be working with Lisa,' said Miss Tyler.

The whole room erupted:

'Unlucky, Lisa!'

'Don't worry, I hear you ain't his type!'

Harry and Ad gave me 'oh crap' glances.

Miss Tyler tried to quieten them down while I went redder than a tomato in a tanning shop. Lisa wouldn't make eye contact.

'You will work in pairs on a special project,' she said. 'You will each be given a baby doll to look after. It is a very advanced doll, which is designed to behave exactly like a real baby. It will cry and need to be fed and have its nappy changed. The aim of the project is for you to understand what a big responsibility a baby is, and for you to demonstrate that you can work well as a team. At the end of your time with the doll, I will analyse the data on the doll's built-in microchip to judge how well you treated it and you will give a talk in pairs to the class.'

Every word was like another clump of dirt on my coffin lid.

'Miss!' said Greeny. 'Does it puke?'

'Yes,' said Miss Tyler. 'It replicates all baby behaviour.'

'Hey, Joe, like father, like son,' he said.

I shot him a sneaky middle finger behind my ring binder.

'OK, now if you'd like to get into your pairs to discuss your plans,' she said. 'And may I remind you that this goes towards your GCSE grade for the year.'

Arse. I want good GCSEs so I don't grow up to be a medical testing subject like Gav. It would be a lot of work to do by myself, but it'd be worth it to avoid the humiliation for both of us.

I saw Lisa getting up on the other side of the room. I quickly changed all the cock and balls doodles Harry had done on my pad into cute puppies. She sat in the seat next to me just as I finished colouring in the last nose.

'Hi,' I said.

She didn't speak, but seemed to be looking at my paper, perhaps wondering why I'd drawn puppies on it. Looking back, the cock and balls would have probably been more normal.

'Look,' I said, turning to a fresh page, 'I'm sorry about this whole thing. You know, Facebook and the *Star Wars* picture and all that.'

'I have never been so embarrassed,' said Lisa.

Ha! Welcome to my world.

« Older posts

'I know and I really am sorry,' I said. 'But I'm just as humiliated as you, if not more! And hey, at least you got to be Leia rather than Jabba.'

Wait a sec, let me understand this, said Derek, pacing up and down and chain-smoking. *Have you, or have you not just implied—to your dream girl, no less—that you want to be a woman in a gold bikini?*

'Tell you what,' I said to Lisa, 'I'll do the project. I'll have the baby, everything. I'll even write your lines for the presentation. You won't have to do a thing and you won't have to embarrass yourself by being associated with me. How about that?'

Lisa made eye contact for the first time. I wish she didn't because it looked like she wanted to rip out my kidneys and use them as earmuffs.

'Whatever,' she said.

'Right,' I said, wondering what the hell to say next. 'Do you think we should meet up just the once though? In case Miss Tyler starts asking questions?'

'All right,' she said. 'But not here. Somewhere else.'

'O-OK,' I said. 'How about the library on Saturday?'

She shrugged and started picking at her nails. Nothing was said. I panicked. The urge to fill the silence began to rise, as it always does, and God knows what kind of crap was going to come out of my mouth. When that idiot Greeny came over, I could have hugged him.

'Hey up, kids,' he said. 'Any plans to make a real baby?'

'Any plans to piss off?' said Lisa.

Greeny laughed. 'Are you gonna make me?'

Before he could say anything else Lisa grabbed his tie and pulled it tight, pushing his second chin over his first.

What a woman. She doesn't take crap from morons like Greeny and Gav. She's strong and gutsy like Beverly Crusher from *Star Trek* or that scary one off *Dragons' Den*.

On the way out of class, she said, 'So, Saturday, then?'

'Yep!' I said, my eye twitching up a storm. 'It's a date!'

She stared at me.

'I didn't mean it like that!' I said. 'It's not a date! Well it is, it's the eleventh, but you know what I mean!' I wiped my forehead. I was sweating like Ad was after he sneaked into a sauna in a gorilla costume for a bet.

'Yeah, see you then,' she said.

I love this time. The period full of optimism before something bad happens and I'm plunged back into despair. I must learn to cherish it.

Wednesday 8th February

My room is disgusting. Well, I say my room, but it's ours now, isn't it? There's crusty pants everywhere, and empty cans and food wrappers scattered around, and I even found a stash of pirate DVDs under my bed. Apparently, Gav gets them off this bloke down the park called Scabby

Barry. I'm not even making it up.

I asked Gav if he would help me tidy. He responded by throwing a can at my head.

9.15 p.m.

In my darker moments, I wonder if we are actually the same person, like in that film, *Fight Club*. Then I remember I've seen his pants, and realized it would take three of me to fit into them.

Syd still not talking to me, and I'm not talking to Syd. We'll see who's the first to crack.

Thursday 9th February

I would have thought the me-and-Lisa thing would have blown over by now, but I'm still getting hassled about it on the corridors.

Even though I know it's down to jealousy, it still racks me off. I thought about spending lunch breaks in a locked toilet cubicle, but the smell in there soon put an end to that idea.

I bumped into Lisa out in the yard. Damian Dunkley from 10d ran past and shouted, 'PUKE AND LISA, SITTING IN A TREE! K-I-S-S-I-S-S-I-S-S-I-S-N-G!'

'Learn to spell, moron,' said Lisa, and stuck her leg out, sending him clattering into a bin.

'S-sorry, Lisa,' I said.

'You don't have to apologize,' she said. 'They're just a bunch of idiots.' She pointed at Jordan Foster who had a Year Seven in a headlock, but got confused and rubbed his knuckles across his own scalp.

She smiled at me. I felt like I was going to burst into flames. Then she seemed to be looking at something behind me. I turned around and there was Gav, staring at us.

Lisa tapped me on the arm. 'How about a hug?' she said.

You'd think Gav watching would have put me off, but come on, I'd have to be an idiot to turn down an invitation like that. Afterwards, I sat down on a bench and couldn't get up for five minutes. I've no idea why she suddenly wanted to hug me, though. Must be her mood swings or something like that. Who even cares, anyway? She actually touched me, with her hands and everything.

10 p.m.

Had a game of online *Epic Warfare* against Harry and Ad when I got home. We talked to each other over our headsets. I am a robot called KillTech 3.0. He took me ages to design and mod. I even sketched him out and everything.

I asked them if they wanted to come over and play my new *Streets of Chicago* zombie expansion pack, but they refused while Gav was there. I was about to point out that Gav was out somewhere, until he walked in, grabbed my headset off me and called the entire *Epic Warfare* online community 'epic benders', earning me a ban for abusive behaviour.

Lying in bed later, the only thing that keeps me from crying is Picard's stern face looking down from the wall. Picard has no time for weakness.

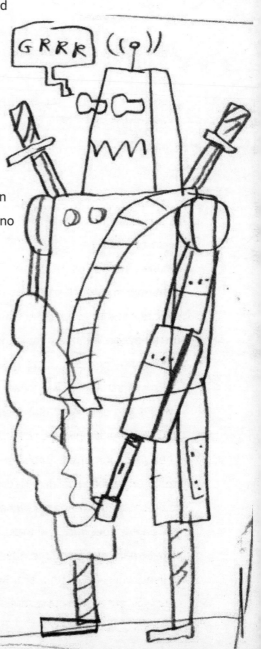

Oh my God!

OH

MY

GOD!

I'm so stressed out I've come out in millions of zits on my forehead. Millions! They look like tiny little heads! It's as if there's a gig happening on my eyebrows! I thought I'd draw it here. It has not made me feel any better.

This is just what I need for my meeting with Lisa tomorrow. I wish I was emo like Natalie, so I could cover them up with make-up or a floppy fringe.

I asked Mum if she could lend me some money for spot treatments. She said I'm perfect just the way I am and kissed my disgusting forehead. I wasn't impressed so she let me borrow her cover-up. The way I see it, it isn't make-up. OK? It just isn't. Don't judge me.

« Older posts

Went upstairs tonight to find Gav smoking on my bed. He laughed and called me 'Brailleface'.

'Nah, man, you ain't Brailleface,' he said. 'People actually wanna touch Braille.'

I turned around and marched to Mum's room to confront them about the spare room, but I heard noises in there that disturbed me to my very core, so I ran straight downstairs and turned the TV up extra loud.

The news showed a report about a drought in Africa, and it made me realize that there are plenty of people out there worse off than me. Then I wondered how much it would cost to send Gav out there. If I hadn't lost my meat van job, I could have saved up for a plane ticket.

Over the noise of the TV, I heard a voice in the kitchen. Calling my name. Gav was upstairs, and Mum and Jim were (excuse me while I fight the urge to vom) upstairs as well, so who could it be?

I crept in, clutching the remote as a weapon. Empty. Except for. No. Surely not? Not after a year of futile effort? Syd isn't finally saying 'Joe's the man'?

'JOE LIKES MEN, JOE LIKES MEN, JOE LIKES MEN' he squawked.

Stupid parrot. Stupid Gav.

Saturday 11th February

Too tired n emotional to right what happned now. Need slep. Hate him so mch.

Sunday 12th February

I sometimes think I must be the unluckiest person in the universe. Where to start? How about yesterday, about four o'clock?

'Oh hi, Lisa,' I said. 'Can I just say you look stunning today? Truly radiant. I picked this flower on the way here, I hope you don't mind, but it was the only thing I could find that could come close to your beauty.'

The mirror steamed up. *You old dog. Even inanimate objects can't resist your charms,* I thought. Before realizing that it probably had more to do with the shower I was running. I threw my Enterprise towel over my shoulder and raised an eyebrow at my foggy reflection.

I'd copied a few chat-up lines from **Men's Domain**. My favourite one was where you get the girl to touch your shirt, and you say, 'Do you know what that is? That's boy-friend material!' A definite winner, I thought.

'Joe!' Mum called up the stairs, ruining my daydream.

I opened the door a crack. 'What do you want?' I was edgy. I didn't sleep at all the night before, so I drank three cans of Red Bull at lunch.

'There's a young lady here to see you,' she called back

« Older posts

in a sing-song voice.

The control room sprang into action. *A young lady? In his house? What the hell's happening? Is it an overeager Jehovah's Witness?*

Blood whacked against my eardrums as I threw my clothes back on and ran down the stairs. The closest thing to a young lady I ever brought home was that Halloween when Ad dressed as Lady Gaga. He had to hide because the neighbour's dog was going mental for his meat dress.

Then I saw her, in my hallway, talking to my mum.

'So, how do you know my Joe, then?' said Mum with a massive never-thought-I'd-see-the-day grin.

'Oh, we're just doing a school project together,' said Lisa.

'Lisa!' My voice came out all high and loud for some reason.

'Hi, Joe,' she said. Sunlight flooded in through the door behind her, making her look like an angel. A sexy angel.

'What are you doing here?' I said.

'Thomas!' said Mum. 'If that's the way you speak to young ladies, it's no wonder you haven't got a girlfriend.'

I ran down the rest of the stairs, giving Mum a 'go away' look. She said goodbye to Lisa then went back into the kitchen, where Syd squawked lies about my sexual preference to all and sundry.

'I got to the library early but it was closed for training or something, so I thought I'd come to you,' said Lisa. 'Hope that's all right.'

'Of course it is,' I said. 'It's cool.'

OK, stop there.

'Coolio.'

OK, but that's enough.

'Too coolio for schoolio.'

Oh sweet freaking Jesus.

Lisa put her hand to her mouth. Men's Domain says you should try to make girls laugh, but not by being an utter moron. I don't think my toes will ever uncurl from the embarrassment. Derek facepalmed.

I led the way upstairs. 'Keep that bedroom door open, Thomas,' Mum called after us. I don't think she likes anything more than embarrassing me. She needn't bother, I'm good enough at doing it myself.

When we stepped onto the landing, TENTACLES OF HORROR SQUEEZED MY RIBCAGE.

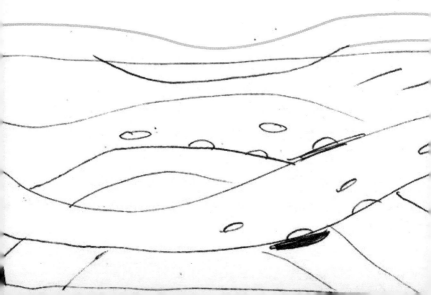

'Actually, Lisa,' I jumped in front of her, 'could you just wait here for a few ticks?'

I bolted inside my bedroom and slammed the door. I got started super quick, kicking cans, pots and other crap under my bed and then cramming the fold-up mattress into the wardrobe, along with pillows, sheets and God knows how many pairs of Gav's crusty pants. It was as if the Red Bull overdose had given me the ability to slow down time.

I opened the windows and sprayed some horrible body spray about. The advert said it's supposed to be a magnet for big gangs of sexy women, but so far all it's attracted is bad luck and, on a field trip last summer, several hundred midges.

Now, I'm not a religious person, in fact you might say the closest thing I have to a god is Captain Picard, but at that moment I prayed to every divine being I could think of.

'God, Allah, Buddha, Vishnu, Jesus, Zeus, Thor, Captain Picard,' I said. 'Please don't let Gav come back while Lisa is here. I'll do anything. Also, if you could do something about my forehead spots, that'd be great. Loving your work, forever and ever, amen.'

I opened the door. Lisa looked weirded out. 'Sorry about that,' I said. 'Just wanted to make sure the place looks presentable.'

'That's all right,' she said, eyeing up my *Star Trek* posters.

'Can I just ask something?' I said, trying to distract her from the bogey-encrusted Picard. 'How did you know I lived here?'

'I have my ways,' she said, with a wink that made me feel like the top of my head was about to spin off. 'No, I saw that Ad kid outside the library. He said he wanted to return an audio book because it wouldn't play anything and had loads of writing on it.'

'It was just a normal book wasn't it?' I said.

'Probably.'

We stood there saying nothing. The one and only **Lisa Hall** was standing in MY BEDROOM! I couldn't do anything but grin. The silence was as potent as one of Gav's farts.

Say something, numbnuts, said Derek. <u>ANYTHING.</u>

Wind blew in through the open window.

'I, um, I like bacon,' I said.

Derek got up from his chair, stormed into the control room bathroom and ripped a sink off the wall.

'Right,' said Lisa.

The silence that followed seemed to last for hours.

'So, do you want to get on with it, or what?'

'Great idea. Let's get down to it!' I said.

Lisa's mouth dropped open slightly.

'Not like that,' I said, my eye twitching. 'I meant in a working sort of way.'

We sat on my bed and started planning the project. All I could do was stare. A real live girl sitting on my bed! And not just any real live girl, **LISA BLOODY HALL!**

She smelt wonderful: like strawberries and ice cream and puppy dogs. Actually no, she didn't smell like a dog, forget that bit.

I tried to slow my heart rate down and relax. I knew I had to play it cool; I wasn't about to do something stupid to impress her like Jordan Foster when he jumped off a shed into a wheelbarrow and ruptured his spleen. I had to demonstrate that I am a sophisticated and trustworthy young gent.

'Lisa,' I said.

'Yes, Joe?' She tucked a stray piece of hair behind her ear.

'Touch this.'

Her mouth dropped open. 'WHAT?'

'My shirt!' I yelped. 'My, my sleeve.'

'O-kay.' She slowly reached over, as if she were petting a pitbull.

'Do you, do you know what that is?' I said, inwardly cursing myself for even starting it.

'What is it?' she said.

Come on, idiot, think. What is it? You just read it on the internet twenty minutes ago, you can do this. Don't just stare at her, it's creeping her out.

'Cotton,' I said. 'And possibly some polyester.'

She stared at me for a second, then laughed. 'You're cute!'

Derek came flying out of the flooded bathroom and joined the other control room men in a conga line. *It's happened! A girl thinks he's cute! Where's the key to the booze cabinet?*

Wait a minute, I said to them. *Does she mean cute like sexy cute, or cute like koala bear cute?*

They stopped dancing and picked their clipboards back up.

We'll look into that right away, said Norman.

I had no confidence in their ability though, especially since they couldn't retrieve a simple chat-up line.

'Ah, thank you,' I said. 'You're not so bad yourself . . . me lady.'

Me lady?

Her laughter shifted up a gear. 'You're like a man from the olden days or something!'

Whatever the hell I was doing, it seemed to be working. My adrenaline was pumping. My nerve endings sparked.

I tried to remember everything I knew about girls, but

« Older posts

other than **Men's Domain** the only advice I'd ever received was from my dad. And that was 'ladies love the bling-bling', which was no use in this situation.

'So,' said Lisa, snapping me out of my daydream. 'Are you looking forward to having a baby?'

'Well, it'll definitely be a challenge,' I said. 'I mean, I've not even had a girlfriend, so . . . '

'Really?' she said.

'No, no, no,' I said, blood burning my cheeks. 'Well, yes. By which I mean, no.'

The control room men punched commands into the system, trying to figure out what the hell I was cacking on about.

Lisa looked right at me. Her eyes were the colour of the ocean. Actually, they weren't, because water isn't blue, it's just an illusion caused by wavelengths of light. Her eyes were the colour of . . . ah, they were the colour of that liquid they pour onto nappies in those adverts, that's it. Nice.

'I find that hard to believe, a nice guy like you,' she said.

I couldn't think of anything to say. My mouth went dry.

'I know you're probably thinking, *Well then why did you turn me down?*' she said.

'Well, maybe a bit,' I said, wondering if it was normal for my ears to be tingling.

'I don't know,' she said. 'I mean, I'd only just finished with Gav, and everything was still a bit weird. I hope you understand.'

Gav. The very mention of his name made my chest go tight. I knew he could come home at any moment and pummel my face into dust with his boulder fists. But that thought just made me realize how different we are: I'm a man of knowledge rather than a man of violence. The Picard to his Kirk. I took a deep breath. The great captain himself gazed down at me from his bogey-infested home on my wall. Make it so.

'Let me tell you something,' I said in the manliest voice I could manage. 'You're too good for him. He treated you like dirt and took you for granted, when he knew there must be a hundred boys who'd give their right arm to be with a great girl like you. He's a scumbag and you're better off without him.'

I was exhausted when I finished. I'd been rehearsing that speech in my head ever since I saw them holding hands on the corridor ages ago. The control room workers slumped back in their seats, shattered.

'Wow,' said Lisa. 'I didn't realize you felt like that.'

'I-I do,' I said. 'I always have. For years, but I never dared to speak to you, because I'd get tongue-tied. I'd see you with these idiots and think—in a just world, that would be me. But the world isn't just. And it never will be.'

She got closer. My heart raced. The control room men downed tins of Red Bull and searched my information banks for all the knowledge I had about kissing. I can't

« Older posts

believe he got through both speeches!

I leaned towards her. The air crackled with tension. *Now is the time. Time to realize your ambition. Time you become a man, Joey boy.*

I closed my eyes and moved closer still. Her breath tickled my face. It was minty fresh.

'WHAT THE—?'

I jumped away. There, in the doorway, was Gav. His face was the dictionary definition of homicidal rage.

'Gav,' said Lisa. 'What are you doing here?'

He stepped further into the room. 'I could ask you the same question.'

'We're studying, Gavin,' I said. 'It's for school.'

'Save it, freak.' He jabbed his sausage finger in my face. 'You were kissing.'

'Not exactly,' I said.

'What the hell would you want to kiss him for, anyway?' said Gav.

'We were rehearsing for a play!' I said. 'We're doing *Waiting for Godot*, the sexy version!'

'You don't have to lie, Joe.' Lisa squared up to Gav. 'Maybe I like Joe, OK? And maybe he likes me.'

I couldn't believe Lisa said she liked me. If Gav killed me there and then, I'd have died happy.

Gav stared at us, his nostrils flaring like a racked-off bull. 'Whatever,' he said. 'You don't know what else I was doing with Leah Burton. That lovebite was nothing.'

I held Lisa back before she smacked him.

'Don't talk to Lisa like that,' I said. 'Not in my room.'

'Oh, but you forget, freak,' said Gav. 'This is my room too, remember?'

Then, as if the council of Gods had considered my request and declined it, the wardrobe door sprang open, sending the fold-up mattress, sheets and pillows tumbling out. Then, as an extra-cosmic middle finger, a pair of Gav's crusty pants arced gracefully through the air and landed on Lisa's shoulder.

'Lisa, wait!' I called to her as she ran from the house. 'Please don't go!'

'I'm sorry, Joe,' she said. 'I need to go. And have a shower.' She turned and ran down the street.

I sat on the kerb outside our house and buried my head between my knees. I could live with the bogey-wiping, the book-farting, the getting-me-banned-from-*Epic-Warfare*, the throwing-Scabby-Barry's-DVDs-on-top-of-my-*Star-Trek*-annuals, the turning-of-my-own-parrot-against-me, maybe even the robbing-me-of-Natalie, but this was a step too far.

I couldn't live in that house any more.

There was only one place to go.

Dad's.

« Older posts

'Hey, son!' he said as he opened the door. 'You do know it's not Scrabble night tonight, don't you?'

I sighed. 'Can I just come in, please?'

I walked in and sat on one of his stupid futuristic chairs while he fetched me a fancy-pants drink with crushed ice. Svetlana sat in her usual place on the sofa with a face like a constipated undertaker.

'So what's happenin' in the hood, my man?' he said. 'Rap with me.'

I looked around the room. Everything in there was white and shiny. Like a classy public bog. It would have to do.

'I'm not happy at home.' My voice came out in a whisper.

'Why?' Dad grinned through his new teeth. 'Is your mother in one of her moods again?'

'No,' I snapped. 'It's not Mum. Well, not exactly.' I rubbed my legs and puffed out my cheeks. 'They've got engaged and—'

'What?' Dad jumped to his feet. Svetlana looked up from her nail-filing. He got this really weird look on his face and then sat back down. *Crap, I wasn't supposed to tell him, was I?*

'I mean, since when?' he said. I noticed his left eye twitching. So that's where I get it from.

'Couple of weeks,' I said, looking at my trainers and feeling like the worst person on Earth.

Dad shook his head and bounced his knees. My stomach

bubbled. He slowly forced a smile.

'Well that's cool beans.' He lifted his glass. 'Here's to them. I only hope they'll be even a fraction as happy as Svet and I are.'

Svetlana rolled her eyes and opened some nail polish.

I tried to compose myself. Talking to Dad is like trying to get through to a brick wall in designer cut-offs.

'But I'm not happy,' I said. 'I want to live here. With you.'

Dad nearly choked on his vodka. Svetlana stopped painting and glared at him.

'You—you want to live here?' he said.

I nodded.

His mouth flapped open and shut. 'Well, you know we'd love to have you, son,' he said. 'But the courts say I can't. You know, custody and that.'

Streetlights twinkled in the dark town outside the window. I felt like I was made of lead.

'And it's not just that—this pad's only got one bedroom.'

'But I could sleep . . . ' I looked for a settee but all I could see were egg-shaped chairs and glass tables. I'd be more comfortable kipping in a junkie's dustbin.

He gave me a thin smile. 'Sorry son,' he said. 'But as I say, the courts.'

The relief on both their faces made me feel sick. *Why did I think this would be a good idea?*

I stood up and made for the door. Dad made a half-arsed

« Older posts

attempt to stop me but I waved him off.

'Just promise me one thing,' I said. 'Don't tell Mum about this.'

He nodded, and without another word, I walked out.

I reached the street in a state of pure misery. I blew out, hoping to see my breath in the air, but it was quite mild for February and I just looked stupid.

I drifted towards the park. Normally, going down there on a Saturday night would be suicide for a kid like me, because of all the dodgy characters hanging around there. But when I remembered that the dodgiest character of all was at home in my bedroom, I stopped worrying.

I put up the hood on my *STAR TREK* hoodie and walked on with my head down.

The old Second World War bunker looked creepy in the dark. Still, if I put some nice furniture in there, bit of Febreze, I could make it a nice home. Even if it is haunted, I'd rather live with an army of ghosts than Gav.

I went over to the lake. Moonlight reflected on its surface. Ducks slept with their heads tucked under their wings. It would have been a nice scene if it weren't for all the used condoms and empty cans of tramp beer lying around.

I picked up some stones to skim across the lake, because that's what you're supposed to do when you're thinking about important stuff.

The first one skipped once then sank. The second one

plopped straight to the bottom. The third one ricocheted off a tree stump and pinged me right in the shin.

A laugh echoed behind me. 'You throw like a bender!'

I turned around to see Greeny sitting on a bench, surrounded by empty cans and burger wrappers.

'What the—?' I said, nursing my shin wound. 'Are you stalking me or something?'

'Nah,' he said. 'To be honest, I didn't even know it was you.'

'So what, you just hang around here, calling random people benders?' I said.

'Well, you did throw like one,' he replied, as if that explained everything.

I cleared some of the crap away and sat down. *This is how bad my life is. I'm hanging out with Greeny.*

'Have you ever thought that your homophobia may just be overcompensation for confusion about your own sexuality?' I said. I remembered reading something similar in one of Mum's women's magazines once.

He got this weird look on his face and his eyes shifted from side to side before that stupid grin finally came back. 'I don't know what half those words mean,' he said. 'But they make you sound bent.'

On the other side of the lake a man who must have been about eighty skipped a stone across the water and it bounced eight times. Yeah well, he probably learned to do

« Older posts

that in the war or something.

'You know,' said Greeny, giving the old boy a salute. 'I've been thinking.'

'Nice to see you're trying new things,' I said.

'I've been thinking that people only pretend to like me because I can make stuff for them on Photoshop. What do you reckon?'

'I think it's possible,' I said. I was in no mood to be nice, and after all he'd put me through, why would I bother?

'Yeah?' he said. 'Cause Gav only ever speaks to me when he wants me to make something for him. Other than that, he just calls me lardy and pushes me around.'

I looked at his stupid sad face and came to the gut-loosening realization that perhaps we weren't that different. The only difference between us was that he tried to impress people like Gav, whereas I'd always known he was a tool.

'The thing is, Greeny.' I held up my hand to refuse a bite of his burger. 'And this is the only time I'm ever going to try and help you out, so listen up. The thing is, you shouldn't try to please people like Gav in the hope that they'll let you into their little club, because they don't care about you.'

Greeny looked like he was about to cry.

'Don't try and be someone else for them,' I said. 'Maybe you could just, you know, try and be yourself? Whatever that is.'

He took a swig from his can and wiped his mouth with

the back of his hand. 'You're dead clever, you know that?' he said.

'Yes,' I said. At least he's right about something.

'Tell you what.' He reached into his back pocket and passed me a business card. 'Take this.'

I grasped it between my little finger and thumb. I didn't especially want to touch something that had been in such close proximity to Greeny's arse.

GREENY'S GRAPHICS
SPECIALIZING IN
DIGITAL PHOTO ENHANCEMENT
AND LIVE HOLOGRAMS

'You've had business cards made?' I said. 'What *are* you?'

'Look, maybe I feel a bit bad,' he said. 'About all the stuff I've made with you on it. The *Star Wars* thing, *The Exorcist* thing, the making-you-look-like-a-tranny thing. I was only following orders, but you know . . . '

'Right,' I said.

'Alls I'm saying is, if you ever need a job doing, I'm your man.' He jerked his thumb into his chest. 'And the first one's on the house.'

I pocketed the card and nodded. 'I'll consider it.'

« Older posts

'Make sure you do, man,' he said, pointing a saveloy finger at me.

I looked into his dumb cow eyes. He seemed genuine, but I'm still not sure.

After I left him, I didn't know where else to go, so I went home.

Loud music came blasting out of my bedroom. I remembered the last album I had on up there was Dark Side of the Moon, but this was definitely not that. Not unless the Floyd had slipped in bonus tracks about 'hoes' and 'getting their drank on' while I was out.

I stomped into the kitchen and found a note on the worktop.

Joe,

Tried calling you but you've left your phone. Jim's mum has been rushed to hospital. They think it might be a heart attack. I don't know when we'll be home.

Love,
Mum

PS. I've left you £20 in case you want to order you and Gavin a pizza.

X

JOE LIKES MEN! JOELIKES MEN! JOE LIKES MEN!

The twenty quid was missing. I eye-balled Syd.

'Did he take the money?'

'Joe likes men, Joe likes men, Joe likes men,' was his reply.

'Yeah well you're so stupid you think the mirror is another parrot,' I said, and ran back into the living room before he could get the last word in. We'll call that one a draw.

I turned on the TV but it didn't cheer me up. BBC Two was showing a documentary about the *Mona Lisa*, Sky One was showing *The Simpsons*, a Lisa episode, and ITV was showing a nappy advert with that blue liquid.

I eventually settled on BBC Four, which was showing a documentary about the Second World War. I was about to text Harry and tell him when I remembered I didn't have my phone. It was in my room. With Gav.

I ran up the stairs two at a time and barged in there. At first I thought it was on fire, until I realized that it was just smoke coming from Gav's and the Blenkinsops' fags. I picked up my phone without a word.

'Hey!' said Gav. 'It's my brother from another mother.'

I extended my middle finger so fast I thought I'd dislocated it.

'Nah, she ain't my mum,' he said. 'And I'm glad 'cause she's a bee-atch.'

« Older posts

I spun round and glared at him, but the Blenkinsops stood up and I realized I was outnumbered. I walked out and checked my phone. The missed call from Mum wasn't on the screen. Someone must have been on it. I checked my text inbox and then my sent box. Two texts had been sent to Lisa:

I tried to count to ten in my head to calm myself down, but couldn't get past three.

RED ALERT! RED ALERT! KILL! KILL!

Please, Joe, don't do anything rash, said Norman, trying to switch the alarms off.

No way, man! Derek screamed. *If there was ever a time to be rash, it's now. Get all over his ass like a rash, baby! Yippee ki yay!*

I hammered on the door, my eye twitching like mad.

'Gav!' I screamed over the music. 'I'm going to murder you, do you hear me? I'll kill you and make it look like an accident!'

The door wouldn't budge, and I could hear them laughing at me inside. I called Lisa. No answer. I pressed redial and waited. It clicked. She answered.

'Lisa!'

'Yeah?' She sounded tired.

'Those texts from my phone,' I panted. 'I didn't write them.'

'Oh, they were from you?' she said. 'I thought it was someone else.'

My heartbeat slowed slightly.

'Oh, OK,' I said. 'It was Gav, anyway.'

'God, I hate him *SO* much,' she said.

'Tell me about it,' I said. I wondered who she thought was sending her abusive texts. Did she have a lot of enemies?

'Can you just promise me something?' I said. 'Can you not tell anyone about the whole, you know, me and Gav thing.'

'Sure,' she said. 'I never want to talk about him again, anyway. Like you said, he's scum.'

'Yeah,' I said. 'And I'm sorry we couldn't, you know . . . '

I thought I heard her sigh. 'Yeah,' she said.

Then she hung up. I closed my eyes. The thudding of the music mingled with the epic migraine forming in my skull. I had to get out and get some air.

Greeny had fallen asleep with his mouth open. I sat next to him. Sitting next to a sleeping Greeny was not how I envisioned spending my Saturday night. But I wasn't about to go home.

« Older posts

I woke up this morning on the settee with Mum and Jim standing over me.

'Aww, look at the little angel,' said Mum.

'That comfy, Joe?' said Jim.

Something felt cold and oozy under my cheek. Turns out I'd been using a kebab as a pillow. I sat up and strips of doner meat clung to my face with dried mayo.

'Why did you sleep down here?' said Mum. 'I told you I don't want this room smelling of boys. Or kebabs for that matter.'

'I couldn't get into my room last night,' I said. 'Gav was having a party in there.'

'Oh was he?' said Jim. 'Well, I think I need to have a word with that boy.' He turned and stomped upstairs.

Mum frowned at me. 'You look awful,' she said.

'Yeah thanks.' I picked a strip of meat off my face and scoffed it.

Mum didn't look too good either: she must have been up all night. She opened the curtains, and I shielded my eyes from the burning light.

'Oh,' I said, blinking hard. 'How's Jim's, er, thing?'

'His mum?' she said. 'She'll be fine. They think it's just her angina, so they're going to discharge her today or tomorrow. It was a bit scary for a while, though.'

'Goody good,' I said, too tired to even laugh at the word 'angina'. Or 'discharge'.

'So she'll be staying here for a while,' said Mum quickly as if she were pulling off a plaster.

I snapped awake. 'What? Bloody hell, why don't you just move the whole family in? This is a house, not a cocking . . . refugee camp.' I shook so much, lettuce fell out of my hair. Mum sat down next to me.

'Look,' she said. 'Doris is an old lady and she's ill. She can't go and live on her own. Not yet.'

'Well, where's she going to sleep?' I said. 'Because I don't think my floor can take another mattress.'

'She'll have the spare room,' said Mum.

So they won't clear it out for me, but they will for a geriatric with chest pains. What a stinking life this is.

'So that means I'm stuck in that room with him?' I said.

'For a while longer, yes,' said Mum.

I looked her straight in the eye. 'Kill me,' I said. 'Kill me right now.'

'You're such a drama queen.' She went into the kitchen. For a second I thought she was going to fetch a knife.

I heard shouting upstairs. Two pairs of heavy footsteps thudded down and out of the front door. The Blenkinsops. I shuddered at the thought of those two warthogs sleeping in my room.

'And they're not welcome in this house again!' Jim yelled.

That was good news, but I couldn't be too happy. I came so close to getting my first kiss. Literally inches. Millimetres if you want to get metric about it. And it was Lisa, too. Whenever I think about her I get this weird feeling in my stomach, like a mixture between excitement and pain and feeling sick. NHS Direct said it was indigestion. But I know better. It's love. No Gaviscon can cure that.

I must have been deep in a daydream because I didn't hear the phone ring, but when I snapped out of it, I caught the end of Mum's conversation.

'Yes,' she said. 'Yes, we're fine. Very happy. Yes, really. Really. OK. Yes, I'm sure. Give my love to Martina, won't you? Oh, yes, Svetlana, how could I forget? Yes, bye.'

My intestines twisted into a knot. Flashbacks from last night burned into my mind's eye. Mum walked in and eye-balled me.

'That was your dad,' she said.

'Oh yeah?' I said, trying to sound natural and failing epically.

'Yes,' she said, giving me that look. 'He was asking about me and Jim getting engaged. Now how would he know about that?'

I gulped and my dry throat clicked.

'I don't know,' I said. 'You know what gossips are like these days, what with the internet and everything. He probably read it on WikiLeaks.'

She put her hands on her hips and my guts churned again.

'All right,' I said. 'I told him.'

How does she do that? Get me to come out with the truth instantly? The CIA should take her on as an interrogator. She's like Jack Bauer.

'I told you not to tell him, didn't I?' she said.

'Yes, I'm sorry,' I said. 'It just slipped out.' It looked like Dad hadn't told her about me asking to move in. What a stupid move that was.

'Sometimes I think you've got Tourette's,' said Mum.

'I wish it were that simple,' I said.

She sat down again. 'Are you happy, Joe?'

'Course I am,' I said, unable to make eye contact.

She gave me that 'I-know-when-you're-lying-because-I-have-special-mum-powers' look again.

'All right, I'm not.'

'Why?' she said. 'Are you having problems with Gavin?'

You don't know the cocking half of it.

'You could say that, yes,' I said.

'I thought as much.' She put her arm around me. 'Do you want to know the truth? I'm not crazy about him myself. He's rude, he's arrogant and he has atrocious friends. But he'll learn. He's grown up with a mother who let him do anything, who didn't care, and didn't give him any boundaries or rules. Now, all of a sudden Jim and I are being firm

« Older posts

with him and he's trying to rebel, but he will learn. Deep down I know he's a good boy, just like you.'

Good boy? Don't make me PUKE.

In the kitchen, Syd started up his daily routine of abuse. Well, Gav has parrot training skills and an anti-social outlook, so maybe he has a promising career as a pirate ahead of him.

'Now I know you're not happy,' said Mum. 'But you shouldn't have gone off and told your Dad about Jim. I didn't want him finding out like that.'

'I know,' I said. 'Sorry.'

She kissed my forehead and came away with a piece of onion on her face which she had to pick off. 'How did he take it?' she asked with a mischievous look.

'Quite badly,' I said.

She laughed. 'Good.'

Jim came back downstairs. He had big bags under his eyes. 'I'm sorry, Joe,' he said. 'He's going to clean all that mess up, don't you worry.'

I wondered what horrors were up there. Poo? Corpses? Corpses covered in poo?

'Who was that on the phone?' said Jim.

'Oh, it was just Keith,' said Mum.

Jim got this strange look on his face. 'Yeah?' he said. 'What did he want?'

'Oh nothing.' Mum shot me a quick glance. 'He just wanted to know if we still had one of his DVDs.'

'Oh. OK,' said Jim, looking at Mum and then me. Before anyone could say anything else, Gav flew down the stairs and out of the door with a slam.

It was at that point I went straight upstairs to visit the crime scene. It wasn't poo-covered corpses, but it was still pretty bad.

After I had a go at tidying it, I went to the park to meet Harry and Ad. They were near a gang of emos playing depressing songs on an acoustic guitar. With all my problems, I should be the one wearing black and whinging all the time. I must admit I did check if Natalie was there, but she wasn't.

I texted Dad and said I wouldn't be coming round. He didn't argue, and I don't think he'll tell Mum I haven't gone. I hope not anyway, because she makes Gav look like a pussycat when she's angry.

'It was unbe-cocking-lievable,' I said to Harry. 'There were fag ends on the floor, burns on the curtains, empty booze bottles everywhere, and what's worse, someone found my **STAR TREK** annuals and drew hair on Captain Picard.'

'Hair on Picard?' he gasped, as if there were no graver crime.

'That's not so bad,' said Ad, eating chips at half ten in the morning like some kind of wild animal. 'Didn't that other **STAR TREK** captain have hair drawn on him?'

« Older posts

'William Shatner wore a wig if that's what you mean,' I said.

'I don't know what I mean,' said Ad.

Harry laughed. 'That one's going on his tombstone.'

'So what have you guys been up to over the weekend?' I said, trying to forget about Gav.

'I discovered that if you play the latest Justin Bieber album backwards,' said Harry. 'It still sounds terrible.'

I laughed, which surprised me, because I seemed to remember telling Greeny that I'd 'never laugh again' on our way to the kebab shop.

'So you've got Justin Bieber's latest album, then?' I said.

'No, it's my sister's,' said Harry, blushing.

'You haven't even got a sister,' I said.

'You've got Bieber Fever!' said Ad, chucking a chip at him.

'Bieber Fever is such a lame catchphrase,' I said. 'If I had it my way, it'd be called the Biebonic Plague and would be treated as such.'

'Anyway, anyway,' said Harry, blatantly trying to change the subject. 'I nearly forgot. How did your study date with Lisa go? Did you boldly go where many men have gone before?'

'Hey!' I snapped.

'Well, come on, old boy, she does have a reputation,' said Harry.

'Yeah, well so does your mum,' I said.

'Good one,' said Ad.

'Look,' I said. 'If you must know, we kind of almost, but didn't quite manage to, kiss, a little bit.'

They stared at me open-mouthed, which was pretty rank because Ad hadn't swallowed his chips.

'What do you mean you 'almost kissed', old boy?' said Harry. 'Did you trip and land on her face?'

'No,' I said. 'We were about to kiss, I think, but something happened.'

'What happened?' said Harry.

'Yeah, tell us, Joe,' said Ad. 'Did you accidentally headbutt her, or something?'

'Did you call her someone else's name?' said Harry. 'Did you show her all your *Star Trek* annuals? Did you fart and follow through? Out with it!'

I sighed. 'Gav walked in,' I said. 'She knows about our . . . situation.'

'Oh bum,' said Ad, laughing.

'You're one unlucky human being, do you know that, old bean?' said Harry. 'So what happened after that?'

'She left,' I said. 'My life is actually, literally over.'

'Careful, you're starting to sound like those jolly fellows over there,' said Harry, pointing at the emos with his pipe.

'I don't care,' I said. 'My whole life is like one massive joke and I'm the only one who's not laughing.'

'Wasn't that on Oh, Inverted World's last album?' said

« Older posts

Ad. Harry laughed and high-fived him. Great, even Ad's scoring points off me now.

'Well, it's nice to see I can count on my friends for support,' I said, which must have made them feel bad, because they stopped laughing. Eventually.

'Look, old bean,' said Harry. 'I've been watching your situation closely these past few weeks and I think it's time we took action.'

'There's nothing we can do,' I said. 'I'm going to die alone, and my corpse will lie undiscovered for months while the mail piles up on the doormat and that stupid treacherous parrot picks my bones clean.'

'OK, now that was definitely on Oh Inverted World's last album,' said Ad.

I could tell Harry was trying to keep a straight face. 'Don't be such a defeatist, soldier,' he said. 'What would have happened if the Allied Forces had just lain down and taken it back in 1939?'

'We'd all be speaking German,' I sighed, having heard that speech about a gazillion times.

'Too right we would!' said Harry. 'Now come on, let's see some fight!'

'But I just can't see a way of changing anything,' I said.

'Oh, there's always a way, old son,' said Harry, holding up the chip Ad threw at him. 'There's always a way.' Then he ate it with a determined look on his face.

'Er, I picked that chip up off the floor, Harry,' said Ad.

After he emerged from behind a bush, looking green, Harry started formulating plots to get rid of Gav. He even drew diagrams in the dirt with a twig.

'How about some more piss balloons?' said Ad. 'They worked last time.'

'It's going to take more than piss balloons to do the trick now, soldier,' said Harry, puffing on his empty pipe. 'This problem calls for precision and cunning.'

'Besides, my room is bad enough as it is without being covered in your urine,' I said.

We sat under the tree and pondered for a bit longer.

'I don't get it, old boy,' said Harry. 'Why are you so bothered about Lisa, anyway? I mean, no offence, but she is a bit out of your league.'

'Yeah,' said Ad. 'I mean, Lisa's like Barcelona, and Joe's like . . . our school football team. Year Seven. No offence, mate.'

'I know, it's just . . . ' I stopped and rubbed my eyes. 'Do you promise not to tell anyone what I'm about to tell you?'

'Certainly,' said Harry.

'I swear on my nan's gravy,' said Ad.

'Don't you mean grave?' I said.

'No.'

'Well, what is it, Joe?' said Harry.

'I've kind of set myself a challenge,' I said. 'And it's that

« Older posts

I'll actually kiss a real live girl.'

Harry and Ad gave each other a look.

'You mean you haven't?' said Harry.

'No,' I said. 'Have you?'

'Oh yeah,' he said. 'Loads.' The stinking liar.

'Well, if you're that bothered, why not try Sam Brothwell from 10d?' said Harry. 'She'll snog anyone for a fiver.'

'Yeah, and she'll show you her boobs for seven-fifty,' said Ad.

'But where's the challenge in that?' I said. 'And besides, I can't afford to spend any Buzzfest money. It's got to be with a girl who actually wants to kiss me.'

'That could be tricky,' said Harry.

'Lisa will,' I said. 'I know she will. I just have to get rid of Gav. Somehow.'

'I never thought I'd say this, but I'm bollocksed,' said Harry. 'Short of firing him out of a catapult, I can't think of a way of removing him.'

'There's loads of girls at Buzzfest,' said Ad. 'You'll defo find one wasted enough to snog you there.'

'But we can't afford to go, can we?' said Harry. 'Because old Safety Queen here won't do Operation Blooper.'

We sat in silence and stared into space. I took my pad out and doodled Gav being fired out of a catapult. I was just getting into the shading when Harry sat up and gasped. Pigeons in the branches above took off in fright.

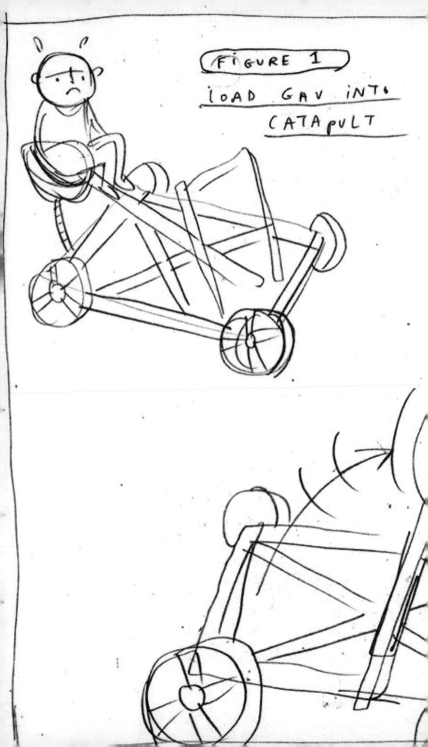

FIGURE 1

LOAD GAV INTO
CATAPULT

Figure 2

FIRE!

INTO

29

'I've got it!' he said. 'I've bloody well got it, old bean!'

He jumped to his feet and threw his hands in the air like he was being held at gunpoint. 'I am a genius!' he yelled. The emos tutted.

'What is it?' I said. Ad looked confused, but then he always does.

'It's easy,' said Harry. 'Why didn't I think of it before? We combine Operation Get Rid of Gav with Operation Blooper!'

I stood up. 'How?'

'We scare him away,' said Harry, pacing up and down. 'You said he's got a mum hidden somewhere. We'll scare him so bad, he'll go running back to her. And we'll film it, send it in, and reap the rewards. Gav will be gone, and we'll be two hundred and fifty quid richer!'

'How can we scare Gav?' I said. 'It's not as if he's a six year old. That's just his reading age.'

'This is the beautiful part,' said Harry. 'We hit him with the scariest thing you can throw at a gullible idiot around here.' He pointed with his pipe at the crumbling bunker on the other side of the park.

'Army ghosts?' I said.

Harry clasped his hands together. 'Army ghosts.'

'But how are we going to do that?' I said. 'It's not as if we can summon spirits from the cocking underworld, is it?'

'I dunno, Joe,' said Ad. 'I mean, my sister got one of them squeegee boards and spoke to some ghosts on that,

« Older posts

once. Later that night, all our lights went out.'

'That was because you plugged two lawnmowers into the same extension lead and caused a power surge,' I said.

'Why did he do that?' said Harry.

'Lawnmower Grand Prix,' said Ad.

'Anyway,' said Harry, after an awkward pause. 'We won't need any squeegee boards for this. I've got a Second World War officer's uniform in my wardrobe. We slap a bit of talc on it to give it a ghostly look and Bob's your aunty, we've got ourselves an army ghost.'

'This is like something off *Scooby Doo*,' said Ad. 'Except we ain't got a talking dog. It'd take at least a few months to train it to do that.'

Me and Harry looked at each other.

'So, are we up for *OPERATION SCOOBY DOO* then, Private Cowley?' said Harry.

I blew out through my lips and shrugged. Deep down I knew it was a bad idea, but the thought of Lisa made me lose all sense of perspective.

'OK, I'm in,' I said. 'Just tell me what I've got to do.'

While Harry and Ad went back to Harry's to prepare the uniform, I called Gav, number withheld.

'Yeah, is that Gav?' I said, trying to disguise my voice.

'Yeah, what do you want?'

'Well, you know Scabby Barry, who gets you the DVDs?'

I said. 'He's on holiday at the minute, so this is his brother. Scabby . . . Steve.'

'Yeah, and?'

'Got some films for you, innit?'

'What films?'

I tried to remember the names of some films that had just come out. The kind Gav would want to watch.

'Well, I've got *G-Man Hustla*,' I said. '*Bionic Soliaz*. And um . . . *Pimpz in da Hood*.'

There was silence on the other end.

Oh my God, he's figured out who it is and he's coming to get me. I knew this was a bad idea; I should have listened to Norman.

'All right,' said Gav. 'How much?'

I started to breathe a bit easier.

'I'll flog you the lot for a fiver,' I said.

'Ah, man, I ain't got that much,' said Gav. 'Oh, actually, I can go home and nick it out of the freak's jar.'

'DO NOT TOUCH THAT JAR,' I said, forgetting I was supposed to be Scabby Steve. 'I mean, it's all right, you can have them for a quid.'

Another silence. 'Sweet,' he said. 'Where can I pick them up?'

'Meet me in the park,' I said. 'In the old army bunker.'

'Why in there?' he said.

'What's up, you scared of the ghosts?' I said.

'Course I ain't,' said Gav. 'I just want to know why it's got to be in there.'

'Well, what it is, right, is the filth is after me, 'cause these films is some high-end stuff, none of that taped-in-the-back-of-the-cinema crap. So I gotta operate somewhere top secret . . . Innit.'

'Yeah, all right, I'll be there in about an hour,' he said, then hung up.

My whole body shook. It was really happening. If it worked, maybe I could be rid of him for good. The thought was too sweet to bear.

Harry and Ad arrived soon afterwards. When I told them Gav was coming, Harry rubbed his hands together.

'This is excellent news, soldier,' he said. 'Now we initiate the final phase of *OPERATION SCOOBY DOO*.'

I glanced at Ad. He grinned back at me as if we were going on a jolly picnic.

'Right, Private Ad, you are the ghost,' said Harry, pacing and taking quick puffs of his pipe.

'Yeah, all right,' said Ad, as if it were no biggy.

'Private Joe, you are Camera One,' said Harry.

'Which camera's that?'

'The one on your bloody phone, old son,' he said. 'And I will be Camera Two. It is important to have two cameras in case of malfunction. One can never be too careful in the theatre of war.'

We crept inside the bunker. It smelled awful. Like an explosion in a urinal. Ad changed into his costume and dabbed talc and mud on his face. He pulled the helmet down as far as he could and folded his glasses away in his top pocket.

The first room of the bunker was about the same size as our shed, but it opened out into a bigger one. We hid around the corner in the second room and waited.

'Are you OK, soldier?' said Harry.

'Yeah, just a bit nervous,' I said.

'Don't be.' He patted my shoulder. 'Once this is over, Gav will be running away to his mum in . . . Where did you say his mum is?'

'Scotland,' I said.

'Scotland,' he said. 'Imagine that.'

'I am. It's sweet,' I said, as images of kilt-wearing caber tossers beating Gav with bottles of Irn-Bru danced through my mind.

'If he's going to Scotland I hope he's got an up-to-date passport,' said Ad.

'I love you, old son,' said Harry.

The tension was unbearable. Things scurried and squeaked in the darkness. I could just about make out Harry and Ad crouched in the other corner, Ad closest to the opening, ready to jump out.

I pressed the light on my Enterprise watch. *He'll be here*

« Older posts

any minute now. Any minute now. Any minute . . .

Footsteps crunched in the dirt outside the bunker. Ad peeped round the corner. I switched my phone to camera mode.

'Go! Go! Go!' Harry whispered.

I pressed record and watched through the viewfinder. Ad jumped out with a ghostly shriek. Something wasn't right. Something wasn't right at all.

It wasn't Gav.

'THE POWER OF CHRIST COMPELS YOU!' Mad Morris boomed, sprinkling Ad with some kind of liquid. 'THE POWER OF CHRIST COMPELS YOU!'

Ad stumbled back to us. 'Aargh, he's throwing cider at me!'

We scrambled back into the third room, with Mad Morris close behind.

'SHOW YOURSELF, SATAN!'

There was an old window at the back of the room. We gave Ad a leg-up out of it as Morris came around the corner. Harry lifted me out before he got out himself.

We went our separate ways without looking back. By the time I got home, my lungs were burning. It looked like Gav was still out. Maybe he was going to find Scabby Steve. God, if only Mad Morris had stayed away for a bit longer.

I went into the kitchen, where I was startled by the sight of an old lady in a Cliff Richard jumper sitting at the table with Mum.

'Oh hello, you must be Joseph,' she said.

'Hi,' I said, trying to normalize my breathing.

'This is Doris,' said Mum, doing her 'be nice' face.

I could hear Jim clearing the spare room out upstairs. Cocking marvellous.

'Now have you seen that grandson of mine?' said Doris. 'I bet he was worried about his nana.'

'Yes, he seemed very concerned,' I said. Luckily the old dear doesn't seem to get sarcasm.

'I heard about his little stunt,' she said, suddenly going serious. 'And he'll be getting a thick ear from me, don't you worry.'

Maybe she's not so bad after all.

I said goodbye to Doris and went upstairs after checking again that Mad Morris hadn't followed me home. My room still smelled a bit smoky, but I was starting to get used to it.

I lay on my mattress, stuck on the last series of *The Next Generation* that I've watched billions of times and scarfed a whole bag of Doritos, cherishing some alone time for once. Then the door swung open.

« Older posts

'What you looking at?' said Gav. His ear looked redder than normal. Doris must have got him.

'*Star Trek*,' I said.

'What's that?' he said. 'Gay Trek?'

'No, Gavin, it's *Star Trek*,' I said. 'Or are you deaf as well as stupid?'

'Who do you think you're talking to?' he said.

'You, Gavin,' I said. 'Because there's no one else here. That is unless one of those Jeremy Kyle rejects is still hiding somewhere. But then, they're both so obese, there's nowhere they could remain undetected.'

He pointed at me with his big meaty finger. 'You ain't gonna get away with disrespecting me much longer.'

'Disrespecting you?' I said. 'Who do you think you are, Tony cocking Soprano?'

'Yeah, you would listen to opera, you boff,' he said.

This is the level of intellect I'm having to deal with here.

'You wanna hear something weird, freak?' Gav sat on the bed and kicked his disgusting trainers off. 'I got a phone call from this bloke saying he was my mate Scabby Barry's brother. But I just saw Scabby Barry in the precinct and he said he ain't got no brother.'

'Yeah, that's spooky,' I said.

He stared at me. My eye twitched. He knows, I thought. But then he lay down and started picking his nose and wiping it on Picard.

I can't believe this is happening to me. I reached into my pocket and found Greeny's business card still in there.

GREENY'S G
SPECIALIZ
DIGITAL PHOTO EN
AND LIVE HOL

Maybe it's something to think about? I don't know.

Monday 13th February

WHAT IS HAPPENING!?

I've gone from verging on tears to grinning like a mental in less than twenty-four hours!

Maybe this is what it's like to be bipolar!

Blargh! Even thought the last thing I want to do is sit here and write, I feel like I have to get it down because today is now officially the Best Day of My Life. Straight in at number one.

TOP FIVE BEST DAYS OF MY LIFE

1. Today.
2. When I met Patrick Stewart and he signed my Star Trek DVDs.
3. When I discovered that you can get two Mars bars of the vending machine down the precinct if you p the button twice quickly.

I'm struggling to think of two more, but who cares? Today is enough to make up for all of them.

« Older posts

I was woken up early by a text. **From Lisa.**

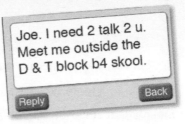

Joe. I need 2 talk 2 u.
Meet me outside the
D & T block b4 skool.

Reply   Back

I jumped up out of bed in my Batman pyjamas and freaked out. I slapped tons of cover-up on my zits, brushed my teeth five times and just about managed to get my hair slightly neater than Mad Morris. All the while, my brain whizzed with questions. What could she want me for?

I'm not sure, said Norman. *But please don't get too excited. Because when you get excited, that's when you start . . . saying things.*

Pfft, said Derek. *Can you believe this guy? You get asked to meet up by the most smoking-hot girl in school and you're not supposed to be even a teensy bit jazzed? Go nuts, my man. It's so obvious she's dying for a piece of the Joe-Joe action. Go give the lady what she wants.*

I set off early and got to the D & T block before she did. I noticed there were still faint yellow patches on the pavement. I think when that careers advisor told us to 'leave our mark on the world' that wasn't what he had in mind.

Then she arrived.

'Hi, Joe,' said Lisa with a smile.

'Hi, L-Lisa,' I said, already turning into a wreck.

'Thanks for meeting me,' she said.

'It's fine,' I said. 'It's not as if I have anything better to do at this time of the morning. Besides eating Coco Pops.

But I'm thinking of ditching them anyway—I should really move on to a more grown-up cereal. Like muesli. I always thought that stuff was like rabbit food, but they're energetic little fellows, aren't they? Always running across roads and reproducing. And the volume of poo they generate is astonishing. In fact, their droppings do look a little like Coco Pops, which if you think about it, brings us full circle.'

The control room men gawped in disbelief.

Why the hell is he talking about cereal and rabbit crap? Derek shrieked.

Lisa didn't say anything and I didn't know what to do, other than grin like an idiot.

'Anyway, the reason I wanted to talk to you is, I've had a rethink,' she said.

The control room men took their heads out of their hands and watched.

'Oh right,' I said. 'What about?'

'About us,' said Lisa. 'I realized that we shouldn't let Gav get in the way of our feelings for each other.'

'R-really?'

'Really.' She held my hands.

The control room men dashed around trying to put out fires in the equipment. *This has never happened before! There is no protocol!*

'Um, great,' I said. 'M-me neither.'

I know! For the first time in my life, I actually have a

girlfriend! The most **beautiful**, **popular** girl in school has asked me out, and it hasn't ended with me waking up in my own bed covered in sweat and/or various other fluids! This kind of thing should not happen.

The day passed by in a haze. My head was filled with sunny meadows and rainbows and hopping bunnies. Who needs school? What use is trigonometry when you're in love? My whole body felt like it had been shot through with a thousand volts.

We met again at the General Studies room to pick up our baby. I reached out and held Lisa's hand. She pulled it away.

'Sorry, Joe,' she said. 'But I think we should keep this between us for now.'

'Oh,' I said. 'OK.'

'Just for a little while,' she said. 'I don't want people thinking I'm on the rebound from scummy Gav, do I?'

She's right. She must be. I don't know how this whole girlfriend thing works, so I'm just going to assume that this is standard procedure, because there is nothing about this on Men's Domain. NOTHING! How can it call itself a 'complete guide to life for the twenty-first century metrosexual male'? And what, for that matter, is a metrosexual? Someone who fancies trams?

In the classroom, Miss Tyler gave us our 'baby'. We have to look after it all the time, except during school hours.

Then, we have to deactivate it. It's got this really weird vacant expression. I tried to think who it reminded me of, then it clicked.

'It looks just like Ad,' I said to Lisa. We looked over at him, trying to fit the tip of his tongue into the end of a pencil sharpener.

'Yeah it does,' she said. 'But like, a girl version.'

I laughed. 'Adwina.'

Miss Tyler did this boring speech about how the project would help us to appreciate other human beings and blah, blah, cocking blah, but all I could think about was how much my life had changed. Yesterday, I was single and lonely, and today I've got a girlfriend and a child! It's as if my life's on fast forward. At this rate I'll be dead by next Thursday.

But what I mainly thought about was how close I am to getting my first kiss and fulfilling my ultimate ambition. Because girlfriend equals kisses, right?

10 p.m.

WRONG!

Lisa insisted that we spend the evening at my house. She reckons it's important that we have some quality time together with our baby.

I walked back with Harry and Ad after school, trying to convince them I was telling the truth.

« Older posts

'So you're going out with Lisa, for real?' said Ad, swinging his doll around by its leg.

'For the eighteenth time, yes!' I said.

'See this?' said Harry, pointing at himself. 'This is my sceptical face.' 'Why would I lie?' I said.

'Because Gav has finally broken your mind and you're suffering from delusions?' said Harry.

As we rounded the corner I spotted Lisa coming towards us with her friends Ellie and Chloe. 'Look, here she is. Hi, Lisa!'

Lisa eyeballed me as if to say 'shut up', then walked off without saying anything.

Harry clapped his hand on my shoulder,

'I am positively tearful at the display of love I just witnessed there, old son.'

'Look,' I said, 'she just wants to keep it on the down-low for now, that's all.'

'The down-low?' said Harry. 'You sound like a granddad trying to be hip.'

'I'll believe you with proof, Joe,' said Ad. 'Like a pair of her knickers.'

'You make me sick,' I said.

'I thought that was the waltzer,' said Ad.

'So what are you doing tonight?' said Harry. 'Are you going on a date to the park, where she sits on a bench and you watch her from the bushes?'

'No, actually, she's coming over to my house,' I said.

'Why your house?' said Harry. 'I thought she couldn't stand to be around Gav. That's rather curious if you ask me.'

'Well, we would go to hers but she says we can't,' I said.

'Why's that?'

'She says her mum doesn't want her seeing any boys.'

'Bit late for that,' said Harry.

I crumpled an old merit card up and bounced it off his forehead.

'So what does this mean for **OPERATION SCOOBY DOO**?' Harry said. 'Is it still a goer?'

'I don't know,' I said. 'I mean, he's still got to go, but there must be a better way of doing it.'

Harry glared at me. To suggest I had better strategies than him is like giving colouring-in tips to Vincent van Gogh.

'Well, what's your plan, oh glorious leader?' He bowed down to me.

'I don't know,' I said. 'But Greeny's offered his services, so . . . '

Harry and Ad gave me an 'are you mental' look.

'Greeny?' said Harry. 'Greeny as in blobby-always-calls-you-a-bender Greeny?'

I nodded.

'I wouldn't trust him, mate,' said Ad. 'Remember what he did to me and Harry?'

I did. He invited them to a fancy dress Halloween party. When they arrived, dressed as Winston Churchill and Lady

« Older posts

Gaga, they discovered that it wasn't actually a fancy dress party but a massive joke at their expense.

'It was a stupid idea having a Halloween party in March, anyway,' said Ad.

'Look, I don't like him much either,' I said. 'But I think he genuinely might be able to help.'

'All right, old son.' Harry folded his arms. 'But don't come running to me when he grasses you in to Gav and he breaks both your legs.'

'Well, if he breaks both my legs, I won't be able to go running to anyone, will I?' I said.

'All right then, don't come wheeling yourself over to me on your motorized bloody scooter,' he said. 'Smart-arse.'

After I left Harry and Ad, I rushed straight into town to buy Lisa's Valentine's card for tomorrow. Missing our first Valentine's would be bad form.

I bought one with a couple of bees on the front. Inside it says 'I can't bee without you.' This is funny because they are bees.

I also bought her a teddy bear holding a heart that says, 'I can't bear to be without you.' This is funny because it is a bear. If this doesn't demonstrate my GSOH I don't know what will.

After dinner, I shut myself in the loft with my torch. I've never written a Valentine's card before. How is it supposed to work?

« Older posts

Dear Lisa,

Happy Valentine's Day,

I can't bee without you.

Love,

Your not-so-secret admirer!

JC xxxxx

PS: JC stands for your boyfriend, Joe Cowley, not Jamal Chauhan. Just thought I'd point that out so as to avoid any confusion.

PPS: Nor does it stand for Jack Cartwright. What am I saying? I've just told you it's your boyfriend Joe Cowley. Please ignore this PPS.

PPPS: Just to reiterate. It's Joe Cowley. Your boyfriend.

I probably should have practised on a bit of scrap paper first.

Once that was done, I went down and activated Adwina. Doris said she doesn't think it's right that schools had boys playing with dolls.

Page 159 of 352 »

'In my day, boys did woodwork, and girls learned how to cook,' she said.

Yeah, well in her day they probably had to stop most lessons halfway through because of Viking attacks.

Adwina started crying straight away. I fed her with this electronic bottle but she still wouldn't stop.

'She wants winding, me duck,' said Doris. 'Give her here.'

Doris put Adwina over her shoulder and rubbed her back. Eventually, she made this little burping noise and stopped crying.

'Thanks Doris,' I said.

'That's all right, Thomas,' she said, cradling Adwina in her arms. 'You know, I never had a daughter of my own.'

'Really?' I said, taking Adwina off her. 'That's dead interesting. Anyway, I've got to go.'

Doris got this odd look on her face then. I don't know why.

I brushed my teeth three more times before Lisa arrived. When she knocked on the door, I ran down the stairs so fast I nearly face-planted the windowsill.

'Hi, Lisa.' I threw the door open and puckered up.

'Hi, Joe,' she said as she walked past me.

'Hello, my love,' said Doris from the living room. 'Are you the baby's mother?'

'Er, it's a doll,' said Lisa.

We went upstairs, taking Adwina with us. Lisa threw her down on the bed.

'Shouldn't we be careful with that?' I said. 'Miss Tyler said something about them having an internal chip.'

'You need to loosen up a bit, Joe.' She walked towards me slowly, like a catwalk model.

I gulped and my eye twitched. 'Oh, I'm loose,' I said. 'I'm loose as a . . . goose. Or possibly a moose. Drinking juice.'

She smiled and put her arms around me. I felt faint. She leaned in close. So did I.

'Is Gav here?' she said.

'Um, no,' I said.

Lisa stopped smiling and relaxed her grip on me. 'So what do you want to do? Shall we watch a film?'

'Yeah, OK,' I said.

'What films have you got?'

'Well, I recently got the *Star Trek: Generations* Director's Cut Japanese import,' I said.

'What's *Star Trek*?' she said.

We just ended up watching telly and taking it turns seeing to Adwina. She kept asking if I knew when Gav was going to be back. Well, I suppose she wanted to avoid him, because she went home at about half eight.

I walked her to the front door.

'So . . . ' I said.

'Yeah,' she said.

'This has been . . . nice.'

'It has,' she said.

The control room men hammered buttons and pulled levers. *Go, go, go!*

I leaned in and closed my eyes. Adwina started screaming upstairs.

'You should probably see to the baby,' said Lisa.

'Yeah.' I opened my eyes again. 'See you tomorrow.'

She smiled and blew me a kiss. I caught it in my hand.

That doesn't count, does it?

No, not really.

11 p.m.

Gav has only just got in! Jim is going MENTAL! 'You're grounded!' he's saying. Great, that's just what I need when I'm trying to romance Lisa. Still, it won't stick. Keeping Gav in this house is like trying to contain a rhino in a playpen made of candyfloss. Just managed to get Adwina off to sleep.

12 a.m.

Adwina woke up crying. Gav sat up in bed. 'What the hell is that?' he said. Gave Adwina another feed, which got her off to sleep. Hopefully that's it for the night.

12.45 a.m.

Adwina crying AGAIN. Fed her but that didn't work. Changed her nappy which did the trick. Gav asked what it is again. His powers of observation are abysmal.

1.20 a.m.

Adwina crying again. Kill me now.

1.35 a.m.

Adwina has stopped crying.

1.55 a.m.

Adwina screaming. For a few seconds, my sleep-deprived brain actually considered taking her to A & E. Gav threatened to take her battery out. I said if he does that I'll fail. He asked why I care about school. I said so I don't end up like him. He didn't say anything else.

4.30 a.m.

Right, I think she may be down for the night.

4.32 a.m.

She isn't.

5.05 a.m.

OK, that's it. She's down. I hereby swear, and let this be the written agreement, I will never ever have kids. Still, I wonder what mine and Lisa's kids would look like? Hopefully they'd have her looks. And my intellect. The other way around would be a disaster.

5.35 a.m.

Adwina crying again. If I fail my algebra test tomorrow, I'm blaming it on lack of sleep, rather than the fact that I haven't done any revision whatsoever.

Tuesday 14th February

Happy Valentine's Day? Pah. Yes that's right, pah.

Woke up this morning feeling like a hung-over zombie. Jim had to drag Gav out of bed to get him to go to school.

'How did you sleep last night, Doris?' said Mum over breakfast.

'Oh, I slept like a baby,' she said.

I can only surmise she means she woke up every ten minutes screaming.

I lifted up Adwina's back flap to deactivate her but Doris stopped me.

« Older posts

'What are you doing, duck?' she said.

'I'm deactivating her,' I said. 'I've got to go to school.'

'But you can't just switch a baby off, my love,' she said. 'Let me look after her.'

I was going to refuse but she looked really sad so I let her have the doll. Plus, giving her something to do might speed up her recovery so she can get out and Gav can have the spare room. That is, if I can't get rid of him first.

The algebra test was a disaster. I'd just hidden Lisa's card and present by her locker and I could barely keep my eyes open. Ad didn't exactly help either, pestering me for answers.

'Here, Joe,' he whispered. 'What's the answer to this one: n equals something?'

'I'm not telling you, it's a test,' I said.

'Ah, come on,' he said.

'No.'

'Please.'

'No.'

'Please, mate!'

'What part of no don't you understand?' I said.

'Well, n obviously,' said Ad.

Even if I wanted to, I couldn't have told him. It all just looked like a jumble of letters and numbers to me. I never did find out what n equalled, but I did find out that F equals FAIL.

Tried telling Boocock that I couldn't do PE because I was too tired, but he was having none of it and announced that we'd be doing rugby, even though it was belting it down.

Before I could shut myself up I pointed out yet again that my human rights were in breach, and he pointed out that if I didn't shut up, he'd exercise his human right to pick me up in the air and drop me. I think we both know that isn't a right.

Out on the field, we were paired up to practise tackling while the rain came down sideways. By some really jammy miracle, Harry and Ad got paired up together. In the end, everyone had a partner except me, Gav and Henry 'Squirgy' Kallow, who's even scrawnier than I am.

'Now then,' said Boocock, 'you'd think that given their similar builds, I'd put Kallow and Cowley together, which would leave James to team with me. But given Cowley's incessant bleating about his poxy human rights, he can go with James, and Kallow can go with me.' I am so reporting him to Ofsted.

From where I was standing, I could see into the swimming pool, where the girls had their PE lesson. Not the worst view in the world. Lisa emerged from the water, looking like a goddess in a tight blue swimming costume. She stood on the side of the pool and hugged herself to get warm.

I looked over at Gav, mud smeared on his face and wearing a rugby shirt two sizes too small. What a contrast. Like

« Older posts

going from a sirloin steak to a mouldy microwave burger in the same meal. He sneered at me and dragged his thumbnail across his throat.

'Now then, boys, pay attention,' said Boocock, pacing around with his hands behind his back. 'James and Cowley here are going to demonstrate.'

My heart sank into my shin pads.

'Now, one of you is going to have the ball, and the other is going to run at him and tackle him for it.' Rain ran into my eyes as my will to live withered like a slug in salt.

'Cowley.' He shoved the ball into my chest. 'You are going to stand there while James tackles you.'

'What?' I yelled while everyone laughed. I swear I could see a little smirk under Boocock's daft moustache.

'Ready, James?' said Boocock.

'Oh yeah,' said Gav, snarling.

'This isn't right, you know!' I cried.

Boocock got into position behind me, probably so he could get a good view of me being obliterated. He blew his whistle.

Time seemed to slow down. Gav ran at me through the driving rain. Clumps of mud flew out behind him. I held the ball tight. As far as I was concerned, that ball was Lisa, a much less sexy version, and I had to protect her. He got closer and closer, picking up speed as he went, all six feet of him.

In that split second, I knew what I had to do. I realized the real difference between me and Gav. He goes charging at things head on whereas I, like Captain Picard, think things through and consider the consequences. To deal with Gav, I don't need to be tough, I need to be clever.

Just as he was about to make impact, I clutched the ball to my chest and dived out of the way. As I hit the sodden, muddy ground, I turned my head just in time to see Gav take out Boocock with a wicked flying spear tackle.

He made me do twenty laps after that, but it was so, so worth it.

Got home this afternoon to find Adwina fully dressed in baby clothes.

'How did this happen?' I said to Doris.

'Oh, my friend Florrie popped round this morning and as luck would have it, she had some spare baby clothes in her bag. She knits them, you see.'

'Right,' I said. 'So, do you want me to have Adwina back now?'

'Ad what?' she said. 'No, her name's Ivy, after my sister.'

'Riiiiight,' I said. 'So, shall I take Ivy off your hands, then?'

Doris pulled her close. 'No, I don't mind having for a while longer, me duck,' she said. 'We're having a nice time together, aren't we, Ivy? We've been listening to my Cliff Richard LPs. Yes we have, yes we have.'

She's loopy, there's no doubt about that, but at least the project will be nice and easy from now on.

« Older posts

Making the most of being baby-free, I took some of Mum's scented candles up to my bedroom. Then I found a Spotify playlist called 'Valentine's Day Love Songs— Perfect for Gettin' it Oooonnn'. Finally, as the icing on the sexy cake, I draped an old red T-shirt over my lamp to give the room a subtle glow.

It only took half an hour, but by the time I'd finished, I'd turned my bedroom from a pants and Pot Noodles dumping ground into a sensual boudoir of delights.

Lisa came over at about half five, wearing this little black dress. God, she's lush. She gave me a hug when she came in, so that's a start. She had this really strong perfume on which made me sneeze.

'Gav's not here, is he?' she said.

'Yeah he is,' I said. 'But he's in the living room watching *World's Wildest Monster Truck Disasters*, so we can get out of his way upstairs.' I couldn't wait to see her face when she saw our love den.

'Oh no,' she said. 'I can't be alone with you in a bedroom because who knows what might happen?' She winked and I nearly passed out.

'Hello, Gavin,' she huffed as she walked in.

'What are you doing here?' he said, not even looking up from the TV, where a monster truck flipped over a flaming caravan in super slo-mo.

'Just visiting my boyfriend,' she said. My cheeks burned.

'I told you, we split up,' he said.

'Not you, you idiot,' she said. 'My new boyfriend, who actually cares for me.'

Lisa held my hand. Electricity pulsed up my arm.

'You ain't serious.' Gav looked at us for the first time.

'Oh, I am,' said Lisa. She had a dangerous glint in her eye as she slipped her arm around me.

Gav turned back to the TV and grunted. 'Whatever,' he said. 'Once you've had me there ain't no way to go but down, anyway.'

I looked at him there, eating a Pot Noodle, his big toe poking out of a hole in his disgusting grey sock, and thought that if I am downhill from that in any way, I might as well just throw myself off a bridge and be done with it.

'You're a pig, Gavin,' said Lisa. 'Joe is a real man. Aren't you, Joe?'

'Um, yes,' I said. 'I think so . . . last time I checked.'

Gav made a 'whatever' noise and slurped the last of the water from his pot. Lisa scowled at him.

'Shall we go upstairs, then?' I said.

'No,' she snapped. 'We'll stay down here.'

She took the seat next to Gav, leaving me with nowhere to go but the chair next to the window. Gav tutted and turned the monster truck show up louder.

'This is nice,' I said to myself.

Mum and Jim came home after a while and Gav had to

« Older posts

turn his show off. Mum was really pleased that Lisa was here, chatting to her about dresses and fashion and stuff like that, as if she had any idea what she was talking about. I mean, she's ancient. She's like thirty-seven. She even came over to me, dug me in the ribs and whispered, 'Nice one, son, you've pulled a cracker there.'

Then Doris came down with Adwina. Lisa asked to have a look but Doris wouldn't let her. God knows what I'll do when we have to give her back.

'So, Lisa,' I said, when Mum and Jim went out for a walk. 'Can we just go upstairs for a sec?'

'Why are you trying to get me upstairs, Joe?' said Lisa.

Gav sniggered. 'He's heard about your rep.'

'Keep out of this, monkey boy,' she said.

'I just, um, want to show you something,' I said.

'Well can't you show me here?'

'Nah, man, I don't want to see that,' said Gav.

'I wasn't referring to my penis, Gavin,' I said. 'I know you're obsessed with it but you're just going to have to let it go.'

'*You're* going to have to let it go,' he said.

Idiot.

We sat in silence for another hour. I doodled Lisa being kidnapped by a giant ape (Gav) climbing up a skyscraper, and me getting KillTech 3.0 to blast him with rockets. By the time I'd finished Lisa decided she was going home. I insisted on walking her, even though she argued for ages

that she didn't want me to.

My pulse got quicker the further we got into her street. Everyone knows that the walk home is always followed by the kiss goodnight. It's the law.

'So,' I said when we got to her house. 'Here we are, then.'

'Er, yeah,' she said.

We stood there for a while. A black cat ran in front of us.

'Been a nice night, hasn't it?' I said.

'Hmm.'

She seemed bored. Maybe she'd been waiting for me to make the first move. Time to be bold. *Control room: commence kiss initiation.*

I leaned forward and tried to kiss her, but she stepped back.

'What are you doing?'

'I don't know,' I said. 'Trying to kiss you?'

'Look, Joe,' said Lisa. 'I don't know what kind of girl you think I am, but we've only been together a couple of days. I'm not ready for that yet.'

'Oh,' I said. 'I'm sorry.'

'Yeah,' she said.

'Anyway, did you get my card and present?'

'Yeah.'

'Did you like them?'

'Yeah, I love puppies,' she mumbled

'But—' I said, and then stopped. I got her a bear. That meant someone else got her a Valentine's present, didn't

« Older posts

it? Who would do that to my woman? Then I remembered that no one actually knows she is my woman.

'Good,' I said. 'I knew you liked puppies. That's why I got you that, erm, thing.'

She didn't say anything.

'So,' I said, trying to sound all jolly. 'Have I got anything?'

'I don't believe in Valentine's Day,' she said. 'I think it's a big con to make money out of people.'

'You're right,' I said. 'Grrrr, bloody . . . Moonpig.'

She wrapped her arms around herself and shivered.

'Can I just ask something?' I said.

'Yeah, but make it quick, it's cold.'

I sighed. 'Why did you want to stay downstairs all night?' I said. 'I thought you didn't like Gav.'

She frowned and bit her bottom lip. 'I don't,' she said. 'But I don't know. Maybe it's because . . . because . . . I don't trust him. I have to know where he is or I can't relax.'

'Oh,' I said. 'OK.'

'Yeah.'

'That's actually a, um, interesting strategy,' I said. 'Similar to one used by Captain Picard in the ***Star Trek: The Next Generation*** episode, 'The Enemy'. Series three, episode seven. You see, what happens is, they take a Romulan on board the Enterprise, and Picard realizes that he's more use to them alive than dead, but the only way of keeping him alive is with a ribosome transfusion, but the only crew member who is a match is Worf and, if you know anything about Worf, you'll know—'

'Goodnight, Joe,' she said and went inside.

I couldn't believe I went to all that trouble for nothing. And it's all down to Gav. If it weren't for him, Lisa would be all over me, I know it. She pretty much said so herself.

I took Greeny's business card out of my wallet and rang him.

'You know that favour you promised me?' I said. 'I'm calling it in.'

'Wicked,' said Greeny. 'What have you got in mind?'

I had an idea. I didn't know if it was even possible, but it was an idea. I didn't tell him what it was, though. I arranged a face-to-face meeting with him for tomorrow, where I can be sure that he's not recording me or anything like that.

10 p.m.

The candles have burned themselves out. While cleaning all the Valentine's junk away, I noticed a card for Gav on the side. It's signed from 'the girl who misses you'. Who the hell would miss him? Must be that daft cow Leah Burton. How stupid can you get?

10.10 p.m.

Mum came in with Adwina and had a go at me for dumping my homework on Doris. I said if I really wanted to give

« Older posts

my homework to Doris it'd be History, because she's been around for most of it. Mum not amused.

3.10 a.m.

This doll must be defective.

Wednesday 15th February

'I've got some bad news,' I said to Harry and Ad over lunch. 'I'm going to see Greeny in a minute.'

They exchanged 'what the hell' looks.

'I can't believe you're actually doing this, old boy,' said Harry. 'You're asking for trouble. You know as well as I do how desperate he is to take up permanent residence in Gav's lower intestine.'

'I know,' I said. 'But have you got any better ideas?'

'I have,' said Ad.

We stared at him, stunned.

'You have?' I said.

'Yeah,' he nodded, as if it were no biggy.

'Well, what is it, old bean?' said Harry.

Ad leaned forward and narrowed his eyes.

'I'm thinking . . . ' he said, 'piss balloons.'

I picked up my tray. 'I'll be off, then.'

'All right, but it's your funeral,' Harry called after me.

Maybe it is. I smiled at Lisa, who was sitting with Ellie and Chloe, but she blanked me. This is all Gav's fault, I know it.

Greeny was waiting for me by the bike shed. Some other kids were there, smoking and playing crap music off their phones.

We turned to leave and ran straight into Gav and the Blenkinsops.

'Sorry, girls,' said Gav. 'But yous two is gonna have to go somewhere else to play with each other's knobs, innit?'

'Girls don't have knobs, Gavin,' I said. 'Except maybe your mum.'

We ran down the school drive to get away. Greeny is surprisingly fast for a plus-size.

'So where are we going?' he said, panting.

I examined his face for even the tiniest trace that he was up to something. If he was messing with me, he was being very clever about it indeed.

'Before I take you,' I said. 'I need you to promise me that this is genuine and you're not setting me up.'

'Yeah, man,' he said. 'Scout's honour.'

'You were a Scout?' I said.

'Yeah,' he said. 'Until we went camping and I got kicked out for supposedly eating all the supplies. Totally wasn't me. It was one of them undercarriages of justice things.'

I led him back to my house, still undecided.

I'd be wary, if I were you, said Norman. *He does have a history of duplicity.*

« Older posts

Yeah, and you have a history of being a pompous ass, said Derek. *Go with the fat boy, Joe. He's your best hope.*

I took him upstairs, but stopped outside my bedroom.

'I need you to promise me one more thing,' I said. 'That you will not tell anyone what I am about to tell you. If it gets out, I'll know it was you.'

'God, what is this? The Spanish Expedition?' he said.

I raised my eyebrows at him.

He puffed his cheeks out. 'Fine,' he said. 'Cross my heart, hope to die, blah, blah, blah.'

I opened the door and walked inside, allowing Greeny to take in the extra mattress, the huge pants, the Pot Noodle cups, and the Hip Hop Honeyz DVDs scattered around. I only tidied yesterday for God's sake.

'So this is the big secret?' said Greeny. 'That you're a slob with a giant pants fetish?'

I shook my head. 'The pants aren't mine, Greeny.'

'Well, whose are they?'

I said nothing.

'No way,' he said.

'Way.'

'Gav?'

'Gav.'

'Crap.'

'Crap.'

'But how?'

I sat him down and explained everything that happened with Mum and Jim and how I have to get rid of Gav. I didn't tell him about Lisa though; I have to respect her wishes.

'But what can I do?' said Greeny. 'I specialize in digital enhancement and special effects, not . . . bear traps.'

'Well, this is the thing,' I said. 'Harry had the idea of scaring Gav off by making him think the whole area is haunted by army ghosts, and I know you can do holograms . . . '

A grin spread across his big moon face.

'So, do you think that's something you could do?' I said.

'Yeah,' he said. 'Easy-peasy, booby-squeezy.'

He started straight away, sizing up the room and planning where he'd hide the projector and if it would be possible to get some atmospheric lights in there. He even said he'd come over after school to set up.

I gave him this sketch of what I wanted the soldier to look like. He said he could do it, and make it a billion times scarier.

I asked Lisa to wait until after six to come over. I told her I had to take Syd to the vet's to see if they could stop him talking. Actually, that might not be a bad idea.

The other problem was keeping Gav out of the room. When Greeny arrived with his rucksack full of equipment, I sneaked him upstairs while Gav watched *America's Most Dangerous Psychopaths* in the living room.

I stood by the door and watched Greeny. It was amazing how quick he worked. He screwed this black, golf-ball-sized thing to the top of my wardrobe and covered it with an old blanket.

'Now it's time to test this bee-atch,' he said. 'I can project any image as a hologram. Check it.'

He pressed something on the screen of his iPad and in a split second, there was Scarlett Johansson, standing in my bedroom.

'Wow,' I said.

'I know,' he said. 'I've had hours of fun with this thing.'

I smiled. 'Hey, Greeny,' I said, 'could you get Captain Picard on that?'

'Who?'

'Captain of the USS Enterprise.'

'But isn't he a bloke?'

'Just do this for me!'

Before either of us could say anything else, footsteps thudded up the stairs. We stared at each other. Greeny's eyes were huge, and his mouth a black hole of horror.

'Quick, turn that off!'

Greeny fumbled with the iPad while I threw myself at

the door.

'What the?' Gav grunted behind the stuck door. 'What you doing, freak?'

'You can't come in!' I cried, as Greeny still struggled. 'I'm, I'm naked.'

Greeny glared at me and mouthed, 'WHAT THE—?'

'Just get out of the way, man,' said Gav. 'I didn't bring my microscope so I ain't gonna see anything.'

'Please, Gav, no,' I said. 'Just let me put my pants on!'

The door heaved open, sending me crashing into the wall at the exact moment Scarlett disappeared.

Gav looked at Greeny, then at me. 'So, you was naked, was you?' he said, shaking his head. 'I knew you liked geezers but I didn't have you down as a chubby-chaser.'

Greeny looked like he was going to pass out.

'What you doing here anyway, fat boy? You better not tell no one you saw me here.'

'Oh, why don't you just piss off, Gav?' I said. I can't be sure, but for a second I actually felt protective of Greeny. The world had gone insane.

Gav punched my arm. Pain flared up to my shoulder.

'That was for saying my mum's got a knob,' he said, before picking up a pack of fags and walking out.

'Sorry about that,' I said to Greeny, holding my arm.

''S all right,' he said. 'It just makes me want to create the scariest ghost anyone's ever seen. I'll get to work on it tonight.'

« Older posts

He left soon after that, telling me to 'plant the seed' with Gav about the ghost. He ran into Lisa on the way out.

'All right, Lisa?' he said. 'What are you doing here? Come to see Gavros Flatley?'

'Never mind that. What are you doing here, lard boy?' she said.

'Just helping Joe with some IT issues,' he said. 'Anyway, goodnight.'

Lisa was off with me all night again, staring at Gav and frowning. I can't wait until he's gone.

10.10 p.m.

Gav is having a row of Biblical proportions with Jim in the hallway; it's brilliant. Oh no, I can hear him coming up the stairs.

10.40 p.m.

Gav is now asleep but has emitted a fart of such stinktitude that it would have suffocated Adwina if she were real.

10.45 p.m.

Adwina started crying, probably disturbed by Gav's lingering air turd. A nappy change soon shut her up. Gav probably needs one as well by the smell of him.

11.45 p.m.

Adwina woke up again.

Gav screamed, 'Will you shut that baby up?'

'I'm trying!' I said. 'And anyway, how come it's me that has to get up? She's your baby, too!'

'Er, no she ain't,' he said.

'That's exactly the kind of thing you would say,' I said. 'Out until all hours, expecting me to stay in and have your dinner ready for you when you get home.'

'What are you talking about, you knobber?' he said.

'I don't know,' I said

1.05 a.m.

Woke up with the wind blowing in my face. *That's odd*, I thought. *I'm sure my bedroom used to be inside.* As my eyes got used to the dark I could see a shape silhouetted against the open window. For a horrible split second, I thought it was a real ghost, but then I realized who it really was.

'What are you doing?' I said.

'Doing what you said, freak,' said Gav. 'I'm seeing to the baby.'

It took a few seconds for my eyes to focus properly, but when they did I nearly died. Gav was holding Adwina out of the window by her leg.

'No!' I jumped to my feet. 'Gav, don't!'

'I hate being here enough as it is,' he said through gritted teeth. 'Without being kept up all night by a doll.'

'Please don't do it, Gav,' I said. 'I'll get in so much trouble.

And Lisa won't talk to me.'

Good move, Joe. Bring up his ex that you stole, that'll get him on your side, said Derek. *You freakin' moron.*

Gav stared at me. He loosened his grip until he just had her between his index finger and thumb. If I made a grab, he could just drop her. There was only one thing for it.

'Wha? What is it?' yelled Doris as I ran into her room. 'Luftwaffe?'

'Much worse than that,' I said. 'Gavin's about to drop Adwi—I mean Ivy out of the window!'

I've never seen an old lady move so quick. She was like Usain Bolt in a nightie.

'Give her to me, you evil sod!' she screeched. Gav handed her over. Doris held her close and rocked her as she screamed.

'It's OK, Ivy, I'm here now,' she said. Then she glared at Gav. 'I'll be looking after Ivy from now on. It's the only way I'll know she's safe.' And with that, she went back into the spare room.

Gav screwed his face up. 'You grassing me in to my nan now?' he said. 'One of these days I'm gonna mess you up.'

'Whatever,' I said. 'You're scared of an old woman with no teeth in.'

'I ain't scared,' he said. 'I ain't scared of nothing.'

'Really?' I said. 'Well, maybe you're right. I mean, you do stay in this house alone quite often, don't you?'

'Yeah,' he said. 'So?'

'Oh nothing,' I said, playing it innocent. 'You're braver than me, that's all.'

He looked me over. 'Why?'

'Well, you wouldn't catch me staying in on my own,' I said. 'Not with the . . . activity.'

'What you talking about?' he said.

I turned and looked out of the window. You can see the park from there, and the bunker. 'There's just some things that live in the neighbourhood,' I said. 'Some terrible things.'

'What things?' he said.

I smiled to myself.

'The army ghosts,' I said.

'That's just crap made up to scare kids, innit?' he said, a little quiver in his voice.

'I thought so,' I said, turning to face him. 'I thought all the bumps, all the cold spots, all those noises were just my mind playing tricks. But then I saw it.'

'What?' he said. Watching him trying to maintain his hard exterior was hilarious.

'A soldier, in this room,' I said. 'Right where you're stand-ing. And he—he spoke.'

'What did he say?'

'He told me to . . . '

'What?' Gav grabbed my arm.

'He told me to get out.'

Gav looked like he was about to poo. I have no idea how I stopped myself from laughing.

I got back into bed and quietly texted Greeny, asking him to make the ghost say, 'Get out!' if at all possible. He texted back straight away, asking if I'd planted the seed.

More like the cocking forest.

Thursday 16th February

'I forgot to ask,' said Harry at break time. 'How did your meeting with that "genius" Greeny go?'

Before I could answer, the man himself came tripping in. He had a mental look in his eyes and his hair stood up on his head at random angles.

'It's done,' said Greeny. 'I was up all night, and I ate a whole pack of fun-size Twixes, but it is done.'

He must have noticed Harry and Ad staring at him. 'All right, lads?'

They ignored him.

'Brilliant,' I said. 'Isn't that great news, guys?'

'I don't know,' said Harry. 'I wouldn't trust him as far as I could throw him.'

'Yeah, and that ain't far,' said Ad.

'Well, what would you say if I told you we had a hologram ghost?' I said, lowering my voice.

Harry glanced at me, then Greeny. 'I'll believe it when I see it.'

'Alright, then.' Greeny pulled his iPad out of his bag. 'Gather round, children.'

He clicked on a file called 'GHOST'. Harry bit down on his pipe and Ad squinted through his glasses.

A window popped up. A figure emerged. At first it was just an outline, but then it got clearer. A soldier in full uniform. Black eyes. Mouth hanging open. I was terrified just watching it on a screen.

'*GEEEEETTT OUUUUUUT,*' it wailed.

'*GEEEEEETTT OUUUUUUTT!*'

'How did you do that?' I said. 'That's amazing.'

Greeny blushed, making him resemble a giant beetroot. 'There was nothing to it, really. Just basic animation. That's actually my voice, put through a modulator.'

'Incredible,' I said.

'To be fair, that is pretty impressive,' said Ad. 'Better than me in a soldier uniform, anyway. What do you reckon, Harry?'

'Well, from a technical standpoint, it's perfectly serviceable,' said Harry. 'But it lacks the personal touch.'

'Harry, I want to get Gav out of my house, not ask him out on a date,' I said.

He huffed and pulled a war book out of his bag.

'So when are we going to do this?' said Greeny with that

« Older posts

crazy look in his eyes. 'Because I am ready to rock and roll.'

I thought about it. 'Well, this might seem a bit soon, but I know for a fact that my mum, Jim and Doris are going out tonight.'

'Tonight!' Greeny threw his hands in the air. 'We'll do it tonight! Boo yeah!'

'Boo yeah?' said Harry. 'What are you, Greeny?'

'Hi, darling!' I said to Lisa. I found her at lunch, re-applying her make-up. She clearly didn't like being called 'darling' by the look of her face.

'Sorry, darling,' I said. 'But unfortunately you can't come over tonight because I'm working on a project with Greeny.'

''S all right,' she said. 'I'm going out anyway.'

'Out?' I said. 'Out where?'

She slammed her little compact thing shut. 'So what, I have to tell you whenever I want to go anywhere?'

'No, of course not,' I said. 'I was just curious.'

'I'm going out with Ellie and Chloe, all right?'

'OK.'

'Yeah.'

Wow, Gav really has got to her.

I was so excited about tonight that I couldn't concentrate at school. I couldn't even come up with an excuse as to why I hadn't done my English homework. So Mr Dalton has gave me a detention! My very first detention! I was hoping to make it through school without one, but now it has come to this. I blame Gav. He's a bad influence. I mean, look, I'm even writing this blog when I should be finishing my essay about *Pride and stupid-arsed Prejudice*.

I met Greeny in the park after school. We went over everything and he showed me how to work the projector remote.

We went to mine the back way and crept in through the kitchen. Gav was in the shower and had left his phone in the bedroom. I hid it behind the bedside table. He was still in the bathroom drying off when Greeny sneaked into the bedroom to synchronize the remote with the projector and hide some powerful wireless speakers behind the drawers.

We crept back downstairs, listening to the movement above us. The car wasn't on the drive so I knew everyone was out.

'Can I just ask something?' I said. 'Why have you decided to help me now?'

Greeny scratched the back of his head. 'I don't know. It's like, I spent my whole life trying to fit in with Gav and them, but sitting down and talking to you made me realize I was wasting my time. They're always grabbing my belly and calling me 'Tits' and stuff like that. Whatevs. I don't need them no more.'

I heard Gav unbolting the bathroom door upstairs. We ran outside through the kitchen and Greeny hid in the shed.

« Older posts

I knew Gav wouldn't go into the bedroom by himself, not after what I told him.

I peered in through the window and watched Gav sit down in the living room. Somewhere inside I felt a little pinch of guilt. Maybe it was Norman. Then Gav picked his nose and wiped it on the cushion and the pinch was gone.

I dialled his number on caller withheld. He sat up and listened. I ran, crouching, over to the shed and got Greeny. By the time we'd reached the kitchen, Gav was upstairs.

We tiptoed through the lounge and up the stairs. Greeny leapt in front of the bedroom door and pulled it shut, holding it tight. He nodded at me.

I pressed play on the remote, and slid around to Mum's bedroom door on the left. After what felt like a month, the wailing started.

'GEEEEEET OUUUUUUT. GEEEEETTT OUUUUUUUUT.'
Goosebumps stood up on my arms.

Gav squealed, actually squealed. The door buckled, but Greeny kept a firm grip, using all his weight to keep it shut.

'Nooo!' Gav screamed. 'Let me out! I'll do anything you want! Just let me out!'

'GEEEEEEET OOOOOOOUUUTT.'

'I'M TRYING!'

'GEEEEEEET OOOUUUUUUUUT, GAVIN.'

The door shook, but Greeny kept his grip, his face turning purple with the effort. Gav screamed again and the door stopped moving. In one horrible second, I realized what he was doing.

'Greeny, get out of the way,' I mouthed at him.

'What?'

'I said get out of the—'

But before I could get 'way' past my lips, Gav ran into the door, shoulder first, knocking it off its hinges and sending Greeny flying into Doris's room. I dived behind Mum's bed. The pounding of blood in my ears almost drowned out the sound of Gav running down the stairs and out of the door.

And then the sound of Doris screaming.

'Get off me, you awful beast! I won't let you hurt my baby!'

I crawled out from my hiding place and peered around the doorway to see Doris slapping Greeny, making his cheeks wobble. He grabbed onto the banister before turning and running down the stairs even faster than Gav. What the hell? Why is she still in?

I picked myself up and approached her carefully.

'Are you all right, Doris?' I said.

'Oh, it was awful, Joseph,' she said. 'I was having a doze on the bed when this great fat lad landed on me out of nowhere! I think he meant to hurt Ivy!'

'It's OK, he's gone now,' I said. 'Let's get you sat down.'

I felt sick. She's got a dodgy heart as it is. How would I have lived with myself if I killed her?

I went downstairs and made her a cup of tea. It was only

then that I saw the note on the side:

> *Joe,*
> *Me and Jim have just gone out because Doris didn't*
> *want to leave the baby on her own (!).*
> *Dinner's in the oven.*
> *Love,*
> *Mum x*

How could I have missed that, for cocking out loud? I took Doris her tea and her nightly pills and went back into my room. I unscrewed the projector and speaker set and hid them in my bag with the iPad. This was partly to conceal the evidence and partly because I didn't want to risk it going off again. Even though I knew it wasn't real, I'd still freak out if it materialized.

I took a bigger screwdriver out of Jim's toolbox in the garage and put the door back on. Not an easy task when you're shaking. It seemed a bit wonky but it worked.

I was still shaking an hour later when Mum and Jim got back. When Mum called me from the bottom of the stairs, it got worse. I went down and faced her.

'Joe,' she said. 'Is this true? Someone broke into the house? Doris is scared to death and Jim's about to go ballistic.'

'W-what?' I said.

'Doris is saying that a kid broke in and jumped on her in bed.'

I looked into the kitchen and saw Jim pacing around while Doris cooed at Adwina.

'Listen,' I said. 'I'm not being disrespectful, but this is a woman who thinks a plastic doll is her dead sister. This could just be another one of her—you know, episodes.'

I am the worst person on planet Earth.

'I don't know,' said Mum. 'She looks really shaken.'

'All I'm saying is,' I said, 'I haven't seen any fat kids running around the house . . . '

'I didn't say anything about him being fat,' said Mum.

Norman spat out his coffee and called for backup.

'Um, um,' I babbled. 'Well, Doris mentioned it to me earlier.'

'So you did know about this, then?' she said.

'Well technically, yes,' I said. 'But I just thought she was having a bit of a turn, you know.'

'Why didn't you call and tell us?' said Mum.

'I, I . . . ' The backup in the control room shrugged. 'Sorry,' I said. 'I didn't think.'

Mum shook her head and joined Doris and Jim in the kitchen. I stood in the hallway, still shaking. So this is what it feels like to be a bad person. It sucks. No wonder Gav is so miserable all the time.

'Maybe we should call the police?' said Mum.

« Older posts

'The police?' Jim snapped. 'What are they going to do?'

'All right, I'm only trying to help,' said Mum.

'Yeah, well don't,' said Jim.

I had caused all this. What with Mum and Jim arguing, Adwina screaming and Syd **SQUAWKING**, it was like some kind of mad house. The kind of mad house I'll end up in if it carried on much longer.

I needed to speak to someone so I called Lisa. She didn't answer. Probably having too much fun with Chloe and Ellie. I wish I was still in touch with Natalie.

I was in the kitchen later trying to figure out how to warm my dinner up when I heard the front door open. Gav. Jim intercepted him in the hallway.

'Where have you been?' said Jim. 'I thought I said you were grounded.'

'Just leave me alone,' said Gav. His voice sounded weird.

'We need to talk,' said Jim. 'In the kitchen. Now.'

I looked around, and for a reason I still can't work out, climbed into the little storage room at the back of the kitchen. It's dark in there and pongs of cabbage. I sat silently and listened.

'Sit down,' said Jim.

'W-why?' said Gav.

'Just do it.'

'What do you want?' said Gav. I realized why his voice sounded weird. He was scared.

'I want to know why you have no respect for me or for this house,' said Jim.

'What?'

'What?' he said. 'Let me say it again. I want to know why you have no respect for me or for this house.'

'Yeah, well you've got no respect for me,' Gav mumbled.

'No respect?' said Jim. 'I give you a place to live when your mum leaves, and you're talking about me having no respect? Helen opens her house to you and you treat her like dirt. And I specifically ask you not to go out and then you just waltz in at half nine. Your teachers have written me letters telling me you're not turning up to your lessons. What is your problem?'

'What's my problem?' said Gav, getting angry as if someone had just flipped a switch on the back of his head. 'You're my problem.'

'Don't talk to me like that,' said Jim.

'Yeah, well this place is like a prison, innit?' he said. 'When I was at Mum's I could stay out as late as I wanted, have the lads round, and she didn't care.'

Jim didn't say anything. Silence. I was getting a dead bum so I shifted slightly. The movement dislodged a bag of potatoes. In my panic I just about managed to keep them upright.

'That's why you're never here, then,' said Jim. 'Where is it you keep going?'

« Older posts

'I dunno,' said Gav. 'Just out.'

'Just out,' said Jim. 'Well tonight, while you were "just out", someone broke in.'

'You what?' said Gav.

'Or so your nan says,' he said. 'We're not sure whether it actually happened or not, but the point is, if you were here, like you should have been, things might have been different.'

'Hold on,' said Gav. 'W-what happened?'

'She said a kid, or a man, jumped on her then disappeared.'

Nothing was said for a while, until Gav whispered, 'It's real.'

'What did you say?'

'N-nothing.'

Silence. I wondered if they could hear my heart thudding.

'I don't know what we're going to do with your nan,' said Jim, his voice getting thicker somehow. 'She's getting worse. Which is why I need you to be strong, son. We can't deal with her and you and Joe. I mean, you know what he's like.'

What? He knows what I'm like? What am I like?

'You've gone quiet,' said Jim.

'I'm just thinking,' said Gav in a faraway voice.

'What about?'

'I've gotta get out of here.'

'Out of the kitchen—why?'

'No,' he said. 'Out of this house.'

Derek made every single control room worker high-five him. Twice.

Jim snorted. 'Where are you going? Are you going to live on the streets?'

'No,' said Gav. 'I want to go and live with Mum.'

'That's really what you want?' said Jim, his voice all tight.

'Yeah,' he said. 'I hate it here.'

'Well, you know what, son?' said Jim. 'If that's how you feel, go. But the minute you miss having all your meals cooked for you and your clothes washed, don't come crying back to me.'

'Why would I?' said Gav. 'You never bothered with me until now anyway.'

Then I heard the door slam.

Could it be? Gav was leaving? I was so excited, I nearly gambolled out of the storage room. I waited until I heard Gav leave before I got out. I went upstairs and found him standing outside the room, his hand hovering over the door handle.

'I saw it,' he said. 'I saw the ghost.'

Brilliant.

Friday 17th February

The last day before half-term! There's been so much going on I forgot.

Harry didn't seem to be in the half-term spirit though. He was acting all weird on the way to school, as if he was narked off about Greeny's plan working. I can't figure him out.

« Older posts

I noticed Greeny wasn't around at school so I gave him a call at break time, just to check that Doris hadn't killed him.

'Yeah, I'm fine,' he said. 'I've got the day off 'cause I told my mum I fell down the stairs when she saw my bruises. That old bird packs a punch.'

'What happened in there?' I said.

'Well, the door sent me flying and I landed on this bed. I reached out my hand and felt something soft. It wasn't until she slapped me that I realized I was touching the old girl's boob.'

I snorted with laughter. 'That's Gav's nan, you know.'

'Wicked,' he said. 'So I made Gav crap his pants and then I groped his granny all in one night.'

At lunchtime, I found Lisa standing outside with Ellie and Chloe.

'Hi Lisa!' I said.

She didn't reply.

'Why's this freak talking to you?' said Chloe.

'It's probably about our baby project,' said Lisa.

Ellie sniggered. 'Oh right, well we'll leave you to it, then. Don't stand too close to him though, Lis. You don't want to get puked on.' They walked away laughing.

'So your friends don't even know about us?' I said.

'I told you, Joe, I want it to be our little secret,' said Lisa.

'But you wanted Gav to know,' I said.

She mumbled something and avoided eye contact. 'So what do you want?'

'I've got some good news.'

She pulled me close and giggled. She smelled like smoke.

'What are you doing?' I said.

'Just trying to be flirty with my BOYFRIEND,' she said. 'God!'

I turned around and saw Gav and the Blenkinsops sloping past like something out of *Planet of the Apes*.

'Anyway,' I said. 'Do you want to hear my good news?'

'Hmm.'

'Gav is going!' I said. My cheeks hurt from smiling so hard.

'Going where?'

'He's leaving my house!' I said. 'Going to live in Scotland! Can you believe it?'

She stared at me as if she couldn't understand what I was saying.

'But how?' she said. 'Why?'

'Let's just say he may have realized that living with me isn't all it's cracked up to be,' I said.

Lisa's mouth dropped open.

'I thought you'd be happy,' I said.

'And why did you think that?'

I blinked hard to try and stop my eye from twitching. 'Well, because I thought he was making you uncomfortable being there, you know, with your history. You said so yourself, you couldn't trust him.'

'God,' she said, 'you don't get me at ALL, do you?' Then she stormed off.

What is wrong with everyone today?

6 p.m.

After school, Mum asked me what I wanted for my birthday. I just asked for money. I noticed a massive bunch of flowers in the kitchen. On the tag, it says,

Helen,
Thank you for being so supportive.
I couldn't do it without you.
I love you so much.
Jim

Excuse me while I bring up my dinner.

I'm not sure when Gav will be beginning his grand voyage north of the border; there's been no mention of it, but there's a weird atmosphere in the house. Mum is being ridiculously cheery, as if trying to make up for it.

9.30 p.m.

Lisa came round later and we watched a film upstairs. She was still in a mood with me, but seemed to cheer up whenever Gav walked in. Maybe the brilliant news of him going is slowly sinking in.

I let her bring the DVD, so we ended up watching this terrible rom-com about a man who falls in love with a ghost, or something like that. I would have thrown myself out of the window had I not had my Lisa snuggled up under my arm. It was lovely. It would have been lovelier if Gav wasn't lying on my bed with his hands down his trousers, glancing around nervously, but beggars can't be choosers.

At one point, Lisa put her face really close to mine, and I thought it was the time, but then Gav walked out and she moved away. Damn him, distracting her as she was about to give me the snog of my life. I don't think I can take the stress much longer.

After the film ended Lisa went home, leaving the house before I could even offer to walk her. Things will be so much better when Gav's gone.

Saturday 18th February

'Joe loves Lisa, Joe loves Lisa, Joe loves Lisa,' I said.

Syd stared back at me with his beady eyes.

'JOE LIKES MEN, JOE LIKES MEN, JOE LIKES MEN.'

I wonder if Gav can take him up to Scotland when he finally goes? Kill two birds with one stone.

I met Harry and Ad at Griddler's.

« Older posts

'So how's the "girlfriend"?' said Harry, doing the airquotes and everything.

'She's "fine" thanks, you "knobber", I said.

'I told you, Joe, knickers or it ain't true,' said Ad.

'For the last time, Ad, I'm not getting you a pair of her pants,' I said.

'But what about—'

'Or my mum's pants,' I said, before he could finish.

'How do we know you're not messing with us, old boy?' said Harry. 'You have to admit, it does seem a bit far-fetched. Like when Ad said he saw a UFO.'

'I did see a UFO!' said Ad.

'It was a bloody Chinese lantern stuck up a tree,' said Harry.

'Oh yeah.'

'Look,' I said. 'I know it seems hard to believe, but it's true. And I'll prove it.'

'How?' said Harry.

'We'll go and meet her,' I said. 'Right now.'

I picked up my phone and dialled.

'Hello.'

'Hi, Lisa, darling,' I said. 'It's Joe. Joe, your boyfriend.'

'Yeah, hi.'

'I was just wondering if you fancied hanging out for a while? Maybe in the park?'

'Is Gav with you?' she said.

I sighed. 'He could be, maybe, if I ask him . . . '

'All right then,' she said. 'But I'm supposed to be meeting Chloe and Ellie, so . . . '

'That's fine!' I said. 'Bring them too, it'll be fun! It'll be a hoot. A . . . hootenanny.'

Harry and Ad creased up laughing and I had to wave at them to shut up.

'Yeah right,' she said. 'But remember, they don't know about us.'

'Righty ho,' I said. 'See you there, sweetheart!' I hung up and looked at them, eyebrows raised.

'I bet that was the talking clock,' said Harry.

I gave him the finger.

'Right, so we going then?' said Ad.

They stared at me. I could tell they wanted me to be lying.

'We certainly are,' I said. 'To the park!'

On the way there, I asked them how their baby projects were going.

'Not bad,' said Harry. 'Turns out my doll enjoys the History Channel. She only cries when Winston Churchill comes on. Which is a bit worrying.'

'How about you, Ad?' I said.

'What?' he said.

'Your baby project.'

'What baby project?'

We waited for him to twig.

« Older posts

'Oh arse!' he said. 'I've left it in my locker!'

Me and Harry laughed.

'Do me a favour, old son,' said Harry. 'Never have children.'

We got to the park to find Lisa, Ellie and Chloe sitting on a bench.

'Afternoon!' I said. 'How's tricks?'

'Tricks?' said Chloe. 'Jog on, freak.'

I looked at Lisa for support and got none. I could feel Harry and Ad's stares burning into the back of my head.

'Just thought we'd join you for a while,' I said, grinning like a tool.

'Oh great,' said Ellie. 'I've always wanted to spend an afternoon with Puke Boy, Pipe Boy, and Thicko Boy.'

'Which one am I?' whispered Ad.

'Come on now, Ellie,' I said. 'There's no need for personal insults.'

'You what?' she said. 'You've got some nerve talking to me like that, you weaselly little . . . weasel.'

'Yeah,' said Chloe. 'Piss off, you freak.'

Lisa shifted in her seat and wouldn't make eye contact.

Rise above it, said Norman. *Remember, sticks and stones . . .*

May break my balls but yada, yada, yada, said Derek. *Enough already. This pair of witches need to know they can't talk to you like that any more, man. You gotta lay down the law.*

'Well, I can't be that much of a freak, can I?' I said. 'I mean, I am Lisa's boyfriend.'

They stared at me like a pair of gargoyles.

'No way,' said Chloe. 'You dirty liar.'

'That's not right, is it, Lis?' said Ellie.

Lisa squirmed. Harry stepped forward.

'Lis?'

'Well,' she said. 'Um.'

I silently willed her to back me up. If she didn't I'd never live it down.

'I didn't want you guys to know yet, but yes. He's right.'

I don't know who was more shocked: my friends or hers.

'Oh,' said Ellie.

'Are you sure, Lisa?' said Chloe.

'Yeah,' she said, staring at the floor. 'I am.'

'Wow,' said Chloe. 'Sorry for calling him a freak, then. I mean, I'm sure he's . . . nice?'

'Yes, I am nice,' I said. 'Very nice, aren't I, guys?'

Harry shrugged awkwardly and Ad said, 'Yeah, and so's his mum.'

'I thought you said Gav was coming,' said Lisa.

'No,' I said. 'I called for him, at the house where he lives that's nowhere near me, but he's too busy packing for his big move.'

'Where's he going?' said Ellie.

'Scotland,' I said.

« Older posts

'Ah, no way!' said Ellie. Then she looked at Lisa as if she suddenly understood something. 'Oh.'

'Actually,' said Lisa. 'I don't really feel like hanging out right now. I might just go home. Maybe see you tomorrow, Joe.'

With that, the three of them got up and walked away.

'See?' I said to Harry and Ad. 'Told you she was my girlfriend.'

'Yes,' said Harry, frowning and chewing the end of his pipe. 'You, um, really showed us.'

I certainly did.

11 p.m.

Gav followed me upstairs to bed tonight. He'd obviously been waiting for me to go because he couldn't face the bedroom on his own.

Revenge is sweet. MWAHHAHAHAHA

Sunday 19th February

Called Lisa and asked if she wanted to come and visit Dad with me. I thought it might be nice to take my mind off the bone-crushing boredom, and also to show Dad that I'm capable of actually having a girlfriend, despite not being into football or Tinchy Stryder. Anyway, she said no because she's got too much homework. Then I asked if she wanted Adwina for the week, as she's technically supposed to, but she said her signal was breaking up. Fine. I probably couldn't have got her off Doris anyway.

Dad was wearing a T-shirt that said 'Pump Up the Jam, You Bad Mother', and playing crap music off his phone like Gav does when he's on the bus. Not only that, he was non-stop questions about Mum and Jim:

Have they set a date yet?

Is Mum's engagement ring nice?

Has she been looking at dresses?

Are you going to be an usher?

The answers to which were:

No.

Don't know.

Don't know.

I thought he was a singer.

Just talking about it makes me feel sick.

When I got home, Gav and Jim were sitting in the living room in total silence. I sat with them for a while. The temptation to speak was so great I had to leave the room before I exploded.

I decided to take the opportunity to finally re-alphabetize my DVD collection and take out Gav's *Hip Hop Honeyz* Volumes 17—27.

« Older posts

When he came upstairs, I tried an innocent line of enquiry.

'So, are you off anywhere this half-term?' I said.

'Shut up, skidmark,' was his reply.

Monday 20th February

So Lisa's gone on holiday. To Spain.

This is the first I've heard about it.

Apparently it was a surprise, some kind of last-minute thing.

But I'm fine with that.

Absolutely fine.

Fine and dandy.

You know what? Maybe it'll be a good thing. Perhaps some time apart will make her yearn for me and we'll snog furiously in the arrivals lounge when she gets back.

Or maybe she'll get chatting to some waiter. Called Pedro. Who's all tanned and healthy and can do that flamingo dancing or whatever it's called. Maybe she'll get chatting to him and he'll be all like, 'Hola, preety lady, d'you wanna dance with Pedro?'

And she'll be all like, 'No, I have a wonderful, devoted, handsome boyfriend at home.'

And he'll say, 'Forget about that muchacho, you're on holiday now. There are no rules on holiday. And there are no rules with Pedro.'

I've got to stop thinking about it. Norman keeps telling me

to do something productive like read a book, but then Derek says stuff like, *I don't know, dude. Chicks dig Spanish guys. I'd be worried if I were you.*

I wish he'd shut up.

Tuesday 21st February

Today, I have done the following things to take my mind off the Lisa/Pedro problem:

- Reread my **STAR TREK** annuals
- Spent four hours unsuccessfully trying to train that idiot bird to say something other than **'JOE LIKES MEN'**
- Counted every star on my ceiling (fifty-seven to the left of the crack, seventy-one to the right)
- Drawn a comic about a hero (Super Joe) vanquishing the evil El Pedro --->
- Restarted work on my screenplay about a gang of space bandits who go for one last big score, but have to fight a giant space octopus first
- Attempted to tidy my bedroom.

Nothing worked. I thought about phoning her, but the call would be too expensive. Still, I'm tempted.

When I was tidying my room, I accidentally dropped a shoe. Straight away, Gav was at the bottom of the stairs.

'What was that?' he said. 'Was it the ghost?'

« Older posts

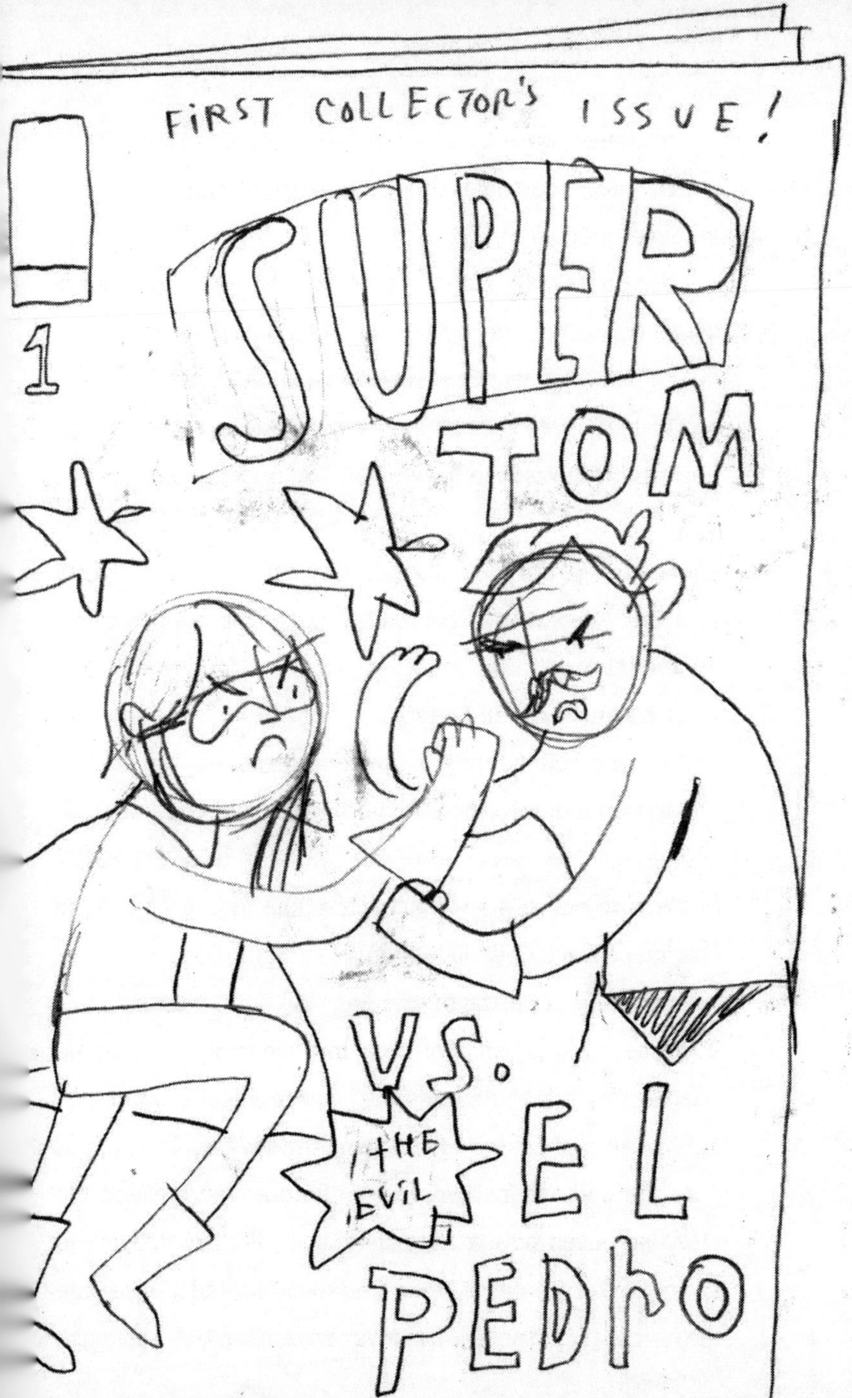
FIRST COLLECTOR'S ISSUE!
1
SUPER TOM
V.S.
THE EVIL
EL PEDRO

I hesitated.

Say yes, Joe, said Derek. *Tell him it just dropped a severed head*.

I don't think that's a good idea, said Norman. *You've got what you wanted: he's going. Leave it at that*.

I closed my eyes. 'Just dropped a shoe,' I said.

'Well, be more careful then, you freak.'

Derek went back to his workstation and sulked.

I called Harry, but he's grounded for calling his dad a 'rap-scallion'. And Ad can't come out because he's been given another chance in the meat van.

In the end, I called Greeny.

'What do you mean?' he sounded confused.

'I mean, I just wondered if you wanted to, you know, do something? I've got to give you your stuff back anyway.' I made sure not to get too specific about the stuff because Gav could have been listening.

There was a pause on the line. 'All right,' he said. 'I—I suppose so. It'd probably be a bad idea for me to come over to yours though. I mean, I got to second base with Gav's nan and I didn't even call her afterwards.'

In the end, we just went down the park and relived the stunt we pulled on Gav. My cheeks still hurt from laughing so much. It's so weird when you think about it. We made the hardest kid in school run away screaming like a little girl.

You know what? Maybe Greeny isn't so bad after all. At least he helped me forget about Lisa for a while.

11 p.m.

Caved and called Lisa. She didn't answer.

11.05 p.m.

That's fine. She's probably in bed by now.

11.10 p.m.

Or she's gone to a flamingo nightclub with Pedro.

2 a.m.

Adwina has got Doris up six times so far tonight. Yes, I'm keeping count.

3 a.m.

Just noticed Gav's awake too. He keeps looking at his phone.

3.10 a.m.

The flamingo club would have to be closed by now, surely.

Wednesday 22nd February

Spending half my time bored and half my time terrified about Lisa. Gav is always hanging around the house, as well. All he does is reply to texts all day. God knows what kind of idiot would want to text him. I would say it's one of the Blenkinsops, but they lack the opposable thumbs.

Friday 24th February

I've never met Pedro. In fact, he only exists as a figment of my imagination, but I hate him. I hate him with every fibre of my being.

I bet the only reason Lisa has gone on holiday is because of Gav. She obviously loves me, but is repulsed by him. I hope she still loves me when she gets back on Sunday.

Anyway, today is my last day as a fourteen year old. So I feel now might be a good time to reflect on the last year:

It was mostly crap.

So that's that, then.

Dad came over with my card and presents. Svetlana stayed outside. She looked miserable as usual, but then so would I if I had to go around in a convertible with Dad in the middle of February.

I had a look inside the gift bag. He's bought me a razor. I don't know why, I can't even grow a bumfluff tash. Not like Conor Savage in 10b, who had a full beard when he was in Year Six. Maybe he bought me it so I can slash my wrists the next time he cacks on about his new stereo, or something.

4 p.m.

Got a phone call from Harry. He's been let off his grounding and the Sound Experience somehow got a last-minute gig.

'Are you coming down, old boy?' he said. 'You can be our roadie.'

'You mean I get to lug your crap around for you?' I said. 'No thanks.'

'That's a shame,' he said. 'Because there's a crisp fiver in it for you.'

I thought about it. I could buy a bunch of flowers for Lisa with that as a welcome home present. Flowers work. Ever since Jim bought Mum that bouquet, they've been revoltingly lovey-dovey again.

'All right,' I said. 'I'll do it. Where's the gig?'

He mumbled something.

'What?'

'Morningside,' he mumbled again.

'Morningside, as in the old folks' home?' I said. 'Are you high?'

'A gig's a gig, old boy,' he said, sounding sheepish. 'Plus, it's thirty quid towards Buzzfest.'

'Yeah, but when you said DJing would mean playing to crowds of hot girls, I thought you meant ones with their own teeth,' I said.

'Look, are you going to help or are you going to make smart-arse comments?' he said.

'Can't I do both?'

The gig was a disaster. Why Harry and Ad thought a load of eighty year olds would enjoy Slayer, I have no idea. When the manager asked for songs that would remind them of the war, I think he meant 'Pack Up Your Troubles' and stuff like that, not songs that sounded like an actual war happening.

The home was depressing, too, and reeked of a mixture of disinfectant and poo. The residents seemed dead sad, and reminded me of Doris.

'Make some noise, party people!' Ad yelled down the mic.

'When's the bingo?' someone replied.

To keep myself busy during the 'gig', I drew a doodle of it. Yes, I was surprised they were able to sleep through the noise, too.

The manager came over at the end and reluctantly handed the money over.

'Oh.' He pointed at Harry's pipe. 'There's no smoking in here.'

'I know, old bean,' said Harry. 'This is empty.'

The manager shook his head and walked away, muttering something about wishing he'd booked the organist.

Got home late to find Gav hanging around in the hall, waiting for me before he went to bed. Had the idea of staying up all night to mess with him. What's he going to do, sleep in the shed?

Saturday 25th February

Happy birthday to me. I have received the following gifts to mark the occasion:

- £70 in cash, a jumper, and a 'Number One Son' mug from Mum, Jim, and Gav.
  I doubt Gav had anything to do with it. If he were to get me a mug, he'd have to have one specially made, as I doubt Clinton's do 'Number One Victim' mugs.

- A razor, some aftershave, and a pair of monogrammed socks from Dad and Svetlana. The card he bought me has a picture of some golf clubs, a football, and a sports car on it. DOES HE KNOW ME AT ALL?
- A fiver from Doris.
- A *¡COJONES!* magazine calendar from Granddad Cowley in Tenerife.
- A ventriloquist dummy from weird Uncle Johnny which is so freaky I've hidden it in the wardrobe.
- A cardigan from Nan and Granddad Arnold. It's got a cow on the front. I've put it with the dummy.
- A copy of Justin Bieber's latest album from Harry.
- A pack of Rich Tea biscuits from Ad.

But all that pales into insignificance next to what I got from Lisa. A text!

> **Lisa**
>
> Hi hun. Happy bday.
> Soz cant txt nemore,
> 2 expensive in spain xxx

There are three kisses on there! Three! I was so happy, I even fed Syd a piece of one of my birthday Rich Teas.

What's better is, I expected to be black and blue from Gav's birthday beats today, but he hasn't bothered me at all. Ever since his encounter with Greeny's ghost, it's as if he's been in his own world.

« Older posts

I saw him on the phone in the garden this afternoon. I strained to hear what he was saying.

'Just leave me alone, yeah?' I just about made out. 'When will you get it into your head that I ain't interested?'

Probably cold callers.

11 p.m.

Mum made a little birthday buffet and invited all my friends (Harry and Ad)

Harry wasted no time plugging his business.

'Congratulations on your betrothal, future Mrs J,' he said to Mum. 'And may I just say, if you're planning an engagement soiree and require some music, look no further.'

He handed her a business card. Why does everyone have business cards except me?

Mum majorly embarrassed me by kissing me all over my face and saying, 'I can't believe my baby boy is so grown-up' all the time.

'Hey, Joe,' whispered Ad, chomping on cheese and pineapple on a stick, 'does that count as your kiss?'

'Of course it doesn't,' I said. 'It's my mum.'

'How about if I kissed your mum, would that count for me?' said Ad.

The worst was when she got my old baby photos out and showed everyone, pointing and giggling at my 'little dinky'. Everyone laughed it up like it was all a big jamboree.

Unbelievable. Would it be so funny if I went around showing naked pictures of her to random people? No it wouldn't. But it would be very weird.

Then she brought a cake out and made everybody sing 'Happy Birthday'. Even Gav. I don't know how she does it.

'Make a wish,' she said.

I did. I hope it comes true.

When Mum went up the loft to get the Twister board down, I insisted we make our escape. Ad was gutted that I was robbing him of the chance of going face-to-face with my mum's arse, though.

We walked around for a bit and ended up down the park.

'Come on, old bean,' said Harry. 'Saturday night in the park? There has to be a girl here willing to snog you.'

'No,' I said. 'Lisa is my girlfriend. She's the only one I want to kiss.'

'And I want a yacht full of gold and naked ladies, but sometimes we have to be realistic,' he said. 'Ad, go over to those girls over there and ask them if any of them want to tickle the birthday boy's tonsils.'

I tried to call him back, but he was already gone. He'll do anything Harry tells him. He's like a sheepdog. He returned about ten seconds later with the verdict.

'The two on the end said no, but that one in the middle said she would if she were drunker, so if you bought her some booze, it could defo be a goer.'

'I am not buying booze to get some random girl drunk enough to kiss me,' I said. 'I do have some dignity.'

The shop wouldn't serve us. Ad even tried going back five minutes later, but without his glasses. When Mr Singh pointed out that he'd already been in, Ad replied, 'Nah, mate, that was my twin brother.' Then, because he wasn't wearing his glasses, he tried to leave the shop via a store cupboard.

So we returned to the park booze-less and I ended my birthday without having a fumble with a random drunk girl. Not that I could even contemplate being unfaithful to my Lisa.

12.45 a.m.

Keep your stinking hands off her, Pedro.

Sunday 26th February

Lisa's flight landed at 13.39, according to the airport's website. Allowing her time to pass through customs and baggage, I sent a welcome home text at 14.29. She replied at 21.00. Must have been tired with all the travelling.

Dad showed me his new tropical fish tank. I looked at this beautiful angel fish and felt real sympathy. I too am imprisoned in a tank of loneliness and dream of one day swimming in the open seas of love. Then a really long turd slid out of its arse and a bit of the romance died.

Monday 27th February

Hooray! Lisa has agreed to come out with me for our very first date! We're going to the Cineworld in Atherworth. I asked why we couldn't just go to the one in town, but she said she heard there was a bad rat problem there, so I agreed we should get the bus to Atherworth. Rats are a definite passion killer.

I was so excited all day at school. At lunch, Harry yelled at me because of my plate and fork drumming.

'What's the matter with you, old son?' he said. 'You're jumpier than a Cossack.'

'Me and Lisa are going on a date tonight,' I said. 'A real one, to the cinema.'

'Congratulations, soldier,' he said. 'But are you fully pre-pared?'

'Prepared?' I said. 'We're going to watch a film, not climb a mountain.'

He shook his head as if he were dealing with an idiot. 'No, I mean have you practised the move?'

'The move?

He nudged Ad in the ribs. 'Can you believe it, old boy? Casa bloody Nova here has never heard of the move.'

Ad laughed, then asked what Casa bloody Nova is.

'The move is older than cinema itself,' said Harry. 'In Eliz-abethan times, men would bust out the move whilst watch-ing Shakespeare's latest snoozefest. In Roman times, men would do the move whilst taking in a gladiator fight. In cave-man times, they'd do it whilst watching some bloke trying to kill a . . . giant pig.'

'For God's sake, just tell me what it is,' I said.

Harry looked around, then leaned forward and lowered his voice. 'It's the yawn-and-grab.'

'Is that supposed to mean something to me?' I said.

'It will do shortly,' he said. 'Observe.'

He sat back in his chair.

'Cripes, all this film watching has made me tired,' said Harry. 'I might have to do a yawn.'

He pretended to yawn and stretched his arm in the air. He kept it there for a second and then lowered it down around Ad's shoulders.

Ad slapped him on the cheek.

'I'm not that kind of girl, Harry,' he said.

'Yeah, but Lisa is,' said Harry.

'Hey!' I said. 'No, she isn't.'

11 p.m.

She really isn't.

After school I bought a bouquet of flowers with my Sound Experience money and gave them to Lisa at the bus stop. She moaned about having to hold them all night and insisted we take them back to my house.

When we finally got to the cinema, I even let her pick the

film, which was a bad move because it was the sequel to that terrible ghost romance thing we watched at mine.

She seemed a bit nervous in the refreshments queue and kept looking around.

'Are you all right?' I said.

'Yeah, fine.'

I scanned the posters in the foyer. Still no films about space bandits. That's a relief.

A couple sat in front of the posters with their arms around each other, and a big tub of popcorn between them. They were laughing at something. The girl tried to throw a piece into the boy's mouth. She missed, but it didn't matter because they were snogging just seconds later.

'Could I—could I hold your hand, Lisa?' I said.

She looked around again. 'Yeah, OK,' she said. So I did. It was nice.

'So, did you have a nice holiday?'

'Was OK,' she said.

'Any Spanish waiters called Pedro?' Shut up, you idiot!

'What?'

'Nothing.'

This massive bloke in front of us ordered two large pop-corns, a large shake, a hot dog, and a tub of nachos.

'So Gav's going up to Scotland in the next few weeks, then?' said Lisa.

'Who told you that?'

« Older posts

'Um, you did, didn't you?'

'I told you he was going, but I didn't know it was in the next few weeks.'

She blushed. 'Oh. I must have dreamt it then.'

Seems fair enough, but WHY IS SHE DREAMING ABOUT GAV?

I looked at the price list on the board. What a rip-off. That fat guy in front must be a millionaire. I thought it might be nice for me and Lisa to share a drink. I mean, it would save money and who knows? We might go for the straw at the same time and anything could happen.

'Do you want to share a shake?' I said.

'A milkshake?' she said, as if I'd suggested we do a bushtucker trial. 'Do you have any idea how many calories are in those things? I'll have a Sprite Zero, thanks.'

'OK,' I said. 'Do you want to share a popcorn, then?'

'No, I had a yoghurt at dinner time,' she said.

'You don't have to worry about what you eat,' I said. 'You're in, you know . . . lovely shape.'

'I know,' said Lisa. 'And I want to keep it that way.'

'Right.'

The narked-off-looking cashier called us forward.

'Two Sprite Zeros, please.'

He snorted. 'Hey, big spender.'

The film was terrible. I thought the first one was the lowest cinema could go, but this took the soggy biscuit. If this can get made, then my space bandits script will be snapped up instantly.

About twenty minutes in, I knew it was time. I'd already drained my Sprite Zero until it was just ice and I had nothing to hold me back. Time for the yawn-and-grab.

The yawning part wasn't a problem. The film was boring me into a coma anyway. I put my arms in the air. Something glowed in Lisa's lap. Her phone. She was texting. Great. I bring her to this piece of cack film and she's not even watching it. I strained my eyes to see what she was writing.

> Yeah go 2 scotland then c if i care. I hope i neva c u again.

It's definitely a good thing she's texting him that, isn't it? Yes, it is.

'Hey, put your arms down!' yelled the fat bloke sitting behind us.

I walked her home from the bus stop, right to her front door. She kissed me. On the cheek. In fact, it was so far around it was almost my ear.

Gav was slumped over asleep on the stool in the kitchen when I got back. I would have left him where he was, but I fancied some toast and his head was on the bread bin.

« Older posts

Tuesday 28th February

I've had worse days. I can't think of one right now, but I'm sure I must have.

'So, how did the date go, old son?' asked Harry on the way to school. 'Did the yawn-and-grab work its magic?'

'Well, the yawning wasn't a problem,' I said. 'It was the grabbing.'

'I see,' he said, and puffed thoughtfully on his pipe.

We trudged on through the rain. My back was killing me. My bag was crammed with my PE kit and cooking ingredients. Whoever scheduled practical Food and Nutrition and PE on the same day deserves to step on an upturned plug every morning for a month.

What was worse was we had to go down to an assembly at the start of the day to listen to this bloke trying to get us to do the Duke of Edinburgh's Award. No thanks. It would end with me getting rolled me down a hill in my sleeping bag, or someone farting into my tent then holding the zipper shut, I could see it now.

We got back to the form room just in time to see my giant bag flying through the air and hitting one of the idiot twins right in the face. Great. I picked it up and heaved it over my shoulder without acknowledging them.

'You got a problem, freak?' Gav mumbled.

'Not for much longer,' I said.

'That was a pretty weak comeback, old son,' said Harry

as we made our way to Food and Nutrition.

'Really?' I said. 'Well, what would you have said?'

'I don't know, something to do with him fiddling with boys' bags,' he said.

Ad laughed. So did Greeny, who was tagging along behind us.

'What are you laughing at?' said Harry.

'That thing about boys' bags,' said Greeny. 'It was funny.'

'Yeah, well it wasn't meant for your ears, Halloween boy,' he said.

I couldn't help but feel a bit sorry for him, but Greeny was the least of my worries once I got to the cooking room.

I put my bag down on the desk. It made a squelching sound, which was odd, because my bag doesn't normally do that.

I slowly unzipped it. My guts dropped. Everything inside was white. I had a pint of cream in there and it had probably busted open on Bruiser Blenkinsop's melon head. What a disaster. All my books were ruined and my PE kit was sodden.

On the bright side though, I got out of practical Food and Nutrition and Mrs Morris wrote me a note getting me out of PE. All I had to do was sit there quietly and watch Ad try and make croissants without blowing the school up. He managed it. Not blowing the school up, I mean. His croissants were a disaster. To amuse myself, I doodled Ad presenting his finished product to that sweary chef on the telly.

« Older posts

We went down to PE afterwards to discover that Boocock was off with broken ribs. Is it wrong that that cheered me up? What was better was our replacement was Mr Fulcrum, who retired years ago but still comes back occasionally.

He squinted at my note from Miss Morris through his re-entry shield glasses.

'That's fine, Tim,' he said. Tim? 'You can be in charge of equipment.' He fetched me a giant sack of rugby balls.

'So what you're saying, Mr Fulcrum,' said Harry, already stripped down to his Superman skivvies. 'Is that you want Joe to hold your ball sack?'

'Yes, that is what I'm saying, Henry,' he replied.

'OK, just so I'm clear,' said Harry. 'Say, Joe, make sure

you don't let Mr Fulcrum's ball sack drag along the floor, or you'll get it dirty.'

I sucked my cheeks in to stop myself laughing.

'And the last thing you want is to have to stay behind to wash the teacher's ball sack.'

I watched the lesson from the sidelines. Gav was different. Normally he ripped into the opposing team, making the most of being able to legally inflict pain. Today, he just stood there and made the occasional half-arsed tackle.

I peered into the swimming pool. Lisa wasn't doing PE either. She sat by the window, messing with her phone.

After PE, we had History in one of the mobile classrooms. I stood outside with Harry and Ad. The wind was so cold it made my ears tingle.

'I can't believe I scored a try!' said Ad.

'Me neither, old son,' said Harry. 'Especially as it was on your own line.'

'Doesn't that count, then?'

I heard a car door shut behind me, then footsteps approach. I thought it was a teacher. But I was wrong.

'Joe!'

I turned around. Oh sweet Jesus.

'Mum! What the hell are you doing here?' I said through gritted teeth.

'Nice to see you, too!' she said. 'Your teacher called and

told me what happened.'

This is bad, Joe, said Derek. You need to get her out of here. Tell her there's a bomb in the school.

'As I was on my break, I thought I'd bring you some lunch.' She handed me a paper bag. I never eat her packed lunches anyway. 'Don't want you going without, sweetheart!'

WHY THE BOILING HELL DOES SHE HAVE TO SPEAK SO COCKING LOUD? I could hear the rest of the class sniggering behind me. I knew that no matter what happened, today could not get any worse.

'Oh hello, Gavin!' she yelled.

No. Oh dear God no.

'I didn't see you there!' she said. 'Chippy tea tonight, darling! See you both later!' Then she got in the car, blew us both a kiss, and started to drive away. Then she stopped. 'Oh, sorry, Lisa, I didn't see you either,' she said. 'Must be going blind in my old age. Let my Joe know if you want anything. Byee!'

I shot Gav a look. His eyes bulged like a couple of boiled eggs. Lisa looked like she was about to faint. Everyone swamped us.

'Oh my God! You're brothers?'

'More like life partners!'

'Is this some kind of weird threesome?'

'ENOUGH!' I yelled, like something out of an old horror film. **'ENOUGH OF THIS MADNESS!'**

They all stopped and stared at me.

'It's time to tell the truth,' I said.

Gav and Lisa both gave me 'what are you doing' looks.

There was total silence. I took a deep breath.

'Me and Gav aren't brothers,' I said. 'Or life partners. I mean, I do have standards . . .' I waited for the laugh but none came.

'Anyway, as I was saying, we're not brothers, or lovers, but we are soon-to-be stepbrothers. His dad is marrying my mum.'

'Lucky bastard,' said Ad.

'And Lisa,' I took another breath. 'Lisa is my girlfriend.'

'Yeah right!' said someone after a stunned silence.

'No way!'

'Maybe in your dreams,' said Pete Cotterill. 'Your wet dreams.'

I caught Greeny's eye. His chin was trembling.

'It's true, isn't it, Lisa?' I said.

She looked at me, shaking. Then Gav. After what seemed like a hundred years, she nodded.

'Oh my God!'

'She must like being puked on, the dirty bint!'

She turned and ran away, down the drive and out of the school gates, while I stood there like a discarded sausage.

I caught some of the other lads looking at me. If I didn't know any better, I'd say they were awed. If they knew me and Lisa hadn't exchanged so much as a peck on the cheek, they might feel differently, but I wasn't about to tell them.

Maybe this is what it feels like to be respected.

After school, I called and texted Lisa but got no reply. When I could take no more I went to her house but no one answered.

Having a girlfriend is great.

Wednesday 29th February

Summary of February

Kisses with real live girls: None

Girlfriends: One

Buzzfest fund: £150

High point: Having Lisa as a girlfriend

Low point: Lisa not kissing me

School has gone weird. Not a single person took the piss out of me today. People like Jordan Foster were actually congratulating me on the corridors.

'You got a fit girl, and some muscle to back you up if things go bad,' he said. 'You got it sorted.'

If only things were that simple. Lisa was off school and still not replying to my texts. Greeny wasn't not talking to me either for some reason.

As well as the Joe-Gav-Lisa thing, school was buzzing with talk of a new girl starting in our year.

'I bet she's fit,' said Ad, to whom I'd just spent fifteen minutes trying to explain leap years.

'How do you know?' I said.

'I dunno, I just bet she is,' he said. 'I've got a fifth sense for stuff like that.'

'Tell you what, old boy,' said Harry. 'She'll be in your set for computers next. See if you can get a photo for us to have a look at.'

'You're a real class act, Harry,' I said.

'Oh, I'm sorry Mr-I-have-a-girlfriend-who-runs-off-in-tears-when-people-find-out-she's-actually-my-girlfriend,' he said.

That hurt more than I thought it would.

We were doing a lesson about medication in Biology. I think. I wasn't really listening to Mr Fuller droning on. Until he said something that made me sit up.

'Anti-emetic,' he said to the class. 'What do you think that is?'

No one said anything.

'It's to stop you being sick,' he said. 'An anti-sickness drug.'

I braced myself for the taunting. Silence. No one said a thing. It was incredible. Could it be that they're scared of me because they think I'm in league with Gav? Or have my cool points been upgraded because of Lisa? Either way, I'm happy.

Towards the end of the lesson, my phone vibrated in my pocket.

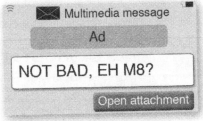

I clicked on the attachment. The first thing I saw was the purple hair.

Cocking hell! Natalie? What's she doing here?

As soon as the bell rang, I bombed down to the IT labs to see if she was still there. No one. Except Ad, being told by Mr Gooch that it is never acceptable to photograph women without their express consent. I went down to the dinner hall, but couldn't see her there, either. Then I remembered that day I went to the crazy nun school with Harry. I headed out to the rear yard. Sure enough, she was there, sitting alone on a bench.

'Natalie?' I said.

She pushed her fringe out of her eyes. 'Oh bloody hell, you come to this school?'

'Unfortunately,' I said. 'Can I sit down?'

'Free country, isn't it?'

I sat next to her. 'It's really nice to see you,' I said.

'Oh really?' said Natalie. 'I thought I was a munter.' The way she spat that last word out made me jump.

'But—but—I never said that,' I said. 'That was Gav, my stupid stepbrother thingy. He's literally the worst person on Earth. Even worse than Shinzon.' I threw in a Trek reference to get her onside.

'Ah, but Shinzon isn't the worst person on Earth, you fool,' she said. 'He's from Remus.'

'I've missed these chats,' I said.

Natalie looked at me sideways and tutted. 'Me too.'

If only talking to normal people was as easy as talking to a fellow Trekkie. It was weird because this was the first time we'd actually spoken to each other in the flesh properly, but I felt like I'd known her for ages.

'So how have you ended up in this dump?' I said.

She sighed and dug the toe of her black Converse into the dirt. 'Well, you know how I was having problems?'

I nodded. 'Yeah, I noticed.'

'Well, I did something about it.'

'What did you do?'

'There was this girl called Rachel Blake—a total bitch—and she'd had it in for me for years, turning all my friends against me, telling everyone I was born a boy, and stupid stuff like that. Anyway, the day after you came to the school, she started a rumour that you and that guy with the pipe were my brothers and that they'd seen me snogging both of you.'

'That is weird,' I said, although was it wrong that I felt

jealous at the idea of her snogging Harry?

'And I went to my locker at lunch and caught her writing "Inbred" on it.'

'Cocking hell,' I said. 'What did you do?'

'I punched her in the face.'

I gasped. 'No way.'

'Way.'

'But she was giving you a hard time,' I said. 'Surely they could have let you off a little bit.'

'Not when her mum is head of the school council, and one of the wealthiest businesswomen in the country,' she said.

'Ah.'

'Yeah. I can't get into any private school in the area now, so my parents had to send me here. They are steaming.'

'Yeah,' I said. 'But it can't be any worse than what you went through at the last place.'

As soon as I said it, Craig Jackaman from 10d came running over.

'Eeeeee-mooooo!'

'Hey!' I said. 'Don't shout at her like that. She's new. Be nice.'

He looked at the ground and scratched his head.

'Now apologize.'

'Yeah, sorry,' he said, before sloping off.

'Wow,' she said. 'I never knew you were so authoritative.'

The control room men became drunk with power.

Especially Derek.

'So what's new with you, other than the fact that you rule the school with an iron fist? Are you, you know, seeing anyone?'

Derek and Norman started arguing,

What are you talking about, you freakin' moron? Of course he shouldn't tell her about Lisa. She hasn't even kissed him yet!

If anyone is a moron, it is you, sir. He loves Lisa. She's his dream girl, remember?

I'll give you dream girl!

Then they started smacking each other with their clipboards.

I screwed my eyes shut. 'Yes,' I said. 'I am.'

Norman won. Just.

'Oh,' said Natalie. 'OK. How long?'

'Couple of weeks.'

Her fringe fell over her eye. 'And how's it going?'

'Great,' I said. 'We get on . . . great.'

'Does she like *Star Trek*?'

'No, she doesn't even know what it is,' I said. 'She thinks Mr Spock is the bloke who owns the Chinese takeaway.'

'That is sacrilege!' she said.

'I know!' I said, and we laughed.

'Joe.'

I looked up and saw Lisa there, staring down at us.

'Hi, Lisa.'

'Who's this?' Her eyes narrowed to slits.

'This is Natalie. Natalie, this is Lisa.'

'Charmed,' said Natalie.

'What?' said Lisa. 'Are you coming, Joe?'

I looked at Natalie, then at Lisa. 'Yep,' I said. 'Be right there, darling.'

'See you, Joe,' said Natalie as we left. 'And remember to pick me up some noodles from Mr Spock's if you're going that way!'

Lisa glared at me as I laughed. Then she turned and gave Natalie the stinkeye.

'Who's she?' said Lisa, walking so quick I struggled to keep up.

'Oh, she's just a friend I know from **STAR TREK** conventions,' I said, which has to be the single geekiest lie ever told.

'Just a friend, is she?' said Lisa. 'Where have I heard that before?'

She sped up and I started getting a stitch.

'How come you haven't replied to my texts?' I said.

'I've got a lot on my mind at the moment. I'm getting so much crap off people.'

'That's funny,' I said. 'Because I'm not. Have you noticed no one has said a thing to you since you started walking with me?'

She shrugged and slowed down.

'It's true,' I said. 'It's as if people are scared of me. It's amazing.'

I spotted Squirgy Kallow walking past.

'Hey, Squirgy,' I said. 'Drop and give me twenty.'

He got down on the floor.

'No, not really,' I said. 'But you would have done it, wouldn't you?'

He nodded.

'See?' I said to Lisa. 'And look, this is just to prove it's not a fluke. Oi, Jack!' I called across to Jack Cartwright, the massive rugby team captain. 'Put your hand on your head and hop!'

He frowned and shook his head, but did just as I asked.

It was <u>BRILLIANT</u>.

'Weird,' she said.

'I know!' I said. 'You're a figure of ridicule, and I'm king of the school. It's like everything is opposite. Oh my God, it's the Mirror Universe from ***STAR TREK!***'

'What?' she said.

'Never mind,' I said. 'But if this is a result of living with Gav, it's almost a shame he's leaving.'

'Well,' said Lisa, seeming to brighten up a bit. 'He doesn't have to, does he?'

We stopped outside the science labs.

'What do you mean?' I said.

'I don't know,' she said. 'I just kind of like this side of you. So . . . powerful.'

She stared into my eyes and licked her lips.

'R-r-really?' I said. 'But I thought you hated Gav?'

'I do,' she said. 'But him being around is worth it when it makes you so sexy.'

'S-s-sexy?' I said.

She nodded. The control room workers stopped slapping each other with their clipboards and watched.

'If you carry on like this, I might just have to snog you,' she said.

I whimpered something and nodded.

That's it. Gav stays.

Thursday 1st March

What a cocking day.

Checked in on Adwina this morning. She was in a cot! Where did Doris get that from? She's getting madder by the second. Earlier, she told me she thought I was Cliff Richard. Isn't he like a billion years old?

I asked Mum for a word before she went to work.

'If this is about that doll, I don't know how you're going to get it off her, either.'

'No, it's not that,' I said. 'Although that is going to be a problem. No, it's Gav.'

She sighed. 'OK, sit down,' she said.

'Is it right what I'm hearing?' I said. 'About him going and living with his mum?'

'Where did you hear that?'

'I overheard Jim and Gav talking,' I said, making sure I didn't tell her it was while I was earwigging in the storage room.

'Well, yes, it's true,' she said. 'He's planning to go up at the start of the Easter holidays.'

'Really?' I said. 'I mean, does he have to?'

'I don't know,' she said. 'He and Jim aren't speaking. I think the fact that Gav would rather stay with that woman than him has upset him. Anyway, I thought you'd be pleased.'

I thought that too. Isn't life weird?

'Not at all,' I said. 'I hate the idea of our little family being

« Older posts

torn apart. Why does he want to leave?'

I might just have to snog you.

'He won't say,' said Mum. 'Just that he has to go. He's been acting very strangely lately, but I haven't been able to get anything out of him. I just can't believe he wants to live with her again.'

'Why?' I said. 'Is she bad?'

Mum nodded. 'She didn't do anything for him. She boozed all day and all night, had all kinds of random blokes round the house. Jim told me he once found out Gav had been having dry Pot Noodles for dinner because they hadn't got a kettle.'

My stomach got all tight. No wonder Gav turned out to be such a monster.

'But why didn't Jim have him, if it was that bad?'

'Courts wouldn't allow it,' said Mum. 'I shouldn't be telling you this, but Jim and Caroline, that's her name, got divorced because she was having an affair with his brother.'

'God, it's like Jezza Kyle or something.'

'I know,' she said. 'Anyway, the divorce devastated Jim. He had a breakdown. And Caroline told all kinds of lies to make sure she got to keep Gavin, and Jim was too depressed to do anything about it. That is the kind of person he'd rather live with than us. The mind boggles.'

Not when you think your house is haunted, I thought.

'You mustn't tell anyone what I've told you,' she said.

'And I mean it this time.'

'Of course,' I said.

'Maybe you could have a chat with Gav?' she said. 'Try and make him see sense? I would have asked you before, but I thought you'd have convinced him to go rather than stay.'

'I'll try,' I said.

I will. There's no way I can tell him about the projector thing, though. He'd kill me and then he'd kill Greeny. I have to try and appeal to him on a human level. Could be tricky.

School is still interesting. At break time, I found Harry and Ad being cornered by Craig Jackaman.

'Are you gonna give me your money, then?' said Craig.

'Do we have much choice in the matter, old son?' said Harry.

'I ain't your son, you muppet.'

'Good,' said Harry. 'Because if you were, I'd be very disappointed.'

'Harry, shut up!' said Ad.

'That's it, I'm gonna do him!' Craig raised his fist.

'Hey!' I said.

He turned around.

'Leave my friends alone,' I said.

Craig stared at me and let them go.

'As soon as Gav's gone, I'm gonna mess you up,' said Craig as he went past.

« Older posts

Harry and Ad gawped.

'What is happening?' said Harry. 'Do you have some kind of weapons cache we don't know about?'

'Don't need one,' I said. 'I've got Gav.'

'Wow,' said Ad. 'Too bad he's going.'

'Hmm,' I said.

Later, Lisa asked me what the Gav situation was. I told her I'd talk to him.

'Make sure you do,' she said, giving me that look that makes my brains turn to jelly and ice cream.

I sat with Natalie at lunch and talked **STAR TREK**. It was great. It comes so easy, it's almost like she isn't a girl. Even though she is. We properly make each other laugh, too.

When I asked her if she'd been having a hard time at this school, she shrugged and said, 'Not really.' So that's good. She told me she'd unblocked me on Skype, too. I don't know if I'd want to risk using it with her, though. Because of Gav. The person I'm now trying to stop leaving my house. My brain hurts.

11 p.m.

I remembered what Lisa said and tried to have a word with Gav after school, when he came in and flopped down on the bed.

'Gav,' I said. 'Could I have a word with you?'

He gave me the finger and said, 'Have a word with this,' before turning over, farting and falling asleep.

I think I'm going to need a different approach.

Friday 2nd March

Tried to make a start on my baby project report, but so far all I have is:

This project has taught me that even if you have a baby and the mother doesn't bother looking after it, you can usually palm it off on an elderly relative.

Needs work.

Gav was snoring like a broken vacuum cleaner last night, so I took my pillow and tried to sneak downstairs. I stepped on my creaky floorboard and he shot up and turned the lamp on.

'Oh, it's you,' he said, breathing heavily. 'Where you going?'

'Downstairs,' I said. 'Your snoring is vibrating my eyeballs.'

'But you can't go,' he said.

'Why not?'

He didn't say anything, but I knew what he meant.

'Look, Gav,' I said. 'Maybe all this ghost stuff isn't true.'

'How can it not be?' he said. 'I saw it! And so did you.'

'Yeah, but maybe we were seeing things,' I said. 'You know what my mum's cooking's like; maybe we were hallucinating.'

'Whatever,' he said. 'I won't have to worry about it when I'm out of here.'

Lisa found me straight away at school, asking me if I'd talked to Gav.

'I tried, but he's still set on going,' I said.

'Well, try harder,' she said, getting closer to me. 'Or I won't be happy.'

Why is she so bothered anyway? Surely she should like me for who I am, and not because I've suddenly become more powerful? Nevertheless, I'm so desperate to snog her that I ramped up my dominance, and managed to get half of Jordan Foster's Twix at break time. Deep down, I know it's wrong, but biting into that sweet, chocolatey, biscuity goodness made me appreciate how nice it is to finally be respected.

Saturday 3rd March

Woke up this morning with a smile on my face. I was having this dream where I was strutting down the corridors at school dressed like a pimp.

I heard Adwina crying in Doris's room. She has to be handed in on Monday. How is that going to happen?

I went downstairs and found Mum and Jim kissing in the kitchen. They stopped when they saw me.

'Morning, sunshine!' said Mum. 'What do you want for breakfast?'

'Funnily enough, I've lost my appetite,' I said. 'No, I've got a problem. It's Adwina.'

They looked at me as if I were mental.

'I mean Ivy,' I said. 'The doll. I need it back.'

'Oh no,' said Mum. She poked Jim in the stomach. 'Can't you talk to her?'

'I don't know what good that's going to do,' he said. 'She and that thing are inseparable.'

« Older posts

We stood there thinking. I considered asking Harry. No, he'd probably have Ad descending through a hole in the roof on a line. And Ad's solution would probably involve piss balloons. Maybe Greeny could design some kind of hologram baby? No, he's still ignoring me.

'I've got an idea,' said Mum. 'Joe, get dressed, we're going shopping.'

'Oh cock.'

'Does this one look like her?' Mum held up a doll in a plastic box.

'I don't know, they all look the same to me,' I said. 'Now can we just buy it and go?'

Mum squinted, examining it closely. We'd been in the stupid toy shop for twenty agonising minutes. 'You don't think she'll notice the difference?'

'Mum, the other day she thought I was Cliff Richard,' I said. 'She doesn't have a clue what's happening.'

'All right,' she said. 'If you're sure.'

I felt a tap on my shoulder. I turned around and saw Natalie, wearing a T-shirt with 'Angels of Death' written on it. My stomach did a little flip.

'Hey, Joe!' she said. 'I didn't have you down as a dolly boy.'

Derek and Norman frantically shouted out their excuses over the top of each other, until it just became a jumble of words.

'Ah ha!' I said. 'Very good. Very funny. No, this is for school. That's why I'm here. On a Saturday. Buying a doll. With my mum.'

'Hello, dear,' said Mum.

'Hi!'

'So, what are you doing here?' I said.

'My mum owns this place,' said Natalie.

Tuft's Toys? How could I not have known? How many Tufts could there be in the Tammerstone area?

'Ah, that must have been nice, growing up around all these lovely dolls,' said Mum.

'Nah, I hate dolls,' said Natalie. 'I remember, when I was nine, I asked my parents if I could have a shrunken head for Christmas.'

The look on Mum's face was priceless. I nearly lost it.

'How . . . lovely,' said Mum. 'Anyway, we've got to buy Joe's dolly, so we'll be seeing you, my love.'

Natalie gave us a wicked grin and made a devil horns sign.

'She seems an interesting young lady,' said Mum on the drive home.

'Yeah, she is,' I said. 'Dead interesting.'

'She's not as nice as your Lisa though, is she?'

'Joe?'

Back at home, we set Mum's master plan into action.

« Older posts

'We need to distract Doris so we can make the switch,' she said with a mischievous look. 'Any ideas?'

'No,' I said. 'She takes that doll everywhere. There's only one thing she likes more than Adwina and that's . . .'

Mum's eyes went wide.

'No,' I said. 'No way.'

'Chriiiiiistmas tiiiime, mistletoe and wiiiiiine,' I sang from the landing, wearing that tragic cardigan from Nan and with my hair swept back into a quiff.

'Ooooh, is that you, Cliff?' Doris screeched from the doorway. She ran out and started kissing me all over my face. No, that doesn't count, she's prehistoric.

Over her shoulder, I saw Mum run into the spare room with Adwina 2 and come back out with the real deal.

I gave her the thumbs up behind Doris's back.

'Now do "Living Doll"!' cried Doris.

Mum beamed at me, but then her expression turned to horror when Adwina started crying.

'What do I do?' she mouthed at me.

There was only one thing for it.

'DA DA DA DA DA, DEEEDUM, DEEEDUM, DAA DA, DAA DA LIVING DOLL!' I screamed, while Mum rocked Adwina and stopped her crying. After that, she threw my bedroom door open and took Adwina inside.

'Thank you, Doris, and goo night!' I said. 'Praise Jesus!' I ran downstairs and quickly de-Cliffed before I could be mobbed by any more pensioners.

A tense night lies ahead trying to keep Adwina quiet.

Sunday 4th March

Not much sleep last night. Spent most of it staring at Adwina.

'I thought that was gone,' said Gav.

'Back for a couple of nights, unfortunately,' I said.

He turned over and mumbled, 'I can't wait to get out of here.'

Doris didn't seem to have noticed the doll switch this morning,

'You were quiet last night, Ivy,' she said. 'Yes you were. Yes you were.'

I somehow managed to convince Lisa to look after

Adwina tonight. I said it would help me talk to Gav. I'm dropping her off before I visit Dad's.

Oh my God. It's just occurred to me. I am being passed between parents too! I am Adwina! Cosmic.

7 p.m.

Do you want to know what the worst thing about your parents being divorced? It's not worrying about whether they still love you, or any of that crap. It's having to visit your dad. Especially when your dad is like my dad.

From the moment I walked in he was acting weird. Even weirder than usual; all smiley and nervous. Today, his T-shirt said 'Witness the Fitness'. Svetlana was the same as normal though, sitting on the sofa brushing Hercules, not speaking.

I sat down and picked up a magazine called Designer Sheds. He lives in a flat, for God's sake.

Dad sat opposite, still grinning like a moron.

'So, Thomas,' he said.

I threw Designer Sheds back onto the coffee table. He never calls me Thomas. It's usually Joe, or Joey. Once, he even called me Snoop Joey Joe. I soon put a stop to that.

'What's up?' I said.

'Well, son, I've been meaning to talk to you,' he said. 'I mean, you don't have a permanent man in your life now . . .'

'There's Jim, I suppose,' I said.

His grin got strained. 'But Jim's not your father, is he?'

I shrugged. 'So what do you want to talk to me about?'

He blinked and clapped his hands together quickly. 'You've . . . got this, um, girlfriend now.'

Oh God.

'Yes,' I said.

'Great,' he said. 'Well done. Your mum says she's a nice looking girl. A babe.'

Understatement of the millennium.

'And I just think I should check that you know everything you need to know. About things.'

His Adam's apple bobbed.

'What things?' I said.

Svetlana rolled her eyes at me.

'You know?' he said, running his hands through his hair. 'The, um . . . the sex.'

'The sex?'

He nodded. 'I just want to make sure you have the four-one-one.'

If it was possible to cringe yourself to death, I'd be writing this from beyond the grave.

'Svetlana, could you fetch me my condoms?' he said.

The control room workers hid their faces in their hands.

'Your condoms?' I said. 'That's really not necessary.'

He waved me off.

'You want the normal or the flavoured ones?' Svetlana

said with that same miserable expression.

'The normal ones.' He laughed nervously.

Svetlana huffed and went into the bedroom. She came back carrying a long, blue strip.

'Oh dear God,' I said.

'There's no need to be embarrassed, dude,' said Dad. 'Hey, Svet, while you're up, fetch me a couple of vegetables we can use.'

Well, at least he wasn't going to demonstrate on himself.

'Don't worry,' he said. 'This is just a quick tutorial, so that if you get into a situation . . . you'll know what to do.'

'But I'm not going to get into a situation,' I said.

'That's what I thought when I was your age.' He lowered his voice. 'But then I met Sharon Hughes.' He whistled. 'I got into a situation with that babe so quick, I didn't know what I was doing. By the time I'd got the thing on, I was no longer good to go, if you know what I mean.'

'I think I may spew,' I said.

Svetlana stood in the kitchen doorway. 'What you want?' she said. 'Carrot or cucumber?'

CUCUMBER?!

'Let's have the carrots, eh, Svet?' said Dad. 'We don't want to give the boy a complex.'

Svetlana tutted and gave him two carrots. 'Do not use those for cooking, Keith.'

Dad held out the carrots to me and winked. 'Choose your weapon.'

This cannot be happening. This cannot be happening. Control room: is this a nightmare?

Negative, sir. This is real.

I chose a carrot and weighed up my options. How could I get out of this?

You could pretend to faint, said Norman.

Don't listen to that horse crap, said Derek. *He'll carry on as soon as you wake up. You need to do something bold. Dive out of the window.*

But we're ten storeys up, you buffoon!

Yeah, but if he lands in the dumpster, he should be OK.

'Now what we're going to do is pop the carrot between our legs,' said Dad, as if he was presenting some kind of dirty version of Blue Peter.

I eyed up the window. Why can't he live on the ground floor? Dad nodded at me. I sighed and put the carrot between my legs. It looked so weird, jutting out like that,

« Older posts

all pointy and orange. Dad had done the same. Without a doubt, this was the most disturbing moment of my entire life.

'Svet,' said Dad, touching the end of his carrot. 'Could you and the Hercmeister give us a minute? It's time for me and Joe to shoot the breeze, mano-a-mano.'

Svetlana did a double take. We must have looked like a couple of perverted Oompa Loompas. She stomped into the bedroom muttering something in Russian.

'OK,' said Dad. 'Now we're ready to groove, but first, we have to take the condom out of the wrapper. How strong are your teeth, son?'

'Um, they're OK.'

'Good, because when you reach the crucial moment, you won't have time to run around looking for little scissors,' he said. 'So what you need to do is tear the wrapper open, like this.'

He put a corner of the wrapper between his teeth and bit it off. He was disturbingly good at it. He nodded at me. I put a corner in my mouth. I tried to bite it open, but it slipped between my teeth and I ended up whacking myself on the carrot.

'See, this is why we're practising,' said Dad. 'Try again. And be careful not to bite through the condom. The last thing you want is a holey sheath.'

I bit down on a different corner and this time it ripped.

'That's my boy,' he said. 'Now what we're going to do is

take the condom out and put it on the carrot. First we'll unroll it just a little bit to make sure that it's the right way round. If it isn't, it will cost you valuable seconds.'

I did as I was told while my stomach tried to jump out of my mouth.

'See, this isn't strange at all is it?' said Dad. 'It's just a father passing down knowledge to his son.'

'Yep, rolling johnnies onto veg, what could be more normal?' I said.

Dad wiped the sweat from his forehead with his free hand.

'OK, now this is the important part,' he said. 'We have to squeeze the air out of it. We're not making balloon animals here, boss. If you don't squeeze the air out, it's liable to split, and that's when accidents happen.'

'Accidents?' I said. 'Are you talking about me?'

Dad wouldn't make eye contact. 'No, of course not,' he said. 'Anyway, what we do to get the air out is we squeeze the tip. No, not of the carrot, Joe, the condom. That's it. And all we do now is we roooooooll it down the carrot. Are you ready? Rooooooooooooll.'

I grasped the edge and rolled it down, watching in horror as Dad did his. I don't care what anyone says, a carrot in a condom is just wrong.

Dad sat there with the sheathed veg poking out between his legs. I had a feeling this was an image I would be talking about in therapy in years to come.

« Older posts

'Now we're ready to rock,' said Dad. 'One thing to remember is to check it hasn't slipped off during the, um, sex. And the best way to do that is to hold the base. Like this.'

'Great,' I said. 'Is that it?'

'Oh, one more thing,' he said. 'Condoms do wear out, so you'll need to replace it after thirty minutes or so. Although at your age, thirty seconds might be a bit optimistic.'

'Right,' I said.

'Here.' He threw me the rest of the strip. 'Keep these in your wallet. You never know when you're going to need them.'

'But Dad . . .'

'Take a chill pill, dog,' he said. 'They're a gift. Besides, Svet prefers the ones with the . . . Well, you don't need to know about that.'

We sat in silence for a minute.

'So,' he said. 'How's school?'

I looked down at my carrot, then at his. 'I think I might go now,' I said.

Wednesday 7th March

OK. I think it's done. It's been two days, I've barely slept and only managed to keep myself awake with energy drinks, but the baby project is done. We didn't even have any Red Bull either, so I had to make do with something called Blue Gazelle which tasted like vom.

I don't mind too much though; throwing myself into the project has helped take my mind off things, e.g. Gav, Lisa, Dad with a condom carrot between his legs.

School is so different now. It's as if I'm one of the big boys. It's liberating, being able to walk down the corridor and not be pelted with sweets or become the target of a stink bombing campaign.

I've also noticed Lisa getting closer to me too, holding my hand on the corridor and being seen with me. The only problem with that is I'm finding it harder to get time to talk to Natalie. We've started exchanging emails again though. Purely on a friendship basis. Nothing more. She's just a friend.

And anyway, me and Lisa aced our presentation. Especially Lisa. She was like a sexy newsreader. Still, my closing talk about how having Adwina had taught us the importance of working together made me feel like a complete faker. I mean, Doris did everything, for crying out loud.

Miss Tyler stopped us on the way out.

'I've analysed the data from your doll's chip and something's been bothering me,' she said.

Me and Lisa glanced at each other, thinking we'd been rumbled.

'Oh,' I said. 'W-What's that then?'

'Your doll hasn't been switched off in weeks. Have you

been bringing it to school with you?'

'Um, well, you see, the thing is,' I babbled.

'Yes, we have,' said Lisa. 'We thought that would be the only proper way to do it. I mean, you can't switch a baby off can you?'

'I see,' said Miss Tyler. 'Well while your dedication is admirable, I hope you didn't disturb any lessons.'

'I wouldn't have thought so,' I said. 'When there's people like Gav James around, a crying doll is the least of your worries.'

Lisa gave me a weird look.

At home, Gav still won't talk. It's like someone's dumped a boulder in the house. Doris still hasn't twigged about the Adwina switch, either.

Thursday 8th March

Decided to call Greeny after school to find out why he keeps snubbing me.

'What do you want?' he said.

'Just thought I'd call to find out what's up,' I said. 'You haven't been talking to me and I thought we were, you know, cool.'

He laughed. 'Cool? Well, we ain't cool, yeah? I thought I could trust you, man.'

And then he hung up. Every day, the world becomes a more confusing place.

Met Natalie at lunch and lent her my copy of William Shatner's autobiography. She was really excited, and not even in a sarcastic way.

Friday 9th March

A weird thing happened at lunch today. I was behind Pete Cotterill in the queue and he'd just had the last of the chips.

'That's all right Joe,' said Pete. 'You can have mine.'

He passed me his plate. I couldn't believe it.

'What have you done to them?' I said.

'Nothing,' he said. 'Please, I didn't really want them anyway.'

I narrowed my eyes at him. 'Thanks, Pete,' I said. 'Thanks a lot.'

'Bloody hell, old son,' said Harry as we sat down. 'It's as if you're a Jedi or something.'

'Nah, he's like that Derren Brown mindreading geezer off the telly,' said Ad. 'Can you tell what I'm thinking right now, Joe?'

I sighed. 'Is it something to do with my mum?'

His eyes went massive. 'Bloody hell, he is a mind reader.'

Lisa came over and stood at the end of the table.

'Y'all right, Lisa?' said Ad. 'We just found out Joe can read minds. He knows everything.'

'No, he doesn't,' she said. 'Anyway, I need to have a word with him, so . . .'

« Older posts

They didn't move.

'We're not stopping you,' said Harry.

She put her hands on her hips and her eyebrows shot up.

Harry puffed out his cheeks. 'Come on, Ad, let's go and sit over there with the bloody Blenkinsop brothers.'

Ad picked up his tray. 'If they start anything, send 'em one of them telegrammic messages and tell 'em to pack it in.'

I gave him a thumbs up as they walked away. Lisa sat opposite me.

'Have you heard?' she said.

'That the bird is the word?' I said.

She shook her head. 'Don't be so childish, Joe,' she said. 'No, have you heard about the Easter prom?'

'Easter?' I said. 'Prom? Since when did we have a prom at Easter?'

'Since now,' said Lisa. 'The hall's booked out for Zumba championships in the summer, so we've got to have it at Easter.'

'Right,' I said.

'You don't sound very excited,' she said.

'Well, proms aren't really my thing,' I said. 'The only prom I've been to was at Blackpool, and that was rainy and full of old codgers eating fish and chips.'

'Well, this prom won't be anything like that.' She leaned in close.

'Oh no?' I said, my voice going all squeaky.

'No,' she said. 'Because if you do what you said you're going to do, I will definitely snog you there.'

She leaned in close and whispered in my ear, 'Tongues. And. Everything.' She took a chip off my plate and put it in her mouth.

I know now I have to dedicate myself to getting Gav to stay put. I can feel my (dirty) dreams are about to come true.

But I realized that to change Gav's mind, I'd need a change of tactic. I'd need to speak to his mum and talk her out of letting him go up. But how to get her number? How?

8 p.m.

Said to Gav, 'Can I borrow your phone for a sec? I've lost mine and need to ring it.' He replied, 'Use the landline then, you tool.'

9 p.m.

Waited an hour for him to go to the toilet and he took his phone with him. Surely he's not making calls in there?

10.10 p.m.

He never puts that thing down! He's always texting. I could wait until he goes to sleep, but he keeps his phone right by his head on the bedside table. If he caught me, he'd make sausages out of my intestines.

« Older posts

10.30 p.m.

Desperation strikes. I told him I could feel the ghostly vibrations coming back. He dropped his phone on the bed and ran downstairs. While he was out I took his mum's number and saved it on my phone. Now I've got to decide what to do with it.

Saturday 10th March

I switched my phone to number withheld and tried to call Gav's mum this morning. It rang out. I don't know what I would have said if she'd have picked up, so it's probably for the best.

I was about to leave for the park. Harry called last night and asked if we could go and try an Operation Blooper and for some reason I agreed. Maybe I feel bad that I haven't been hanging around with them as much as I used to. Harry keeps making whipping noises whenever I mention Lisa.

I stepped out the front door and nearly cacked myself. Lisa was standing there.

'Oh, am I that hideous?' she said when I did a little scream.

'No, not at all,' I said. 'It's just I didn't expect to see you there. On my doorstep. On a Saturday morning.'

'Where are you going, anyway?' she said.

'I'm meeting Harry and Ad.'

'No you're not,' she said.

'Oh,' I said. 'Why's that then?'

'Because we're going shopping,' she said. 'We need to have you looking good for the prom.'

'But that isn't until the end of the month, is it?'

She shook her head. 'No, but if we don't start now, all the good tuxes will be taken.'

'Tuxes?' I said. 'I'm not really a tux kind of person.'

'So what, did you think you could just turn up in your jeans and that stupid *Star Trek* T-shirt?'

'Of course not,' I said. I was lying. That's exactly what I was planning to do.

'Well then, come on,' said Lisa. 'And bring plenty of money.'

'But I haven't got money,' I said.

'Yeah you have, I've seen it in that jar.'

I scratched my head. 'But that's the Buzzfest fund,' I said.

Something weird happened then. All she did was tilt her head forward slightly and look up at me under her eyelashes and unzip her jacket. But it was enough to make me lose my mind.

'I'll get the money!' I cried as I ran back in the house.

On the way into town I called Harry and told him I wouldn't be coming.

'Why?' he said. 'And it'd better be a bloody good reason, like you're dead or something.'

I didn't say anything.

'It's Lisa isn't it?' he said.

I still didn't say anything.

When I hung up two minutes later, he was still swearing.

When we got into town, Lisa took me to a suit hire place that her older sister works at. Sarah, that's her name, is nowhere near as pretty as Lisa and is always chewing gum with her mouth open, which makes her look like some kind of cow. She looked me up and down.

'So this is him, yeah?' she said.

'Joe,' I said. 'Pleased to meet you.' I held out my hand and she put a suit in it.

'Go and try that on in there, yeah?' She pointed to a black curtain at the back of the room.

'But, but, I don't even know what this is,' I said.

They stared at me until I gave up and went into the changing room. It took me ages to get it all on. It wasn't the same as throwing on a pair of trousers and a shirt; there were cufflinks and all these extra buckles I had no idea what to do with. Plus they were way too big for me so I just ended up looking like a little kid who'd put on his dad's clothes for a laugh. I felt a right knob when I walked out.

Sarah laughed behind her hand.

'Shut up, Sarah,' said Lisa. 'I think he looks cool.'

Cool? Me?

'OK,' I said. 'So are we going for this one?'

Then both of them laughed.

I must have spent the entire afternoon trying on tuxedos

of all different types and colours. At one point I was even stood there in a pink one, looking like a broken stick of rock.

Luckily after what seemed like several years of trying, Lisa picked a black tux. Then Sarah measured me and I parted with a hundred quid of the Buzzfest fund. And that was with a staff discount. I feel like crying. How will I tell Harry and Ad? It's terrifying how Lisa can get me to do literally anything, and I don't realize until afterwards. If anyone's Derren Brown, it's her.

Sunday 11th March

Knackered. When I was sure Gav was asleep last night, I crept downstairs and Skyped with Natalie. I know. I feel like I'm committing virtual adultery. Maybe this is how Dad started with Svetlana. One minute it was all innocent chatting and the next it was all swanky flats and flavoured johnnies.

Harry Skyped me earlier. He stayed on long enough to give me the finger then hung up. Maybe if he had a girlfriend he'd understand. Not that that's likely to happen any time soon.

Me and Natalie had been chatting for what felt like only ten minutes, but when I checked, it was nearly two o'clock.

'God, have you seen the time?' I said.

'I know,' said Natalie. 'Time flies when you're debating Trek.'

'Well, weirdly, we actually seem to agree on a lot of things.'

'You're right,' she said. 'I mean, I even listened to a Pink

Floyd album the other day, and do you know what? It was pretty good.'

'Really?' I said.

'No,' she laughed. 'But you should have seen your face.'

The door opened behind me. I got ready to close the lid. I couldn't have Gav insulting her again. But it was Doris.

'Don't mind me, duck,' she said. 'Just getting a drink for the baby.'

IT'S A DOLL!

As she passed behind my chair, she noticed the screen.

'Oooh, are you watching a vampire film?'

Bloody hell. With a nan like that, no wonder Gav's such a charmer. Luckily, Natalie saw the funny side.

'I vaaant to suck your blooood!' she said, sounding like the Count from Sesame Street.

'Yes, Doris,' I said. 'It's one of those interactive films you can talk to. Say hello.'

Doris leaned towards the screen. 'Hello?' she said.

'Hi!' said Natalie. 'Bloody hell, Joe, your girlfriend looks rough with no make-up on.'

Doris walked away, muttering something about how films these days are cheekier than they used to be.

'That was brilliant,' I said through my laughter. 'I love you.'

Natalie looked at the screen and then to the side. The control room night shift man nearly choked on his microwave pasty.

'As a friend!' I spluttered. 'As a friend! Ha ha! Silly me! Wooooh, is that the time? It's been lovely chatting to you. I'll see you Monday. Actually tomorrow, because it is now technically Sunday. The Lord's day! Hallelujah! Have a good Sabbath.'

Yes, I actually said all those things.

8 p.m.

Went round Dad's for a Sunday roast. I didn't touch the carrots.

Monday 12th March

I didn't go and see Natalie today. I thought things might be a bit awkward, and the way my mouth is running away with me lately, I'd have probably ended up proposing or saying I like to fondle badgers or something like that. Breathing space was what was needed.

Harry was still off with me, but I agreed to do an Operation Blooper after school on Wednesday and that nothing will stop me. Maybe the next time Lisa tries to convince me to

« Older posts

do something, I should shield my eyes, or wear sunglasses. Maybe I can say I was temporarily blinded in a paint-balling incident. No, that won't work, I've vowed never to go paintballing again since last time when Harry made us dig a trench and take up sniping positions.

6 p.m.

Jim and Gav still aren't speaking to each other.

'The trouble with them,' said Mum to me, 'is they're so alike. That's why I'm glad you take after me and not your father.'

I was about to argue, but then I remembered the rap albums, convertible, and collection of bizarre contracep-tives and realized I should be grateful.

Tuesday 13th March

Managed to say hello to Natalie at school today. She smiled and said hello back. Then neither of us spoke, and I pretended I had to go and see the school nurse because of my frenetic elbow. I should not be allowed to speak to people ever again.

Nevertheless, I had another go at calling Gav's mum. This time she answered.

'Yeah?' she said.

'Yeah hello,' I said, in my best thug voice. 'It's your son, Gavin.'

She didn't say anything for a while. 'You sound different.'

'That's 'cause you ain't spokes to me for a bit, though, innit?' I said. 'Me, erm . . . bredren.'

'Who is this?' she said. 'You're not Gav—he doesn't sound like a gerbil.'

'You're breaking up, Mum, I is going now, innit? Laters,' I said.

It couldn't have gone much worse. I mean, a gerbil.

Lisa called me later and I told her what happened. She didn't even seem to appreciate that I tried.

I keep thinking about epic snogging to motivate me. Trouble is, I've got a History essay due in tomorrow and I need to forget about things like that so I can get it done. What's the un-sexiest thing I can think of? Ah, Doris in a bikini. Maybe if I sketch that, I'll calm down.

Yep, that's done it.

Wednesday 14th March

Best Maths lesson ever today. Mr Shenko was off sick so for some reason they got old man Fulcrum to cover us. He came in, sat down at the desk, and fell asleep.

We didn't know what to do. I checked his pulse.

'He's still alive,' I said. 'But he stinks of booze.'

This meant we had an hour to kill. Harry told me off for starting on my trigonometry homework.

'This is a once in a lifetime opportunity, old boy, and you're wasting it by doing Maths?' he said.

'But if I get it done now I won't have to do it at home,' I said.

'You make me sick, old son.' He grabbed my pen off me and threw it towards the front of the room. In one heart-stopping moment, it arced through the air and pinged off Fulcrum's nose. He stirred slightly, but didn't wake up.

'All right, all right,' I said. 'What do you have in mind?'

'I say we compile a list of songs,' said Harry. 'With the word "heart" in the title.'

'Good idea,' I said. 'I've been thinking of making a mix CD for Lisa, anyway.'

'I'll say it again,' said Harry. 'You. Make. Me. Sick. You didn't let me finish. We should compile a list of songs with the word "heart" in the title, but with "heart" swapped out for the word "arse"'

Ad laughed. 'Arse.'

'All right,' I said. 'It's on. How about "Set the Controls for the Arse of the Sun", by the Floyd?'

'Not a bad start, soldier,' said Harry. 'Write it down in your folder.'

By the end of the lesson, after consulting Google on our phones, we had our final list:

- Set the Controls for the Arse of the Sun
- Sgt Pepper's Lonely Arse Club Band
- Jar of Arse
- My Arse Will Go On
- A Good Arse These Days is Hard to Find
- Something's Gotten Hold of My Arse
- Achy Breaky Arse
- Can't You Hear My Arse?
- Groove Is in the Arse
- Quit Playing Games with My Arse
- Hand on Your Arse
- Arse on My Sleeve
- Try Sleeping with a Broken Arse
- Total Eclipse of the Arse
- Don't Go Breaking My Arse
- There Must Be an Angel (Playing with My Arse)
- Thunder in My Arse
- My Arse Has a Mind of Its Own
- I Left My Arse in San Francisco
- Pain in My Arse
- Stop Crying Your Arse O
- Goodnight Sweetarse

Best. Lesson. Ever. My face still hurts from laughing so much.

I've just realized we didn't wake Fulcrum up afterwards. He's probably still there. Ah well, I'm off out for Operation Blooper now. Fulcrum could do with sleeping it off.

8 p.m.

Well, that didn't pan out quite how I expected. I'm now thirty-five quid poorer and look like a hipster idiot.

I met Ad in the park. He seemed pretty relaxed considering he still has the scars from all our other Operation Blooper attempts.

Harry arrived soon after and we went through our Arse list again.

When we finally stopped giggling about ten minutes later we headed over to the kids' play area where Harry had planned the Operation Blooper attempt. I'd developed hiccups in the meantime.

'There's nothing funny about the end of days, boys!' yelled Mad Morris, but that just set us off again.

'Right, old bean,' said Harry, after we'd got a grip. 'All you need to do is sit on the swing and, um, swing.' He took his pipe out of his top pocket.

'And?' I said. 'That (hic) can't be (hic) it, surely?'

'Not exactly,' he said. 'When you get as high as you can, you'll jump off and land on Ad.'

Ad grinned and gave me a thumbs up. He's down at A & E so much he's probably got a loyalty card.

I was about to refuse, but then I remembered how I punked out on them the other day. I felt like I owed them. I sat on the swing and started kicking my legs while Harry filmed. I must have looked such a nerd. I waited until I got as high as I could and went to jump, but I just couldn't do it.

'Is there a problem?' said Harry.

'I can't do it,' I said. 'I'm scared of heights.'

'It's two metres off the ground, old son,' said Harry.

'I know, but . . . maybe I'm scared of, you know, breaking my legs.'

Harry tutted. 'You'd be useless in the trenches, soldier. All right, if you don't want to do it, I will. I must lead by example. You film.'

I got off the swing, relieved. The fright cured my hiccups at least. I felt in my pocket for my phone and remembered I left it in my room. Bum. Harry let me use his.

He sat on the swing and got some momentum going. I filmed him, being careful not to get Ad. The element of surprise would be crucial.

When he got to the peak of the swing, I heard a voice behind me.

'JOE!'

It was so urgent, I spun round.

'Oh hello, Lisa.' I heard the sound of Harry smacking

into Ad behind me. I turned back and saw them lying in a twisted heap on the floor.

'Why aren't you answering your phone?' She looked fierce.

'Sorry, I, um, left it at home,' I said.

'Jesus Christ, Joe.'

'Don't mind us, chaps,' said Harry from the floor. 'No broken bones here.'

'Is that your pipe sticking in my thigh or have you got a stiffy?' said Ad.

'Anyway, are you coming?' said Lisa.

'Coming where?'

'Duh! To the hairdressers!'

'Why are we going there?'

'Because look at you,' she said. 'You can't go to the prom like that.'

'Why?' I said. 'What's wrong with my hair?'

'Don't get me started,' she said. 'Come on, I promise you'll look really *handsome*.'

'All right,' I said. I went over to Harry who was sitting up with a dazed look in his eyes and gave him his phone back. 'I'll see you guys later.'

'Of course you will,' he mumbled.

Lisa took me to this place near Dad's called Lars Dulphgren's Salon and Spa. It was nothing like Roger who I usually go to. It was all shiny black surfaces and the hairdressers had wonky haircuts and tattoos. Roger's

Barbers is a shack up an alley where the man himself will give you a short back and sides whilst puffing fags and keeping an eye on Countdown playing on a portable telly in the corner. I'm used to Roger. This salon business was like a different world.

We sat in a waiting room listening to boring techno music. Lisa flipped through a book of men's haircuts. She pointed one out and said she thought it'd suit me. I nodded while sirens screamed in my head. It kind of went up on one side and down on the other.

Maybe you should ask to see an alternative style, Joe, said Norman. *I'm not sure that one is entirely you*.

Derek slammed his clipboard down. *What are you talking about, man? This chick's gonna kiss him. Tongues and everything. Hell, I'd get the word 'buttmunch' shaved into my head if I thought I was going get some tongue action*.

This tattooed bloke came over.

'Hi, I'm Lance, I'll be looking after you today, would you like to come through?'

I followed him into another room, where I thought I'd be having my hair cut, but it was just a series of chairs leaning back into sinks. He put me in this robe and pointed at a chair.

I sat down, wondering what the hell was happening.

He started rinsing my hair with a shower head and rubbing some kind of shampoo into it. I tensed up. *A man is washing my hair. A man is washing my hair. A man is washing my hair.*

« Older posts

Calm down, Joe, said Norman. *He's just doing his job. It doesn't make you a girl.*

I'm not gonna lie to you, Joe. This looks bad, said Derek. *Try butching it up a bit. Even things out.*

'So,' said Lance. 'Are you going anywhere nice on holiday this year?'

'Oh, I don't know,' I said, making my voice all deep. 'I might go rock climbing or potholing or something manly like that.'

'Cool,' he said. 'If you don't mind me saying though, you didn't strike me as the outdoorsy type.'

'Oh, I'm outdoorsy, all right,' I said. 'Not indoorsy at all. Whenever I'm indoors I'm always thinking about the next time I can get outdoors. Outdoors is definitely the best . . . doors. If I had to pick.' *Why can't I ever STOP TALKING?*

'Wicked,' he said, and then started massaging my scalp. Massaging! And I'm going to let you in on a secret, it felt nice! I even closed my eyes for a second. Picard would never stand for such a thing. I mean, he's bald anyway, but still.

Lance then towel-dried my hair while I went as stiff as a board (not like that, I mean I was tense) and took me to a girl called Indie who cut my hair to Lisa's exact specification. I looked at myself in the mirror. Is this what cool looks like? Because it doesn't look cool to me. And having to pay thirty-five smackers for the privilege wasn't great either.

The Buzzfest fund is getting smaller by the day.

'I was right,' said Lisa after I walked her home. 'You do look really handsome.'

'Do I?' I said, getting closer to her.

'Yeah,' she said, before letting go of me and walking away. 'See ya!'

I thought maybe I did look handsome after all, until I got home and Mum took one look at me and said, 'Oh God, it's A Flock of Seagulls!'

I don't know what that means but it doesn't sound good.

11 p.m.

OK, I've just googled A Flock of Seagulls. They were a band from a billion years ago and they had really bad hair. Why must my mother be so abusive?

'OK, two things,' said Harry when I came to the door. 'One, you look bloody ridiculous, and two, I wouldn't have minded you wimping out on us last night, if you'd have actually filmed it. You turned around before I went into Ad. I now have this for nothing.'

He pulled his trouser leg up and showed me this enormous purple bruise on his knee.

'Well, maybe Operation Blooper isn't such a good idea,' I said. 'I mean, it's a bit dangerous, isn't it?'

Harry shook his head. 'Can you think of another way to raise money for Buzzfest?' he said. 'Or do you not want to go now you've got a "girlfriend"?'

'Are you ever going to stop doing air quotes around that word?' I said.

'Yes,' he said. 'When she stops treating you like a bloody dog.'

'Bollocks, Harry,' I said. 'I'll go to school on my own.'

'Ah, come on, lads, don't be like that,' said Ad.

'No, let him go,' said Harry. 'He can walk to school with his "girlfriend". That is if she brings his lead.'

I turned and walked the other way. It meant taking a longer route, but I didn't care. How can he say Lisa treats me like a dog? Do people take their dogs to have their hair cut? Actually yes. Bum.

I walked into school feeling really self-conscious. I knew

people were staring and secretly laughing, but no one would say anything to my face. Except Gav, who said I looked like, and I quote, 'a tramp's armpit'.

'Whatever, Gav,' said Lisa. 'You're just jealous you're not gorgeous like my Joe.'

He shrugged and walked off.

'Do you mean it?' I said. 'You really think I'm gorgeous?'

'Yeah,' she said. 'Why not?'

I can't make her out.

I told her about mine, Harry, and Ad's Arse list. I thought it would make her laugh. It didn't.

'Why do you hang around with those losers anyway?' she said. 'You're way more mature than them.'

You know what? She's right. I'd never try and hurt myself to have a chance of winning some money. I'd never have the idea of throwing piss balloons at people. Maybe I won't hang around with them any more? I don't know.

Lisa had a prom committee meeting at break time so I took the opportunity to go and see Natalie.

'Hello, stranger,' she said. 'Haven't seen you in a while. What have you been up to? Cutting your own hair?'

I sat down. 'This cost me thirty-five quid,' I said.

'They must have seen you coming.'

'Probably did,' I said. 'All those mirrors.'

We sat and talked for a while. I told her about the Arse

list and she proper laughed. When she proper laughs, she gets these little red patches on her cheeks. Just something I've noticed.

She came up with 'Arse-Shaped Box', by Nirvana. I'll add it to the list later, but I won't tell Lisa. I'm too mature for that sort of thing now, apparently. Neither of us mentioned the whole I love you thing, but it was hanging there in the air, somehow.

Lisa came and stung me for more cash later on. It never ends.

'We're getting a limo,' she said.

'A limo?' I said. 'The school's five minutes away. Why would we need a limo?'

'For glamour? For style?' she said, as if she were trying to explain quantum physics to a snail. 'For the fact that I'm going to be wearing my gorgeous new prom dress and I don't want it getting wet if it rains, you know, stuff like that?'

I sighed and pulled out my wallet. Something fell out of it. Before I could catch it, it hit the floor and lay glinting in the sunlight. The strip of condoms.

'What the hell, Joe?' Lisa shrieked.

The control room men were tearing their hair out at this point. I scrabbled around on the floor trying to pick them up, but they seemed to shuffle away, as if they had tiny legs. Eventually, I managed to stuff them back in my wallet.

'So you think I'm some kind of slag, is that it?' said Lisa.

'Oh, no, no, no,' I said. 'Not at all. They're just . . .'

'Just what?' she said. 'Are you seeing someone else?'

'No,' I said. 'My dad gave them to me.'

Lisa stared at me for ages.

'Your family is weird, Joe,' she said.

Despite this mishap, she still came over after school. We sat in the lounge. I tried to hint that we should go upstairs, but we ended up staying on the settee for the whole night. Me, Gav, Lisa, with Mum and Jim in the two chairs. Gav didn't look up from his phone all night.

Friday 16th March

Harry and Ad called for me this morning. To begin with, Harry was silent and just stared at the floor. Then Ad poked him.

'Harry,' he said. 'Have you got something you want to say to Joe?'

Harry looked up, still frowning. 'Yes, I'm . . . sorry,' he mumbled. 'For saying you're like a dog.'

'And?' said Ad.

Harry sighed. 'I'm sorry for putting air quotes around the word girlfriend.'

'Oh,' I said. 'Thanks, Harry.'

All this stuff makes me so uncomfortable. We don't do feelings; we do computer games and lists of songs where you can swap the word heart for the word arse.

« Older posts

'I'm, uh, sorry too,' I said. 'For messing up the blooper thing. And you know, I'll make time to spend just with you guys now. Promise.'

It was going well until break time when Lisa came and stood with us. It felt like the longest break ever.

'So,' said Ad, during an awkward silence. 'How hard do you reckon you'd have to punch a rhino to put it on its arse?'

Lisa tutted.

'Pretty bloody hard, I'd imagine, old son,' said Harry. 'What do you reckon, Lisa?'

'I reckon if you spent less time thinking about stupid things like that, you might have a chance of actually getting a girlfriend,' she said. 'It's pathetic.'

Harry and Ad eyeballed me and I could only shrug.

'Right then, Ad,' said Harry. 'We'd better go if we want to get to our next lesson on time.'

'But we've got ten minutes yet,' said Ad.

'Then we'll walk slow, come on.'

'You, um, seem a little tense,' I said to Lisa as they left.

'Well, can you blame me?' she said. 'Us being socially acceptable depends entirely on Gav staying here, and you don't seem to want to take care of it. Sometimes I wonder if you want to be my boyfriend.'

'Oh, I do,' I said. 'I really do. Don't worry, I'll get on it.' I have no idea how though.

I sat with Natalie at lunch. She's clever; I thought she might have some ideas.

'Are you going to this stupid Easter prom thingy?' I said to her.

'Yeah,' she said. 'I don't want to, but my mum's got herself on the stupid PTA already and heard about it that way. She thinks going will help me make *friends* and that I should *make the effort* so I don't *get into trouble* again. I mean I'd rather stay at home smacking myself in the face with a mallet, but she and Dad are dead set on it. How about you?'

'Yes, I'm going,' I said. 'I'm going with Lisa.'

'Lisa.' She smiled. 'You know, when you said you had a girlfriend, I wasn't expecting her to be like that.'

'Why?'

'Well, she's a bit blonde, isn't she?' she said.

'Yes,' I said. 'And you're a bit . . . purple.'

'I'll have you know this is my natural colour. My mum has red hair, and my dad has . . . blue hair. So it's a mixture.'

'Next thing you'll be telling me your lips are naturally black,' I said.

'They are,' she said. 'They've been this way ever since I snogged that chimney sweep.'

Is it wrong that I was hit by a wave of envy, and wanted to punch Bert from Mary Poppins in his stupid face?

'Ah, ha, ha, ha!' I said, trying to seem amused. 'So have

« Older posts

you done much snogging? You know, in your time? Is that a weird question?'

She laughed. 'No. I went to an all girls' school so there was no snogging there, unless I decided to bat for the other team.'

'Imagine that!' I laughed, and crossed my legs.

'No, to be honest, I've only ever kissed one boy,' she said. 'On holiday in France last year. His name was Guillaume. I thought he was really enigmatic and moody and French, but turns out he was just dull. And he stunk of fish. It wasn't very nice.'

Is it wrong that I cursed Guillaume? The snail-eating, fish-ponging moron?

'How about you?' she said. 'I bet that Lisa's a right goer.'

I nodded so hard it gave me neck ache. 'Oh yes, all the time. Like the clappers.'

I don't know what the clappers are, but it's something I've heard Doris say. Natalie looked at me weird and I got the sense she wasn't buying it.

'All right,' I said. 'Can I let you in on a secret?'

'Of course.'

'We've never actually kissed.'

Natalie frowned. 'And you've been going out for what, a few weeks?'

'More like a month.'

'Right,' she said. 'That's a bit weird.'

'Is it?'

'Yeah,' she said. 'If you were my boyfriend, I'd have snogged you ages ago.'

Those patches on her cheeks flashed bright red and she looked away.

'Well, um, that's nice to know,' I said.

A breeze picked up from across the field, blowing over a smell of cut grass and mud.

'Anyway,' she said. 'Do you want to know something interesting about me?'

I nodded.

'I can read palms.' She twinkled her fingers at me.

'Really?'

'Yep, just call me Gypsy Rose Tuft,' said Natalie. 'Actually, don't, because that sounds terrible.'

I laughed. 'Could you—you know—read mine?'

'All right,' she said. 'But I hope they're clean.'

'Always,' I said.

Natalie took my hand and laid it on her lap with the palm facing upwards. It was red from the cold.

'My aunt taught me how to do this.' She gently straightened my fingers out.

'Is that right?'

'Yeah, we were really close, but she died.'

'Oh. What happened?'

'She was hit by a lorry.'

'Surprised she didn't see that coming,' I said. Norman bit his knuckle. 'I didn't mean it like . . . sorry. I . . . I just say stuff sometimes.' My temples throbbed.

Natalie smiled and bit her bottom lip. 'I know you do.'

My mind flashed back to our Skype chat and the throbbing got worse.

'Anyway,' she said. 'Let's see what the palm has to say.'

Natalie moved a couple of centimetres closer and traced her finger along a crease in my palm. Sparks seemed to shoot all the way up my arm and into my neck. Her fingernail was as black as her lips.

'Ah, this is interesting,' she said. 'See how long your head line is? That means your mind is clear and focused.'

'OK, now I know this is a load of rubbish,' I said.

'Don't doubt the palm, Joe.' She scooched a bit closer. I could smell her perfume. It was nice. Like strawberries.

Natalie slid her finger to a crease near my thumb. 'Now, this is your lifeline,' she said. 'Notice how it's broken?'

'Oh God, I'm going to die young, aren't I?' I said. 'That'd be just my luck.'

She laughed. 'No, you silly arse.' She ran her finger along the line again. 'It just means there's been a sudden change in your life.'

'Oh,' I said.

She stuck her tongue out at me. 'Told you not to doubt the palm.'

'What's this one?' I said, pointing at the line nearest my fingers.

'That's your heart line,' she said. I glanced up and saw her looking right at me.

'O-oh,' I said. 'And what's that for? Does it tell me how long it is before I have a coronary?'

She slapped my shoulder. 'I'll tell you what it means.' She slowly traced her finger along the line, pressing slightly harder than before.

'Your heart line is touching your lifeline,' she said. 'That means—that means you fall in love too easily.'

I gulped.

'That's, um, interesting.'

Natalie pushed her fringe out of her eyes. 'Do you love Lisa?' she said.

'I—I don't know,' I said. 'I suppose so.'

She took her hand away, leaving mine still flopped on her lap. I tried to pick it up, but it felt like it weighed a ton.

'Just be careful, hey?' she said, looking out across the field. 'I'd hate it if she was using you for something. Because, underneath your stupid haircut and you constantly talking rubbish, you're not a bad guy.'

I smiled. 'Don't worry, I'll be fine.'

That sour mud smell from the field mingled with her perfume.

'She is beautiful,' said Natalie. She reached down, folded

« Older posts

my fingers into my palm, and put my hand on my own lap.

'Yes,' I said. 'Yes she is.'

She smiled sadly. 'No one's ever told me I'm beautiful.'

All I could hear in my head was buzzing, like a swarm of bees or a badly tuned radio. I opened my mouth but the words wouldn't come.

'Oh,' I said. 'Sorry to hear that.'

7 p.m.

After school, I was just settling down for my first online game of Epic Warfare since my ban was lifted, when I heard a bang on the front door. I went downstairs and opened it.

'Oh, hi, Lisa!'

She stormed past me and went upstairs. I followed her, running up two stairs at a time.

'Oh, she's not here then, is she?' she said.

'Who?'

'That emo freak.'

'Well no, of course she's not.'

'Don't lie to me!' she yelled as she opened my wardrobe and checked in there. She reached in and pulled out Uncle Johnny's freaky dummy.

'What the hell is this?'

'It's my, um, dummy,' I said.

She shuddered and threw it back in with a thud. 'People say they've seen you talking to her. And that you were holding hands!'

'Lisa!' I said. 'She's just a friend. You're my girlfriend. I'd do anything for you.'

'Anything?' she said.

'Anything.'

'I don't want you seeing her any more.'

It was as if I'd been kicked in the stomach.

'But why?'

'I just don't,' she said. 'I mean, what does she have that I haven't got? I'm prettier than her, aren't I?'

'O-of course y-you are,' I said.

'Well then stop seeing her,' she said. 'You're different now. You shouldn't be with freaks like that. You should chuck those stupid friends of yours as well.'

'Harry and Ad?' I said. 'But I can't! They're my best friends!'

'I'm your best friend,' she said.

I was frozen to the spot.

'OK,' I said.

I heard footsteps on the landing. Lisa grabbed hold of me. When Gav walked in, she jumped away.

'Oh, it's you,' she said. 'Can't we have some privacy?'

Gav shrugged and went back out again.

What is happening?

9 p.m.

I found an article on Men's Domain called 'What to do when you have the pick of two women'. It said that a useful thing to do, right after thanking your lucky stars, is to write a list of the pros and cons for each girl. Here's what I've got so far:

LISA: PROS
- SHE'S LISA HALL, MY DREAM GIRL SINCE FOREVER.
- SHE WILL DEFINITELY SNOG ME IF I CAN GET GAV TO STAY.
- TONGUES AND EVERYTHING.
- GOING OUT WITH HER WILL HELP RAISE ME IN THE COOL STAKES A MILLION PER CENT.
- SHE'S LISA HALL, MY DREAM GIRL SINCE FOREVER.

LISA: CONS
- SHE WILL STOP ME FROM SEEING NATALIE, AND MAYBE EVEN HARRY AND AD.
- SHE'S MOODY A LOT OF THE TIME.
- SHE'S NEVER EVEN HEARD OF STAR TREK.

NATALIE: PROS
- WE HAVE LOADS IN COMMON.
- SHE'S DEAD FUNNY.
- SHE WENT TO A PRIVATE SCHOOL, SO YOU KNOW, KER-CHING.
- I THINK SHE IS BEAUTIFUL. (THEN WHY CAN'T YOU SAY IT, IDIOT?)

NATALIE: CONS
- ANY RESPECT I GAINED WOULD BE LOST.
- I'M NOT EVEN ENTIRELY SURE SHE WOULD ACTUALLY GO OUT WITH ME.
- SHE'S NOT LISA HALL, MY DREAM GIRL SINCE FOREVER.

It's still no clearer. If I didn't have all this crap going on in my head, maybe I could make a decision. I wish I was a Vulcan, so I could just use pure logic.

10.40 p.m.

If Gav can have two girls on the go at once then why can't I? Oh that's right, because I'm not a monster.

Tried talking to him again. Still no response. I'm running out of ideas.

Saturday 17th March

If Gav is going to stay here, I'm going to have to be bold and try something radical. I'm going to have to call his mum again.

I sat in the kitchen, stuck a cloth over Syd's cage, and worked on my strategy. I'd have to convince her that Gav has properly gone off the rails. But how? I couldn't just call up as myself. I had to be someone with a reason as to why he can't come. And then it hit me: school. I went out to the shed and made the call.

'Ah, hello, Caroline, you don't mind if I call you Caroline, do you?' I said in the best Scottish accent I could manage. It was terrible. I sounded like Shrek.

'Who's this?' she said.

'Who's this?' I said. Crap, I forgot to invent a name. 'This is, um, Jockey. Jockey . . . Horse.'

'Are you having a laugh, mate?' she said.

'No, no, no, my dear,' I said. 'I'm the head teacher of your local high school.' I probably should have found out the name of it.

'Yeah, and what do you want?' she said. ''Cause I ain't got no kids.'

I stopped and wondered if I had the right Caroline.

'Oh,' I said. 'But I understand that your son, Gavin, will be moving to the area soon and is looking for a school.'

'Oh, Gav,' she said. 'Yeah, he's coming up, but I haven't been looking for a school for him.'

'Right,' I said. 'The enquiry actually came from a Mr James.'

'Yeah, that sounds like Jim,' she said. 'Anyway, go on.'

'The reason I'm calling is I'm afraid we will be unable to offer Gavin a place at our school. His disciplinary record is just too poor,' I said. A hot, needling feeling stung the back of my head but I closed my eyes and thought of Lisa, while Derek cheered me on.

'That doesn't surprise me,' she said. 'As I keep telling Jim, school is a waste of time for Gavin. He can't learn anything, so why bother even going?'

I was genuinely speechless.

'OK,' I said. 'Sorry.'

'Yeah,' she said. 'And anyway, if you're a headmaster, why are you ringing me on a Saturday?'

'Goodbye, then,' I said, and quickly hung up.

As scary as it sounds, I'm starting to understand how the monster that is Gav was created. It is not pretty.

And what if he does go off to Scotland? He'll become ten times worse. And then he might come back one day, like some kind of tartan Incredible Hulk, and twist my head off my neck.

He can't go.

GAV

SMASH!

Sunday 18th March

Svetlana was out with Hercules this afternoon, so I had to spend the day at Dad's with just him. He was wearing shorts and flip-flops with a T-shirt that said 'I got 99 problems but a bitch ain't one', on it. I beg to differ.

'So, my little dude,' he said, passing me a non-alcoholic cocktail. 'It's been a while hasn't it? Since it was just me and you.'

'S'pose,' I said, twiddling the umbrella.

He swished his drink around. 'Do you miss it?'

'Miss what?'

'Us,' he said. 'And your mum. The family.'

I didn't know what to say. I mean, who wouldn't want their parents to be together? I try and think of the good times: holidays, Dad getting me into *Star Trek* and the Floyd, my birthdays, but then I think of the bad times. The shouting, the tears. Those silences. The way I'd hide under my duvet and look at the stars on my ceiling. How unhappy we all were. What's the point of being with someone if you're not happy? I mean, I'm really happy with Lisa. I'm ecstatic.

I really am.

It got a bit awkward after that. It turns out we don't have that much to talk about any more. The only relief came when Svetlana came thundering in.

'This bloody dog, Keith!' she yelled.

'What's the matter, Svet?' he said.

'He's crapped in my handbag!'

I never used to like Hercules, but now he's my favourite dog in the whole world.

Monday 19th March

Started the day listening to Mum puking in the toilet. Put me right off my Cheerios.

She said she must have eaten something dodgy. I don't know, I think it might be all this stress with Gav.

Lisa called for me before school, even though my house is out of the way for her. Then Harry and Ad turned up.

'Morning, old bean!' yelled Harry. 'Hello, Lisa.'

'Yeah, whatever,' she said.

She held my hand all the way to school, and walked slowly so we were way behind Harry and Ad.

At lunch, I had to go and stand with her up by the bike racks. Then she started smoking.

'I didn't know you smoked,' I said.

'There's a lot you don't know about me.'

'I suppose there is,' I said.

'Besides, doesn't your mate smoke that stupid pipe?'

'No, it's empty,' I said.

'What a weirdo,' she said.

« Older posts

I could see Natalie sitting on the bench, reading. She looked so lonely. Why hasn't she made any friends yet? Then two girls walked over to her. Chloe and Ellie.

'What you reading, emo?' said Chloe.

Natalie didn't look up.

'She asked you a question,' said Ellie. 'That's just rude, innit?'

'Let's have a look, then.' Chloe grabbed the book off her. 'William Shatner? He looks about a hundred. Sad bitch.'

'Hey, give that back,' said Natalie. I could see her face going red.

'Hey, Ells, catch.' Chloe threw the book at her.

'Nah, I ain't touching that, I don't want to catch freakitis,' said Ellie, and let the book fall into a puddle.

I went to go over but Lisa held me back.

'Where are you going, Joe?'

I looked at her, then back at Natalie. 'Nowhere,' I said.

'Too right you're going nowhere.'

As Chloe and Ellie walked away they gave Lisa a look. Natalie picked my book up and shook it. I wanted more than anything to go down there and give her a hug, but I couldn't. I wasn't allowed.

8 p.m.

Just tried to Skype her but she's blocked me again.

Tuesday 20th March

Mum was chundering again this morning. Doris told her to stay in bed, but she still went to work. She hasn't had a sick day since before I was born. I hope she gets better soon.

A weird thing happened in PE today. I actually scored a try in rugby. It was as if everyone was too scared to tackle me. I didn't know what to do when I got to the line, so I just placed the ball on the ground and walked away. Old busted-ribs-Boocock looked flabbergasted.

Afterwards, I saw Natalie on the corridor. I said hello but she ignored me. Balls.

I got home to find Doris pushing Adwina 2 around the street in a pushchair. I eventually coaxed her inside with the promise of a cup of tea and a biscuit.

When Gav came upstairs for the night, I decided to put on a film from Jim's collection, called Trainspotting, about a load of drug addicts living in Scotland. I thought it would put him off, but he thought it was the coolest film he'd ever seen. Damn.

Wednesday 21st March

You know what I hate about Harry? You want to know what I really hate about him? He can't stand the idea of me actually being happy for once.

When stuff was going wrong, like me spewing on Louise Bentley, he was right there. Now, when I've got a girlfriend and I'm sorting myself out, he has to cause problems.

Here's what happened:

This morning, Lisa called for me early. I suggested waiting for Harry and Ad, but she pointed out quite rightly that there's no point waiting for them because they walk off ahead anyway. Sounds reasonable enough, right? WRONG!

Harry came and found me at lunch with Ad trailing behind.

'Do you think we call for you for the good of our health, old son?' he said.

'Well, the walking is good exercise,' I said.

'No, we call for you every morning because we are supposed to be mates.'

His hands were shaking.

'Well I'm sorry,' I said. 'But you walk off ahead of us anyway.'

He smiled and shook his head.

'Do you know why the three of us started walking to school together in the first place?' he said. 'Safety in numbers. So you wouldn't keep getting picked up and shoved in the big bins by Paphlos's kebab shop, remember?'

I didn't say anything.

'But now you're some kind of big man, I suppose you don't need us any more, do you?' he said. 'Well good, because I can't be bothered with you. That's it. You can walk to school with your "girlfriend".'

'What did I tell you about air quotes?' I said.

'Oh come on, old son,' said Harry. 'She is playing you and using you and you're the only one too stupid to see it. Even Ad knows the score, and he's Ad. No offence, son.'

Ad shrugged.

'That haircut and that tux,' said Harry. 'How did you pay for them?'

I didn't answer.

'I've kept quiet up until now, but you need to wake up.'

The control room started buzzing. Lights flashed.

'I need to wake up?' I said. 'I'm wide awake "old boy". It's you that needs to wake up. You just can't stand the fact that I'm not a freak any more and that people actually respect me. All you want to do is drag me down into your freaky circle of weirdness forever.'

I was shaking when I finally stopped. Harry stared at me then stormed off. Ad gawped for a while before joining him.

Yeah well who needs Harry anyway? Lisa's right, his pipe is stupid. And after what I'd just done for him as well. The DJ who was supposed to be doing the prom had to cancel and the prom committee couldn't find a replacement at such short notice, so I suggested the Sound Experience. I gave them Harry's phone number and told them to leave a message. It pays £250. The same as a *You've Been Framed* video.

« Older posts

There's a few reasons why I wanted them to DJ the prom, partly because I felt bad about blowing the Buzzfest fund, partly because I wanted to do them a favour, and partly because maybe deep down, I want them to wreck the stupid prom with their freaky music. But now I wish I hadn't bothered.

Whatever. I don't need them. Any of them. Once I've snogged the fittest girl in school, they'll be nothing but a distant memory. A footnote.

I felt like I didn't have anyone to talk to, so I went outside to see Natalie. Lisa had a dentist appointment so I knew it would be safe. I went to her bench but she wasn't there. Chloe and Ellie were though.

'Looking for the wicked witch?' said Chloe.

'She ain't here,' said Ellie. 'And you'd better go before we tell Lisa we saw you, you get me?'

I nodded and walked away. My new powers don't really work on girls. I wish they did.

Thursday 22nd March

I had to wait until Gav was asleep until I could go to the toilet last night or he would have followed me there. By the time he'd started snoring, I thought I was going to burst.

On the way back, I heard talking in Mum and Jim's room, which I thought was a bit odd as it was half one in the morning, but at least they were just talking and not doing anything else. I slowed down and listened, using my ninja stealth.

'But you're his father, Jim,' said Mum. 'If you can't stop him from going, no one can.'

'Maybe it's what he needs,' said Jim. 'A short time up there will make him realize how good he has it here.'

'But what if it doesn't?' said Mum. 'The reason he acts like he does is he needs something to rebel against. If his mother doesn't create boundaries for him, he'll get worse and worse, maybe even get into crime. And it'll be all for attention. He didn't have enough growing up, you know that.'

'Thanks, professor,' said Jim. 'How much do I owe you for your analysis?'

'Oh for God's sake, Jim,' she said. 'Stop being so bloody proud and do the right thing. He's got a chance here. Who knows what might happen if he goes to Caroline's?'

He won't be going to school, I know that much. I stayed there until I heard Mum saying something about needing to be sick, so I ran back to the bedroom before she caught me. This whole thing is really affecting her.

Gav woke up with a start.

'It's only me,' I said as I got into bed.

I waited for Harry and Ad this morning but they didn't show. Good. I'm glad they didn't, because as I've already made clear, I don't care.

« Older posts

At break time, Lisa told me the committee had booked the Sound Experience for the prom. 'Are they really any good?' she said. 'I mean, how do you know them?'

'Oh, I've seen them around,' I said. 'They'll do a good job.'

Harry is so angry he's bound to play Swedish grindcore like he did at the Year Seven Christmas party.

Then Ellie and Chloe ran over.

'Guess what, Lis?' said Chloe. 'We just locked that freak in the toilet for fifteen minutes. Oh my days, it was brilliant.'

'What freak is this?' I said.

They all just glared at me.

9 p.m.

Heard Jim and Gav having a row earlier.

'I can't stay, all right?' said Gav. 'And you can't make me. I'm going next week.'

I can remember a time when hearing that would have been the best thing ever.

Friday 23rd March

It's the day before the prom and everyone's gone mental. Anyone would think it was the Oscars or something. The decorations are insane.

I was at the urinal at break when Ad came and stood at the one next to me.

'All right, Joe?' he said.

'Hello, Ad, how's things?'

'Not very good, mate,' he said. 'I hate it when you two ain't speaking.'

'That's good news about you getting the DJing gig though, isn't it?' I said.

'S'pose so,' he said. 'I don't know why they called us, but whatever, it's money, innit?'

'So what kind of stuff are you going to play?' I said. 'And can you not look at me—it gives me stage fright.'

'Oh sorry,' he said. 'Harry wants us to play, like, normal stuff.'

'Normal stuff? But you're the Sound Experience!'

'That's what I said,' he replied. 'But Harry's just going on about how he wants to show you he can be normal and not weird and all this. He's even put his pipe away.'

I didn't know what to say to that, so I didn't say anything.

When I left the toilet, I saw Natalie walking down the corridor. I called after her but she carried on walking. I ran and tapped her on the shoulder.

'What do you want?' she said, glancing around.

'I just wanted to see how you were,' I said. 'We haven't spoken in a while.'

'Yeah,' she said. 'I know.'

'So how's things?' I said.

'Pretty bloody awful,' she said. 'Turns out everyone hates me here as well.'

'I know how you feel,' I said. 'Things used to be like that for me but then . . .'

'You changed?' She narrowed her eyes at me.

'No.'

'Yes you have, you've got that . . . ridiculous haircut and everyone kisses your arse. You have changed,' she said.

I didn't know what to say. 'But it worked,' I said. 'Maybe you could try . . .'

She folded her arms. 'No way,' she said. 'This is who I am and if people can't deal with that, they're idiots. I don't care about being cool or respected, because what's the point if the people who respect you are morons?'

I looked around. Jordan Foster gave me a thumbs up then walked straight into a locker.

'And do you know something else?' said Natalie. 'The minute you lose that respect, they'll come for you, even worse than they ever did before.'

I gulped. Gav really is the only thing keeping them from turning on me.

'Anyway, I'm not supposed to be talking to you, so I'm going,' she said, and walked away before I could ask why. I consulted the control room but they were useless as usual.

When I got home, Mum was downstairs with a suitcase.

'What, you're not leaving too are you?' I said.

She smiled. 'No, Jim and I are just going away for the

weekend.'

'But Gav's going next week,' I said.

'I know, love,' she said. 'But Jim has insisted we get away. Says this place is stressing him out.'

He should try being me for a day.

'If anything happens while we're away, just give us a call. I've told Doris the same, but she'll probably forget.'

10.30 p.m.

As it happens, Gav didn't do anything tonight. He didn't have the Blenkinsops over or have a party or anything like that. He just sat and watched *Star Trek: Generations* with me. The whole thing. Afterwards he told me it was 'crap as'. Yeah well what does he know?

Saturday 24th March

The day of the prom. My pillow was damp with sweat this morning.

I picked up the Buzzfest jar and scraped the last of the money out for the corsage. Ellie ordered me to buy Lisa one for the prom. 'And make sure it's pink, to go with Lisa's dress, yeah?'

I stared into the empty jar and sighed. Looks like I'm never going to Buzzfest. Not that I've got anyone to go with, anyway.

A framed photo on the window sill seemed to be staring

at me. I picked it up. It's me, Harry, and Ad at my eighth birthday party. I'm looking off to one side, freaked out by someone dressed as Laa-Laa. Harry is in the middle, in soldier costume, saluting the camera. Ad is standing there grinning, his front teeth missing, and his arm in a sling.

I got this heavy feeling in my throat so I threw the picture in a drawer. I kept telling myself there's no point living in the past. Look to the future. Bigger and better things. I'm not a loser any more.

I went straight to Lisa's from the florist's, where I bought the best corsage I could afford.

I knocked on the door and a woman who looked like an older version of Lisa answered.

'Hello, Mrs Hall,' I said, trying my best to be charming. 'Is Lisa in?'

'Yes, she is, dear,' she said. 'I don't mean to be rude, but who are you?'

'I'm Joe,' I said. 'I'm her boyfriend.'

She frowned at me for a few seconds. 'OK, Joe,' she said. 'Come in.'

I sat down in the living room.

'Lisa!' she called up the stairs. 'Your boyfriend's here!'

Heavy footsteps clomped down the stairs, and a man stood in the doorway.

'Oh good,' he said. 'You're not that horrible Gavin kid.'

I stood up.

'Harry Hall,' he said. 'Pleased to meet you.'

'I'm Joe,' I said. 'I have—' I stopped and corrected myself. 'I had a friend called Harry.'

'That's nice,' he said, giving me the world's firmest handshake. 'Well, hopefully, we can be friends, too. Although at the rate she gets through them, that won't give us much time.' He winked and chuckled. I laughed too, but I didn't find it funny. 'Ah, here she is. Morning, princess!'

Lisa came down in her dressing gown with her hair everywhere, but still looking gorgeous.

'Joe?' she said. 'What are you doing here?'

'Just popping by to give you this.' I pulled the corsage out of the bag.

'Ooh, isn't that lovely, Lisa?' said her mum. 'What a nice young man.'

Lisa grunted and rubbed sleep out of her eyes.

'You'd never get Gav the chav making the effort like that,' said her dad. 'Stick with this one, my girl, he's not an idiot.'

He put his hand on my shoulder. 'You're not an idiot, are you, son?'

'No,' I said, although sometimes I do wonder.

'See?' he said. 'Still, I shouldn't get too pally with you. It's probably your fault I've been lumbered with such a massive phone bill!'

Lisa suddenly woke up. 'Oh shut up, Dad.'

'A hundred and eighty quid!' he said. 'Texting from Spain,

I ask you!'

'I'm sure Joe doesn't want to hear about that,' she said as she pushed me out of the door. 'Thanks for the flowers.'

'But, Lisa,' I said.

'Bye, Joe.' She slammed the door in my face.

'You only text me once when you were in Spain,' I said to the closed door.

I walked home, trying to consider the facts carefully, but my brain was a crazy whirl of thoughts.

It's OK, Joe, said Norman. *She was probably just texting her friends.*

Do you really believe that, man? said Derek. *She was texting some guy and you know it.*

Hold on a minute, said Norman. *Weren't you the one saying how he had to stick with Lisa because she was going to, and I quote, 'give him some tongue action'?*

Hey, dude, I just call it like I see it, said Derek. *What about all those times you saw Gav texting? And what you saw at the movies? You've gotta find Gav and ask him what the freakin' deal is.*

Don't listen to this idiot, Joe, said Norman. *He's got you into enough trouble already.*

I felt sick.

Hey, you wanna make something of it, old man? said Derek.

Please, I was here before you and I'll be here after you,

said Norman. *Just pipe down.*

Oh yeah? Derek threw down his clipboard and ripped off his lab coat and T-shirt. *Well what do you wanna do, huh? You wanna piece of me, old timer?*

That's it. Norman threw his clipboard down and ran over.

The other control room men gathered around and cheered them on as they disappeared into a whirl of fists. A red light blinked on and off.

Must find Gav.

Must find Gav.

The front door left a dent in the wall.

'Gav!' I yelled. 'GAV!'

'Did you want me, duck?' called Doris from upstairs.

'No, Doris, I want GAV!'

The TV was on, but he wasn't in the lounge. The back garden was empty. Then I saw him. In the kitchen. With Syd on his shoulder.

'What do you think you're doing?' I said. Syd took off and landed on top of the fridge.

'None of your business, you freak,' said Gav.

« Older posts

'JOE'S LIKES MEN, JOE LIKES MEN, JOE LIKES MEN,' squawked Syd.

'Come down here and say that, you treacherous bird!' I yelled.

My temples throbbed as the control room fight became a riot.

'What's your problem, man?' said Gav.

'What's my problem? What's? My? Problem? I'll tell you what my problem is, you creator of human misery. You and my girlfriend have been texting each other.'

He shrugged. 'Yeah? And?'

I screamed and pushed him. He stumbled back a couple of steps and stared at me.

'What the hell did you just do?'

'OH, DO YOU NEED A REMINDER?' I screamed and pushed him again.

Gav's look of disbelief turned to one of rage. He picked me up by my collar and threw me through the door. My back smashed into the old record player cabinet, sending glass everywhere. A box of Dad's old vinyls slid off the shelf and onto my lap.

Gav stomped over to me, glass cracking under his trainers. He grabbed me around the throat and squeezed. I couldn't breathe. I brought my foot up quick and kicked him in the balls. He let go and screamed. Seizing the opportunity, I slammed the box of vinyls down on his head, sending him down to his knees. I was about to strike again, but he grabbed me by the shirt and threw me across the lounge. For the briefest of milliseconds, I actually enjoyed the feeling of weightlessness. Then I slammed onto the coffee table and skidded into an iron candlestick, before ending up sprawled against the radiator.

Gav staggered across the room, wheezing. His fists curled into massive spheres. As he got closer, I reached up to the window sill for something I could use. Anything. He had me around the neck again before I found it and smashed it across his face. I looked down and saw what it was. A framed photo of Mum and Jim. A piece of glass from the frame had cut Gav across the face.

Gav stood up straight and touched the wound. It was thin and shallow looking but it bled heavily.

'You cut me,' he said, his eyes wide. 'You cut me, you little freak.'

Before he could do anything else, I pushed away from the radiator and skidded through his legs. Then I sprang to my feet, kicked him on the arse, and ran into the hall. He was behind me straight away.

'Pack the bugger in,' Doris shouted from upstairs. 'You'll wake the baby.'

But Gav had no intention of packing anything in as he threw me against the front door. I cried out as the door handle cracked against my spine.

« Older posts

He walked backwards to the other side of the hall, his eyes locked onto mine. He was going to charge me. I couldn't let that happen. If it did, they'd be picking bits of me out of the letterbox for weeks. *This is it. This is how you're going to die.*

He started running. I remembered something. That day on the field with Boocock. My hand found the door handle. I turned it quickly and opened the door, flattening myself against the wall. I saw the look in Gav's eyes turn from rage to panic, but he couldn't stop himself and went flying outside, flipping over the knee-high fence and landing face first on the lawn.

I ran out and turned him over. I knelt over him and raised my fist, trying desperately to stop it shaking.

Do it, Joe, finish him! yelled Derek, himself bruised and bloodied.

No! cried an equally banged-up Norman. *If you do it you'll become as bad as he is. It's not you, Joe. It's not you!*

Gav's face was a mess of blood, grass, and dirt. I couldn't do it. Could I?

I'll never know because a streak of blue going past distracted me.

'Oh crap,' I said. 'Syd!'

I looked again and saw Syd flying full pelt down the road.

'Wha?' Gav mumbled.

'It's Syd, he's escaped,' I said.

Gav got some recognition back in his eyes and threw me off him as if I were a doll. He staggered to his feet and ran down the road.

I climbed up off the lawn and went after him, pain thudding in my back.

'Where is he?' I said.

'I dunno, I lost him,' said Gav. 'He went towards the park.' He looked genuinely upset. We ran as fast as we could through the park, calling Syd's name like a pair of morons. We reached a clearing by the side of the lake and Gav stopped me.

'Did you hear that?' he said.

'No.'

'Listen . . .' He cupped his hands around his mouth. 'Syd, who likes men?'

There was a second of silence, before we heard the voice calling softly, 'Joe likes men, Joe likes men, Joe likes men.'

I scanned the trees. Nothing. Then I saw him. At first I thought it was a big pigeon, but then I realized it was Syd, sitting on top of a statue. It's a statue of two weird blob people hugging, with a plaque underneath saying 'Working towards a peaceful community'. It's surrounded by a spiked fence.

We crept over, being careful not to make any sudden moves.

'Here, Syd, come down from there, there's a good boy.'

« Older posts

'Come on, Syd. Yes, that's right, I do like men.'

After sitting there staring at us for about five minutes, he flapped his wings and left his perch. He flew around the statue twice before settling on the fence in front of us.

Gav nodded at me and went around the side. I crept forwards, millimetre by millimetre, slowly reaching out.

'Good boy, Syd, good boy.' My fingers were centimetres away. I could feel my heart pounding all the way up in my neck.

'Ready to make the grab,' I whispered. 'In five . . . four . . . three . . . two . . .'

'HE IS COMING!'

Syd took off and landed high up in a tree above our heads.

'Oh bloody hell, Morris!' I said as he waddled up behind us.

'What's your problem, man?' said Gav.

'The Lord is coming! Repent!'

'I'll repent my foot up your arse if you don't jog on, geezer,' said Gav.

Syd flapped his wings and took off again, across the lake and into the dark slit on the side of the old bunker.

'Oh bum,' I said.

Gav was already running over there. I followed him. He hesitated before he went in. We used the light from our phones to find our way around. It didn't smell any nicer in there.

'Syd?' I yelled. 'Syd?'

A squawk echoed from further down in the bunker. Behind the matted blood and grass on Gav's face, I could tell he was scared. I led the way through the bunker. Eventually, we found another small, square room.

We stopped and called out again. He sounded close.

'How far down do you think this goes?' said Gav.

'Pretty far,' I said. 'Harry says it was built to withstand bombings.'

We shone our phones around the walls. The fact that we were beating the crap out of each other not five minutes earlier didn't seem to matter. We had to find the stupid bird.

'This place is creepy,' Gav muttered.

'Just an old building,' I said. 'Nothing to worry about.'

'Yeah but this is where the ghosts come from, you said.'

There was silence. Syd stopped squawking.

'Look,' I said. 'Maybe I was lying about that, OK?'

'How could you be lying?' he said. 'I saw it.'

I knew I had to tell him at some point. Ideally, it wouldn't have been in an underground tunnel where you could easily hide a body, but still.

'That ghost wasn't real,' I said.

'What d'you mean?'

The control room was silent.

'It was a special effect,' I said. 'I made it to try and get rid of you.'

« Older posts

I could have dropped Greeny in it too but I decided against it.

Gav didn't say anything, but I could hear him breathing in the dark. Without another word, he grabbed me and slammed me up the wall.

'What were you thinking? I've been living in fear for weeks now. Thinking that thing could be waiting for me around every corner.'

'Yeah, well maybe you know how I feel,' I said. My back spasmed with pain.

'What d'you mean, freak?'

'I've been living in fear of you for the past four years,' I said. 'Only I used to be able to get away from you at home, but now I can't even do that.'

'Why don't you just grow a pair?' he said. 'Can't you take a bit of banter?'

'It's not banter though, is it?' I said. 'Banter is when Ad says he fancies my mum or Harry says Kirk is better than Picard. What you did was more than banter. I mean, why me?'

He huffed out through his nose like a bull.

''Cause you don't know how to keep your mouth shut, all right?' he said. 'You could have just taken it like everyone else, but you had to have the last say, didn't you?'

'So what? If you give it out, you should be able to take it,' I said. 'And anyway, why would you text my girlfriend? Can't you stand the idea of me being happy?'

'Hey, she was texting me,' he said. 'And all she kept going on about was how happy she is with you and how you're so much better than me.'

I didn't understand it. If I'm so great, why's she always off with me? And why did she have to keep telling Gav?

'Anyway,' said Gav. 'You ain't got to worry about it any more, 'cause I'm going. This time next week I'll be in Scotland and you'll never hear from me again.'

'But that's the thing,' I said. 'Maybe I don't want you to go. Not now.'

I couldn't believe what I was saying.

He laughed without smiling and pushed me further into the wall. 'You've changed your tune, ain't ya?' he said. 'And I know why. It's 'cause being in with me is giving you a good rep, innit? People ain't messing with you no more.'

I shook my head. 'Look, at one time, it was that. Or at least partly that. But it's different now. I don't want you to go because I can't live with it on my conscience. I know what your mum's like.'

'Don't you diss my mum or I will KILL you,' he said.

'I'm not "dissing" anybody,' I said. 'Let me put it another way. Since you've lived at my house, have you ever worn the same clothes for weeks at a time?'

He sighed and shook his head.

'Have you ever had to eat dry Pot Noodles for dinner?'

'Nah.'

« Older posts

'Have you felt safe?'

'Yeah,' he said. 'Until you convinced me the place was haunted with mental ghosts.'

'I know, and I'm sorry,' I said. 'But after what you've put me through, I should be glad to see the back of you. But I can't do it to you, and I can't do it to your dad and my mum. This whole thing's even making Mum ill. They love you. God knows why, but they do.'

I'm sure I could see tears in his eyes. He raised his fist.

I clenched my jaw and waited for it.

A shadow moved across the ceiling. Wings flapped. Something landed on Gav's giant fist.

'Sqwaaaawk, Joe likes men, Joe likes men, Joe likes men.'

We looked at each other. Then at Syd. Then we both broke up laughing. What can you say to that? Gav let go of me and put Syd on his shoulder.

'Look, if you can't stay for me, stay for Syd,' I said. 'I mean look at how much you agree on.'

Gav laughed again. It's a weird sound, him laughing.

'Lisa wants you to stay as well,' I said. 'Which doesn't seem right to me, but what do I know? I mean you cheated on her for God's sake.'

'You wanna know something, man? I never cheated on her. Not even once. Jo's just a mate.'

'What?' I said. 'But why didn't you deny it?'

'Dunno,' he said. 'It's . . . weird. The thing is, I got a rep, you know what I mean?'

'Kind of.'

'And I've gotta keep it up, 'cause in that place, your rep is the only thing that matters.'

'I think that's why Lisa wants you to stay,' I said. 'Because you being here has given me a rep, which looks good on her. But now, I don't think I care. I'm not sure it's as important as you think.'

We stood in the dark for a while; I think both of us were thinking things over.

'Anyway, let's get out of here,' said Gav. ''Cause it's dark and stinks of piss.'

'All right,' I said.

Gav got Syd in a firm grip and we headed for home.

'You know,' I said. 'I tried to leave as well.'

He raised his eyebrows. 'Yeah?'

'I wanted to move in with my dad,' I said. 'But he wouldn't have me.'

Gav rubbed his eyes.

'I think what we both need to realize is, if you're forced to pick one of your parents, you should go with the one who cares the most. Do you know what I mean?'

He nodded.

'So are you staying?'

Gav's eyes were all red. 'Yeah,' he said. 'I'm staying.'

« Older posts

I smiled and clapped him on the back. 'Good,' I said.

'Never touch me, freak,' he said.

'Right you are.'

I called Lisa and told her the news. She sounded really happy.

'I'm going to give you such a snog tonight,' she said.

This should be the best night of my life.

So why doesn't it feel like it?

Sunday 25th March

Well, blog, if you were capable of sentient thought, you'd probably be wondering what happened at the prom last night. So I'm going to tell you.

After we got back, Gav and I tidied the living room together, vacuuming up glass and replacing vases. Nothing could be done about the cabinet or the picture frame, so we're going to have some explaining to do when Mum and Jim get back. It was a weird atmosphere, kind of awkward. It was as if we were cleaning up after someone else, and it hadn't been us trying to kill each other.

Afterwards, I put my tuxedo on, spending ages getting the cufflinks done up right. When it was all on, I looked in the mirror. I looked like a moron. I took it all off and shoved my favourite *Star Trek* T-shirt on. Then I put the tux back on over the top and it somehow made me feel better.

Gav came in and laughed. 'Hey, man, you look like something out of that film.'

'Which film?' I said. 'The Godfather?'

'Nah,' he said. 'March of the Penguins.'

Just because he's staying doesn't mean I have to like him.

Then his phone rang. He left it for a while and then answered it.

'Hello, Dad,' he said. ''S all right. I was just calling to let you know I want to stay.'

I decided to leave him to it and go downstairs. Doris sat there with Adwina 2 as if nothing had happened.

'Oh, don't you look smart?' she said. 'Where are you off to?'

'The prom,' I said.

'Blackpool? Oh how lovely. Bring me back some rock, won't you?'

A horn beeped outside.

I went out, hoping none of the neighbours were watching, and climbed into the bright pink limo. Lisa, Ellie, Chloe, and their dates, Pete Cotterill and Jordan Foster, were inside.

'Hi, sweetheart,' said Lisa. She looked stunning in her dress. She kissed me on the cheek. I burned up.

'I'm so glad he's listened to you,' she whispered in my ear.

'Wicked tux,' said Pete. 'You look cool, man.'

I had an urge to rip my shirt off and show them my *Star Trek* tee and then see how cool they thought I was. It was

« Older posts

only a few months ago that Pete was calling me a freak. I couldn't believe I'd blown the Buzzfest fund on this. I don't even like limousines. Especially not pink ones.

After we'd done seven excruciating laps around the block to get our money's worth ('Ooh look! Paphlos's kebab shop again!'), we arrived at school. The hall had been decorated in blue and red bunting and glittery crap.

Harry and Ad were playing some background music while they set up their lighting equipment on the stage. Harry was frowning at a plug while Ad inspected a bulb that wasn't working. Then Harry changed the plug to a different socket and the light came on and nearly blinded Ad. I nodded at Harry. He didn't nod back. He looked weird without his pipe.

'Oh my God, they are the Sound Experience?' Lisa looked like she was going to be sick. 'Why didn't you tell me?'

'You never asked,' I said. Which seemed like the best explanation.

We sat down in our six. The others talked about stuff like music and telly shows I've never heard of, and I barely got a word in.

'Oh my God, can you believe that is here?' said Chloe.

I turned around and saw Natalie sitting next to Greeny. She was wearing a black dress and looking at her made my chest go all tight.

'You'd think she'd get a different colour lipstick,' said Ellie. 'She looks like a witch.'

'Witch,' I laughed to myself. 'Hundreds of years ago, people used to persecute women and accuse them of being witches. For no reason, most of the time.'

'What are you on about?' said Lisa.

'I just want to know why any of you care what other people look like? Why not keep it to yourself? I mean Jordan clearly has a bogie hanging out of his nose but I haven't mentioned it.'

Jordan rubbed his nose and wiped his hand on his trousers. There was an awkward silence.

I glanced over at Natalie and half-smiled. She walked away.

'Who are you looking at over there?' said Lisa, all icy.

'Oh, um, Greeny,' I said. She looked over to see Greeny with his finger in his ear.

'Weird,' she said.

I was disappointed at how normal the Sound Experience's choice of music was. All the kinds of stuff you hear on Radio 1. I didn't know they even had these songs in their collection. Harry looked disgusted with himself.

Mr Pratt and Mr Fuller stood in the corner, watching everything like tennis umpires. Mr Fulcrum was in the opposite corner. From where I sat it looked like he was asleep standing up.

'Are you OK?' said Lisa. 'Looking forward to later?'

I gulped. 'More than anything.'

« Older posts

She smiled. 'So is Gav coming tonight? I haven't seen him.'

'Um, yeah I think so,' I said, wondering why she cared.

The night wore on. All the cool kids around me laughed and bitched while I got bloated drinking Coke.

This is what you wanted, I thought. To be respected by these people. Does it feel good?

I tried to shut my brain up and remember all the stuff I read about kissing on Men's Domain: not to be overzealous with the tongue, don't grope unless they ask, stuff like that, but that voice wouldn't go away.

Lisa grabbed my hand and squeezed it. I smiled. Maybe this was going to be fun. I noticed her eyes focused on something behind me. I turned around and saw Gav walking in, wearing a shirt and actual shoes which I recognized as being Jim's. He nodded at me and walked past.

'Why has he got a cut on his face?' said Lisa.

'I don't know,' I said. 'Maybe he did it shaving or something.'

I looked at the people around me: Jordan, Pete, and the others. I could tell they secretly hated me but were pretending not to, especially now Gav had arrived. As if I could unleash him on them at any moment. It was like having a pit bull. As long as I live, I'll never understand school.

Lisa got up and went to the toilet,

'I might be a while—having a pee is a nightmare in this dress,' she said.

After she went, I found myself sitting next to Jordan Foster. He's even denser than Ad, but at least Ad isn't a dick. While I was sitting there, Jordan grabbed Squirgy Kallow, farted on his head, and then laughed until he dry-heaved. Pete Cotterill seemed to think this was the funniest thing he'd ever seen.

I decided that their intellectual repartee was too much for me, so I got up and had a wander around. Greeny stopped me.

'Having a good prom?' he said, holding a big bowl of crisps.

'Yeah, it's a right barrel of giggles,' I said. 'How about you?'

'Fff, whatever.'

'OK,' I said. 'Well I'll be off, then.'

'Nah, you won't,' he said. ''Cause I got some stuff I need to say to you.'

He steadied himself and gulped.

'You're a hippogriff,' he said.

'A hippogriff?' I said. 'Isn't that something off Harry Potter?'

'Nah, you say one thing but do another: a hippogriff.'

'Oh, you mean a hypocrite,' I said. 'Why?'

'Well, all that crap you said about how you should be yourself,' said Greeny. 'And you ain't even doing it.'

'What do you mean?'

'Well, I've started being myself and everyone hates me even more, and you've started being someone else, and everyone loves you.'

« Older posts

'I'm not being someone else,' I said. 'I'm still me.'

'Are you?' he said. 'For one thing, you've got that mentalist haircut, and then there's the fact that you've been sitting with that lot all night. Do you know how many years I was trying to get in with them? A lot. A—very lot. You ain't the same person at all. I hate them now, and I hate you.'

I caught a glimpse of myself in the mirror and looked away quickly.

'You don't mean that,' I said.

'I do though, Joe, and I wish I didn't because I liked you,' he said. 'Proper liked you.'

He looked at me really weird. I didn't know what to say.

'Hey,' a voice from behind came to the rescue. I turned around to see Pete Cotterill standing there with that smug grin on his face. 'Don't get eating all them crisps, fatty.'

Greeny sneered at him.

'What you doing talking to him anyway, Joe?' said Pete, before walking away.

'See? This is who you are, now,' said Greeny. 'You're like him.'

'No I'm—'

'Don't eat all the crisps,' Greeny interrupted. 'Stupid . . . this is what I think of your crappy prom.'

He grabbed loads of crisps out of the bowl and licked them before dropping them back in. 'That's what I think of all of you.'

'Look, Greeny,' I said. 'You're obviously a bit emotional so—'

'Yeah, yeah, walk away,' he said. 'You know, I wouldn't care about any of this if you'd been straight with me about Lisa.'

'What?'

'We worked on that job together and it was brilliant, but all the time you were hiding it from me,' he said. 'I thought we were on the same page, but we weren't even in the same . . . the same . . .'

'Book?'

'Yeah,' he said. 'Book. See, you are clever.'

Ellie came over.

'Hey, can you pass me them crisps? We've run out.'

I could almost see the cogs whirring in Greeny's brain.

'Oh,' he said. 'Oh no. No you can't. Sorry.'

'Yeah, I knew you'd want them all to yourself, you fat freak,' said Ellie.

Greeny huffed. 'You know what?' he said, thrusting the bowl at her. 'You can have them. Bon appétit.'

Ellie took the crisps and went back to the table. It was a huge effort not to laugh.

'Look, I'm sorry, Greeny,' I said. 'But the only reason I didn't tell you was because Lisa didn't want anyone to know. Not even her best friends.'

Greeny frowned at me then started laughing.

« Older posts

'Actually, I take it back. You ain't clever at all,' he said.

'What do you mean?'

He went to speak, but then shook his head and walked away. 'Forget it,' he said.

I shrugged and walked out of the hall, into the corridor. I didn't know where I was going, but I just needed to get out of the prom for a while.

It was weird, walking around the school after hours. It was as if I shouldn't be there and had sneaked in when everyone had gone home. Greeny's words kept echoing around my mind. I tried to ignore it and convince myself that he was an idiot that didn't know what he was saying, but I couldn't quite do it.

I walked so far I ended up on the Science corridor. Even at night, it still smelled all stinkbomby.

I could hear a voice inside the girls' toilets. It sounded like Lisa.

'I thought I warned you to stay away from him,' she said.

I couldn't make the other voice out, it was just a murmur.

'Yeah, but I saw you looking,' said Lisa.

Another murmur.

'If you don't there's gonna be trouble.'

Another murmur, but louder and angrier.

The door burst open. I dived behind a bin. I couldn't have Lisa thinking I was stalking her. The first thing I saw from my stinky hiding place was Lisa tumbling out of the toilet.

Then I saw who was following her. Natalie.

Natalie grabbed Lisa and threw her up against a locker. The control room men, already on high alert, leapt out of their seats.

Two girls are fighting, possibly over Joe. This is unprecedented. Code Blue!

Are you kidding me? This is AWESOME! said Derek. *Who wants popcorn?*

I didn't know what to do. Should I jump out and stop them? If Harry were there he'd have suggested hot oil.

'Get off me, you bitch,' said Lisa.

'Not so tough now, are you?' said Natalie.

'Just let go,' said Lisa.

'Why should I?' said Natalie. 'After what you've done why shouldn't I smack you?'

My head pounded and my eye twitched.

'Because if you do, you'll get expelled from here as well, just like you were from that last place,' said Lisa. 'Then where can you go?'

Natalie stared at her for a few seconds, then let go, and walked outside.

'Yeah that's right, run away,' said Lisa.

She stared after her then went back towards the hall. When it was clear, I got out from behind the bin. I looked at the exit, then the corridor leading to the hall. I went one way. Then another. My head buzzed with white noise.

« Older posts

'Joe, where have you been?'

'Sorry, Lisa, just went to the toilet,' I said.

The Sound Experience started playing slow songs. Lisa was still immaculate. You wouldn't know she'd just been in a fight.

'So,' she said. 'Are you ready?'

I took a deep breath and nodded.

Lisa held her hand out and I took it. She led me to the middle of the dance floor. I could feel people staring. The Sound Experience played a song called 'Jar of Hearts'. I laughed to myself. 'Jar of Arse'. Number three on the list. I glanced up at Harry. I could tell he was trying not to laugh.

'Are you OK, Joe?' said Lisa.

'Yeah,' I said, trying to concentrate on not messing up the dance. 'Just a little nervous.'

She smiled. 'It'll be fine.'

People started pairing off. Jordan and Ellie, Pete and Chloe, Greeny and a plate of cakes. Gav stood on the edge of the dance floor, talking to one of the Blenkinsops.

'I'm sorry,' said Lisa.

I shook myself out of my daze. 'What for?'

'For being so off with you,' she said. 'I just . . . really like you and I'd hate for anyone to take you away.'

I looked into her eyes. You know when you can tell if someone's eyes are smiling? Hers weren't. They were blank.

We held each other and swayed to the music. She led us

away from the centre of the dance floor, over to the edge.

'OK,' she said. 'It's time.'

My heart thudded against my chest so hard I bet she could feel it against hers.

The control room men held hands and watched. Some of them even wore party hats.

Her eyes darted around the room. Eventually they stopped and she looked at me.

'Sorry,' she said. 'Now are you going to kiss me or what?'

This is it, my man, said Derek. *The moment you've been dreaming about and practising for since you were still digging Pokémon. You are about to kiss a real live girl. Strike that, you are about to kiss Lisa freakin' Hall. Can you believe it? I sure as hell can't. Good luck, dude. And for Christ's sake, don't screw this up for us.*

I closed my eyes and leaned towards her. I felt her breath on me. It smelled like smoke. There was silence in the control room. The lean took longer than I thought,

but eventually our lips met. Against all advice, I opened my eyes. Hers were open too. I drew back and saw she was looking at something behind me. I turned around and saw who it was. Gav.

Boom. The sound of everything falling into place.

The moods.

The way she insisted on coming to my house when Gav was there.

The way she kept going on about how I had to stop Gav from leaving.

How Natalie stopped seeing me. And the fight. The other day when she said she wasn't supposed to be even talking to me.

The way she tried to stop me seeing Harry and Ad.

All the texts to Gav, supposedly bigging me up.

Gav's Valentine's card? Oh my God.

How could I have been so stupid? Harry, Natalie, Greeny, and even Ad could see what was happening. Maybe I just didn't want to believe it. The fog in my head lifted.

'Sorry, Lisa,' I said. 'I can't do this.'

'It's OK,' she said. 'It's normal to be nervous.'

'No, I don't mean the kiss,' I said. 'I mean the whole thing.'

Her eyes went massive. 'Hold on a minute,' she said. 'Are you dumping me?'

'Yes,' I said. 'I am dumping you.'

'But why?'

'Because you were only ever with me to make Gav jealous,' I said. 'I can see it now.'

Her mouth opened, then closed. 'Yeah, but,' she said, 'so what? I mean, if you get to be with me, does it matter what the reason is?'

'Goodbye, Lisa.' I took my arms from around her and walked away. People stared after me.

'I ALWAYS knew he was bent,' said Pete Cotterill.

I climbed onto the stage. Harry wouldn't look at me.

'I'm sorry,' I said.

'WHAT?' shouted Harry, staring out at the dance floor.

'I'M SORRY!' I screamed. 'I'VE BEEN A DICK!'

'You need a dick?' yelled Ad.

I grabbed a track list and pen off the side and wrote them a message:

Harry and Ad,
I'm sorry about everything that's happened. I can see now
that Lisa was using me, just like you said. I hope we can
mates again, despite my extreme
dickishness. You guys are the only real friends I've ever h
and I'd be honoured to be allowed back into your circle o
weirdness.

I went to give it back to them, but then I added something else:

« Older posts

And I, you know, love you both and all that bollocks.

I passed it to them and they read it by the light of Harry's torch. After they'd finished, they looked at each other, then at me.

'Come here, old son,' Harry screamed. 'Let's hug it out.'

We put our arms around each other, and stood there in the middle of the stage, sharing an awkward, three-way man hug, with plenty of embarrassed backslaps thrown in.

I looked out onto the dance floor. Lisa was already talking to Gav and touching the cut on his face. Looks like she got over me pretty quickly.

'This is crap, isn't it?' I said to Harry.

He nodded. 'I feel like we've sold our souls, old boy.'

'It's not too late,' I said.

Harry and Ad gave each other a look. Harry reached into his top pocket and pulled out his best pipe.

'Swedish grindcore?' he said.

I nodded. 'Swedish grindcore.'

He gave me a wicked grin and clamped the pipe between his teeth.

'Let's wreck this "prom",' he said.

I took off my jacket. Then my tie. Then my shirt. All I had on was my trousers and Star Trek T-shirt. I ruffled my stupid haircut until it was just messy and not 'cool-messy'. Ad gave me a thumbs up.

I returned the gesture and left the stage. I chuckled to myself when I saw how close Mr Pratt was standing to the speakers. And I burst into full-on laughter when I saw Ellie and Chloe go back to the table and eat crisps from the bowl. I walked out of the hall, down the corridor, and out into the freezing night. I probably should have brought the stupid jacket with me.

The sound of thrashing guitars and Scandinavian screaming burst through the doors. I almost wished I was still in there to witness the carnage.

I walked around the edge of the school, past the D & T rooms, and into the yard. I couldn't help but wonder if I'd done the right thing. I'd come so close to fulfilling my biggest wish and I'd walked away. After all those years of dreaming, I had been given the chance to make it come true and I'd turned it down.

Opinion in the control room was divided. Norman thought I'd acted wisely. Derek announced that he was disowning me and looking for vacancies in Gav's control room.

I looked at the sky. It was a clear night and the millions of stars made my bedroom ceiling look crappy by comparison. I thought about the Enterprise, zooming across the galaxy, bringing order where there is chaos. It reminded me of my favourite Star Trek quote.

"'Someone once told me that time was a predator that stalked us all our lives,'" I said to no one, doing my best

Picard impression. "'But I rather believe that time is a companion who goes with us on the journey—reminds us to cherish every moment because they'll never come again. What we leave behind is not as important as how we've lived.'"

"'After all, Number One, we're only mortal,'" said a voice around the corner. 'Captain Picard: Star Trek: Generations.'

I saw her sitting there on the bench, hugging herself against the wind. My chest felt like it was going to burst. I walked over and sat down.

'Hello, you,' said Natalie.

'Hi,' I said.

The field stretched out ahead in the dark.

'Didn't think I'd see you out here,' she said. 'I thought you'd be inside with that girlfriend of yours.'

'Ex-girlfriend,' I said. 'She never was my girlfriend, really.'

'Really?'

'Yeah, you were right. She was using me. I'm sorry.'

'Hmm.' She shifted away from me and folded her arms.

'No, I really am,' I said. 'About everything. Literally everything that's happened since we met. Gav calling you a munter. Me making you so angry you punched a bully and got expelled and ended up in this hole. Not doing anything when I should have known Lisa was giving you a hard time. Even suggesting that you should change in any way when you don't need to even one tiny bit because you're like, perfect and stuff. You're beautiful. I can say it now. You are beautiful. And I'm sorry I've messed things up. I'm an idiot. No, not just an idiot, a stupid idiot. A cretin. A—'

Before I could think of another word for knobhead, Natalie grabbed me by the collar of my *Star Trek* T-shirt and kissed me. I mean properly kissed me.

The control room workers cheered, hugged, and popped open bottles of champagne. Derek shook hands with Norman and withdrew his resignation.

He's done it! The little moron's done it! Let's order a pizza!

The kiss was amazing. Soft and warm. I tingled all over. She pulled away.

'Wow,' I said.

'Well, it was the only way I could think of to shut you up.' She looked at me sideways and smiled.

'M-maybe I should talk crap more often,' I said.

'That's not possible,' said Natalie. 'By the way, you've got black lipstick on now. It totally suits you.'

'I don't know, maybe you could have it back,' I said, and this time I kissed her. I mean, what kind of person am I becoming? A SMOOTH operator, that's what.

Afterwards, she rested her head on my shoulder. I pretended to yawn, stretched my arm in the air, and put it around her.

'Did you really just do the yawn-and-grab?' she said.

'I did a bit, yes,' I said.

'Brilliant.'

People started spilling out of the school, moaning about the disco.

'What was that? It was like a mad tramp and a drum kit falling down the stairs.'

'Oh my God, my ears are bleeding.'

I'm so proud of the Sound Experience.

We got up and I walked her home. I think the last thing either of us wanted was all the prom idiots seeing us. When we got to her door, we kissed again. That's three in one night. I am literally an animal.

I skipped on the way home. Actually skipped. Instead of pretending to be happy, I really was! Yes, I wasn't in the cool crowd any more, but I never was, really. I felt like Picard must have after he survived being assimilated by the Borg. I'd been sucked into the hive and come back against all odds.

I know I'm not cool, and I'm OK with that. I'm different. I own an extensive collection of (defaced) Star Trek annuals, and sometimes, actually a lot of times, I say the wrong thing. But who cares? I have friends and a girlfriend who like me despite all that.

I saw Mad Morris on the way through the park and I hugged him. He was so stunned, he actually stopped ranting about Jesus.

Just before I got home, my phone rang.

'Hello, Mum,' I said. 'Don't worry, I'm nearly home now.'

'That's OK, darling,' she said. 'Did you have a nice time?'

'I did, actually,' I said. 'Anyway, it's late, what's up?'

'Well, we were going to wait until we got home, but now we've had the good news about Gavin, we couldn't wait to tell you.'

'Tell me what?'

I heard her take a deep breath.

'I'm pregnant!'

The control room men stopped their conga line and ran back to their workstations.

'Pr-pregnant?' I said.

'Yes! I just found out today! Isn't it exciting?'

'Yeah,' I said. 'Br-brilliant.'

So our house now has me, Mum, Jim, Gav, Doris, Adwina 2, Syd, and soon, some kind of freakish me/Gav hybrid?

Just my cocking luck.